MINERVA

THE LIAR

Page Turner

Minerva
The Liar

Psychic State Book 3

Published By: Braided Studios, LLC

https://braided.studio

ISBN: 978-1-947296-10-7

A special thanks to my Patreons

Poets

Elan L.

Jason S.

Katrina W.

Michael S.

Praisers

Annabelle P.

Don S.

Eternal O.

Heather N.

Jess B.

Julie H.

Michael D.

Sherpas

Alex B.

Andrea

Avery F.

Becki

Christin O.

Edith M.

Georg

Hillary J.

Jamie L.

Jasper A.

Jitesh M.

Kat

Kirsten J.

Kit L.

Larissa R.

Lisa R.

Michael C.

Nada J.

Samuel T.

Sharon M.

Stephanie G

Tiana S.

Wesley E.

Other Supporters

Adam A.	k k
Alexander M.	Kat O.
Alicia M.	Kate S.
Allyson L.	Kathleen D.
Amanda N.	Lady Mediocrity
Amy	Lani D.
Andrew T.	LennaLeFay
Anna K. C.	Marion L.
Bekah	Maureen S.
Bex	Mayra
Bionyx	Melissa
Chelle	Menachem C.
Christina B.	Michael H.
Clarita D.	Mx. Killian
Coleman S.	Nicki K.
Emz J.	Paul John S.
Endre H.	polymerase
Gunter G.	Pour V.
Heather K.	Rae G.
James A.	Riki S.
James H.	Sara D.
Jane	Tamara W.
Jason D.	Tris S.
Jenny B.	Twyla S.

For those who weren't believed when they were speaking the truth

Exit Strategy, Exit Wounds

In the land of liars, truthtellers are heretics.

-Darren Delvecchio, Beautiful Liars International

"We need to talk exit strategy."

Minerva Cantor startled at the sound of her supervisor's voice. She looked up from her stack of reports. Exit strategy? That was an overly serious thing to say. If she weren't so busy, it might even be concerning to hear. That sounded like termination talk.

But a person who is buried in work doesn't exactly have the emotional or attentional bandwidth to worry properly, so Minerva didn't. Instead, she interpreted this dire pronouncement as a joke.

"I don't have time to get fired today," she said and smirked.

"That's not funny, Mini," her supervisor replied.

Minerva cringed at his use of that nickname. She'd been called Minnie as a kid. That was her dad's name for her. Well, when they'd still been talking anyway. Minnie always sounded particularly wrong coming out of the mouths of her male coworkers.

As the only woman in her department, she'd put up with a lot and had tried to be understanding of the fact that she would likely always be an outsider, especially in a male-dominated industry like marketing. While her coworkers had never been openly sexist with her, they did seem to like finding reasons to pick on her. One reason was her height. It was curious because this was the first time Minerva had ever encountered this form of teasing. At 5 feet 4 inches she was fairly average height for a woman, but on a male-dominated team with most of the members easily over

6 feet tall, she was suddenly considered short for the first time in her life.

Highlighting this, her colleagues spelled her nickname "Mini." That was how her supervisor even wrote it on the team sales printouts, ever eager to remind her that she was the miniature member of the team.

Perhaps if that had been all, she might have been able to move past it, to laugh it off with the rest of the team, but the perception of her as small didn't seem to stop at height. Sometimes they treated her as though she were practically invisible. Over the past year, she'd pitched three separate initiatives to her colleagues that were all met with crickets in the boardroom only to be resurrected a few weeks or months later by another member of her team to great applause.

But that's my idea, she'd think, seething every time it happened. She fumed every time someone spontaneously got a great "new" idea that was actually hers.

When she'd tried to open her mouth to protest, the voice that had come out was quite small. In those moments, she'd felt tiny yet again. Miniature. The incredible shrinking woman.

The first time someone had stolen her idea, it was on the Melrose Cigars campaign. She'd gone directly to her supervisor then, who regarded her with bewilderment. "I have no idea what you're talking about," her supervisor had said in the exact tone that indicated to her that he did but just didn't want to admit it and thought she was being a nuisance by coming to him.

"It was my work. That storyboard looked just like mine," she had said, more firmly.

Her supervisor had shrugged noncommittally. "All storyboards look alike if you really think about it."

Minerva had groaned. "But it was my catchphrase, too." She put up her hands and moved them apart as though spreading out an invisible banner. "All smoke, all fire."

"Brilliant, right?" her supervisor had said.

"But it was my idea! That was my line!" Minerva had protested.

Her supervisor had shaken his head. "No, yours was something different, wasn't it?" He rubbed his chin. "No smoke, no fire, I think it was."

"No," Minerva had said. "All smoke, all fire. I have the old drafts in my desk if you'll just take a look at them. I have proof. I can show you."

"That won't be necessary," her supervisor had said. "I don't want to foster that kind of work environment, where people are afraid to put ideas forward since it might have a passing resemblance to something they've seen in the past." He'd shrugged. "There are no new ideas, after all."

"Well, I don't think it fosters a good environment if people are passing other people's work off as their o–"

"Calm down," her supervisor interrupted. "There's no need to get so upset."

She gritted her teeth together. She wasn't losing her cool, but now she might. Telling someone to calm down might just be the best example of reverse psychology in action; as a directive it nearly always has the opposite effect. "Calm down" has a way of hitting people squarely as "hey there, please lose your shit – with a quickness."

Minerva struggled against this, knowing all too well that if she lost her cool, she'd be immediately labeled as too "sensitive" or "dramatic," words that her coworkers never used on one another but easily slung her way.

"Look, Mini, you need to be a team player. Stop being so sensitive."

Yup, there was the S-word. *Sensitive.* She quietly seethed, hoping her rage wouldn't boil to the surface where it could be detected and punished. Outwardly, she assured him she wasn't bothered. She was only just saying. Of course she wasn't bothered.

And as she backed out of the office after this failed attempt to address the first creative theft, it dawned on her that in an effort to defend her emotions – and by extension her sanity – she had lost the ability to address what she had gone in there to talk about in the first place: The plagiarism of her ideas.

She'd learned an important lesson that day. She wasn't going to get the credit she deserved on this team. While her supervisor was typically polite and professional with her, he wasn't someone she could turn to when she needed someone in her corner to fight for her.

She was on her own.

And now here he was, years later, standing in her office, stony faced and throwing around that dire phrase – "exit strategy." He was in fact being more dramatic than she'd ever been, although he'd thrown the D-word at her many times. There was a Bingo card in there somewhere, in the predictability of the criticisms he and her other male co-workers levied against her. Criticisms, Minerva noted, that she'd never heard before on a more co-ed work force.

This jokester couldn't have picked a worse time to be hovering over her talking about "exit strategy." The nerve. As busy as she was in the face of all this "exit strategy" nonsense, however, something else dawned on her as she kept her head down, trying to ignore the interruption: Her supervisor *had* invited her to a meeting a bit earlier, one scheduled for the end of his workday – she often stayed much later, something he rarely acknowledged—but she'd turned the request down. She had too much to do today. No time for a check-in.

And now here he was, lingering uncharacteristically, talking about exit strategy. Coupled with the earlier request for an end of the day meeting, it was concerning. A bolt of fear coursed through her. Could it be? Could this be it? Was she getting fired?

No, she thought. *Stop that. Keep your cool. It's probably nothing.*

"I'm just trying to get the job done," she said.

He said nothing.

She was right to be afraid, Minerva realized. There was something off about this whole situation. Playing it cool wouldn't cut it. "You're serious," she said. "When you say exit strategy... you... you really want me to leave."

It had to be something else. A joke gone too far. A miscommunication that could be worked through. After all, she'd been with the firm for several years now and had always done good work. In addition to not being credited for her ideas, she was making less than her colleagues, something she wasn't supposed to know but had figured out on her own via sheer resourcefulness.

She wasn't just overworked and underpaid. She was a bargain really, a steal. A steal who had been repeatedly stolen from and had hardly complained despite the unfairness.

How much lower maintenance could you get?

She had voiced her fear, hoping he would reassure her. But that didn't happen. Instead, her supervisor nodded, and her stomach leapt.

He *was* serious. He *did* want her to leave.

"That's the most ridiculous thing I've ever heard," she said. "Why?"

"You've seemed unhappy here for an awfully long time," the supervisor said.

I didn't know happiness was in the job description, Minerva thought. Aloud she said nothing and just stared at him.

Her supervisor stared back.

"I'm not a quitter," Minerva said finally.

"No one thinks that," the supervisor replied, sliding a paper to Minerva across the desk.

Notice of Termination.

"Security," he said, one quick word spat into a phone. In one smooth movement, the supervisor turned around on his heel like a swimmer making a wall turn.

As she followed Security down the hallway, Minerva sized him up. He was a pokerfaced man the size of a vending machine.

Whatever would you buy from him though? She wondered. *Something strong. And bad for your digestion.*

"What?" Security said.

"I didn't say anything," Minerva replied.

"You laughed."

"Did I?"

"You're way too cheerful for someone who was just let go," Security said.

"Have you ever been fired?" Minerva asked him.

"Let go," he corrected her.

"Let go?" she said. "No, I wasn't let go. I was *fired.*" Normally, she wouldn't have argued, but today was different. Being let go – damn it, *fired* – had altered her perspective. She was out of fucks.

"People aren't fired. Guns are fired. Not people."

"Is that what you think?"

Security didn't respond.

Minerva suppressed the laughter brewing in her throat, and the tension from holding it in became more and more powerful as she stepped into the open air, the laugh scrambling to escape from her like a rogue hiccup.

And as it did, she missed the sudden wall that came out of nowhere and hit her.

Cotton. Expanding further. *Can sweaters grow?* Minerva wondered as whatever was sitting in her mouth continued to yawn and pull at every nerve and yanked at fibers even further down into her throat.

She thought of those strange toys made of superabsorbent polymer that children dropped into water and watched grow. It was an uncomfortable feeling, visualizing one of those toys pushing down her throat and out to the walls, fed by her saliva, filling her, suffocating her.

In the distance she heard a band practicing. Fourth graders probably, judging by the skill level. Invested more in making noise than establishing a cohesive arrangement.

On the other side of her, she heard a mix of murmuring voices punctuated by metallic clanging. Someone was moving furniture maybe. But light furniture. They weren't dragging bureaus across an apartment floor. No, they were moving smaller objects perhaps, or items on wheels.

Then her nerves sang, drowning out what she heard in her
ears. So many nerves singing that she couldn't isolate where the
sensations were coming from. She felt a mix of pain and pressure.

Pain.

Pressure.

Which one is pain? Which one is pressure?

Her basic proprioceptive sense whirred to life, letting her know
that she was lying down. Not a lot of information, but it was
something.

And there was light. But not enough light. There was the
suggestion of light, what a person might perceive if they'd been
told about light in passing but had never had the opportunity to
experience it firsthand themselves. The shadow of a form cast
across a lit screen.

Pull back the screen.

I can't.

Is it really a screen?

It wasn't a screen, she realized. It was more of a muted sun. A
yellowed fabric stretched tightly across a drumhead.

The screen was her... eyelids.

Those she could pull back. And so, she did.

She didn't see anything at first because the room was so bright,
but as her eyes adjusted, Minerva knew exactly where she was.

A hospital room.

I've been in an accident, she realized. She glanced over at her arm.
An intravenous line was inserted and active. Dripping pain meds
and normal saline most likely.

A nurse walked in. "Good morning, Miss Cantor. I see you're finally awake."

Minerva nodded.

"I'll let the doctor know. He'll be very pleased. We weren't sure whether you'd come out of it," the nurse said.

Come out of what? What happened to me? Minerva thought. She looked purposefully at the nurse, hoping her eyes would convey the message. Speaking was out of the question with her mouth and throat otherwise occupied.

"Oh right, your pain meds," the nurse replied, misinterpreting the look. "I imagine that's why you're awake at all. You're completely out."

What happened to me? Minerva thought again. She was doing her best to broadcast it at the nurse. Minerva certainly didn't believe in psychic powers, or anything woo-woo or spooky like that, but she'd heard of magicians called mentalists who could powerfully affect people with the power of suggestion. A mentalist could get someone to pick a certain option simply by silently moving their own lips to prime words in the subject's imagination.

Perhaps, if she focused her intent powerfully enough, she could do something similar with her eyes. Especially with a nurse as the target, someone who was used to dealing with patients who couldn't communicate. Surely, there was no one better equipped to receive such a message.

The nurse nodded as if she understood. She hung a new bag on the stand next to Minerva's bed. "Nighty night, Miss Cantor," she said.

Nooooo, Minerva thought, as she slipped back under the influence of the sedative, violently blanketed by sleep, feeling very much like a parakeet might if you draped a towel over its cage in the middle of the afternoon while he still had an awful lot on his birdbrain and more trilling yet to sing about his birdly concerns.

Sailing on a Sea of Man Children

For several days Minerva slipped in and out of consciousness. For several days she tried to communicate with her caretakers using what she hoped were meaningful facial expressions.

And for several days she failed.

She reflected sourly in the few waking seconds she had before the next plunge into the mental darkness of sedation that she seemed stuck in a cycle that wasn't hers to break. It was like she was strapped to the back of a thrashing beast that had its own plans. Willful ones.

It wasn't for her to control this creature. The only thing she could do was keep from getting thrown off and trampled under its hooves.

So, Minerva stopped fighting. She let herself become passive and rest. If she fell off the back of this beast, she fell off. She wasn't in control anymore.

And then one afternoon, after many days of up and down and many days strapped to this terrible riotous beast, she opened her eyes and found that her mind was clear. She had little pain. There was no longer anything disconcerting shoved into her mouth or her throat.

And she had a visitor. A familiar one.

"Chad!" she said, genuinely surprised. He was frankly the last person she'd expected to visit her in the hospital.

True, they'd been dating for two years. Some would refer to him as her live-in boyfriend. Perhaps most people would call him that – as they had an ongoing sexual relationship, and he'd been shacked up at her place for the entire time they'd known one another. But Minerva didn't dare refer to him that way herself, especially not in front of Chad. She wasn't going to use the B word.

Chad wasn't one for labels. At least not applied to him. Minerva often saw that Chad had no qualms pressuring other people to use labels when they suited his own needs, when they were used to quell his own anxiety about uncertainty.

He was the sort of man who wanted firm commitments from others without the expectation that he should ever reciprocate in kind. Chad wanted security without obligation.

And he was the sort of man who got away with it.

"I would have gotten you something from the gift shop," Chad said. "But everything they had was lame."

"That's okay," Minerva said.

"Anyway, you didn't leave me any money before you went and got hit by that truck," Chad said.

"Is that what happened to me?" Minerva said.

Chad frowned. "You don't remember?"

Minerva shook her head. "I remember getting fired and stepping out into the street. Next thing I knew I was here."

"You got fired?" Chad said. "Woah. What did you do?"

"What do you mean what did I do?" Minerva said.

"You must have done something really awesome to get fired. Did you kick your boss in the nads?" Chad asked.

"No, I didn't kick my boss in the nads," Minerva replied.

"Then what did you do?" Chad asked.

"I honestly don't know," Minerva said.

"People don't get fired for nothing," Chad said.

"That's what I used to believe, too," Minerva said *sotto voce*. She felt tired, and she was starting to slip into Chad Mode. She had a way that she acted around him, a way that she spoke, one that lined up better with his expectations of her and less with how she actually was.

She found herself changing into that old lie, slipping on the mask of the impostor, acting out the role of the person that Chad wanted to be with.

Normally she would have already had the costume on, if she hadn't been so groggy still, wiped out from sedation and healing from whatever physical trauma she had suffered. It occurred to her that she still didn't know what exactly had happened to her body, only that it hurt and she felt exhausted.

"What are we going to do?" Chad asked. "What are we going to do for money?"

Minerva considered suggesting that he get a job. That was the solution that common sense dictated, and what she would have concluded herself if their roles were reversed. Chad was able bodied, reasonably intelligent – and an extremely attractive man. Someone would hire him. People were always projecting positive qualities on him, his good looks serving as a halo that distracted strangers from his flaws. It wouldn't be that hard for him to get a job. All he'd need to do is apply.

However, the last time she'd suggested such a thing to Chad – as he'd emptied her bank account while complaining that their apartment wasn't as luxe as his friend Steve's – Chad had wrinkled up his nose as though he'd smelled something nasty and called her a "miserable old bitch."

Back into her shell Minerva had gone, a small part of her cursing at the reflex to recoil the entire time. *You're better than this*, a shred of her feminist conscience had scolded her.

No, I'm not, the rest of her had responded. *I don't want to be alone... and have you looked out there? It's a sea of man children. It's not like I'm going to do any better than this one.*

Anyway, the hop from boat to boat could be quite expensive indeed, she'd noted, watching once-friends, now distant acquaintances, divorce one man child and promptly marry another, stuck each time with the court fees and with paying off the debt that had piled up during those disappointing marriages.

No, it was better to stick with the problem she had, even if that problem could be rather petulant and frustrating at times.

Minerva inhaled slowly, gathering her composure. "I'll file for unemployment," she said. "And we can look into some kind of settlement. If a truck hit me, there are probably options there for help."

Chad nodded. "That lawyer guy who's been by said something like that."

"What lawyer guy?" Minerva asked.

"He was there when it happened," Chad said. "Works at the firm across the street from where you work. Or, um... where you used to work now. Guess he left his office just in time to see you get creamed. He left his card." He pulled the card out and waved it in front of Minerva's face but so quickly that she couldn't read it.

"Well, there," Minerva said, forcing a smile. "You see, we'll be fine. You won't have to worry."

She noted uncomfortably that while she was the one in the hospital bed, she was comforting Chad and not the other way around. As usual.

That was the way their relationship normally worked, she reflected. His stress had a way of whining its way to the top of the queue, a fact that Chad seemed completely oblivious to. If you had asked him, he would have told you in no uncertain terms that Minerva was the sensitive flower in their relationship. He would have told you that she was like any other woman – emotional, dramatic, forever doomed to broadcast her worries in an inexorable melodrama spun from estrogen.

Chad was quite self-deluded in this way, in the stories he told himself. It was true that he possessed a perfectly square jaw befitting a GI Joe figurine or a superhero. By an accident of biology, his body had flawlessly mimicked the appearance of paragons of masculinity that had been flaunted before him in youth.

But the six-pack abs and bulging neck veins were a mirage, a misleading disguise. There was nothing internally steely about Chad. He had been bullied extensively by other kids in the years before puberty bestowed his current form, and because of those early experiences, Chad was quite sensitive to perceived insults or slights. He simply could not tolerate being criticized.

Nor could he seem to weather the natural ups and downs of life. Stoically—or at all, really.

He also seemed particularly adept at making other people's misfortunes all about him.

Whenever this happened, he'd appeal to Minerva for comfort, imploring her to soothe him. Usually this didn't happen overtly but played out in smaller gestures. A hopeless look. A desolate tone of voice. A display of helplessness that was nonetheless still subtle enough to have plausible deniability. Because he was a manly man, after all, he'd reassure himself privately, puffing up his chest.

Minerva had experimented with not responding to these bids for support from Chad but had found if his despair were left untended that Chad would punch something in anger, necessitating costly repairs or replacement.

Which wouldn't do at all either.

No, it had become quite a bit easier over the two years they'd been together to simply respond to his unvoiced expectations, to help him in ways that were largely invisible to him.

Chad responded to this not with gratitude but the continued belief –and occasional pronouncement – that he was tougher than Minerva. Made of stronger stuff. If you had asked him, Chad would have insisted that Minerva required a lot more emotional support from him and not the other way around.

That was because Chad was a kindness miser. It was something Minerva had learned long ago: People who advertise that they engage in prolific selfless acts actually do not do them that often. However, they feel like they do since they're kindness misers. A kindness miser puts great significance on every little thing they do that is not done out of self-interest, precisely because it is not in their nature. This leads kindness misers to feel as though they are "always doing things for other people." But they really aren't.

In contrast, people who do a lot for other people don't usually advertise it. Truly giving people frankly are often unaware that what they're doing is unusual in any way.

Like any other kindness miser, Chad had an overly heightened sense of awareness of the benevolence of his actions on the rare occasion that he did anything nice for anyone else. This would lead him to overestimate the frequency that he took those same actions. A single act of kindness could convince him, rather fully, that he was incessantly kind, someone who always went beyond the call of duty.

However, anyone other than Chad could see that this was plainly not true.

Most liars do not wake up one day dishonest. Instead, becoming a liar is a gradual process, whereby nascent liars are rewarded by society for convenient dishonesty and punished when they are inconveniently honest.

One great example of convenient dishonesty comes in the form of self-monitoring, a practice in which people pay attention to their own behavior and modify it according to the particular social context they find themselves in.

Self-monitoring is incredibly common and by itself typically no cause for concern. However, research has shown that high self-monitors are more likely to engage in other dishonest behaviors – for example, unethical business decisions. High self-monitors are typically well meaning and only seek to build positive relationships with others. However, somewhere in the well-meaning dishonesty, they're prone to losing their way. Perhaps this is what is meant when it's said that the road to hell is paved with good intentions.

-Darren Delvecchio, Beautiful Liars International

The discharge process was a whirl. Everything had to be signed in triplicate. Minerva didn't bother to read anything that was handed to her. She just knew she wanted to go home.

But before they could leave, they needed to make a stop at the hospital pharmacy downstairs to pick up her pain prescriptions.

"I'll just tough it out," Minerva said, feeling exhausted.

"No, you won't," Chad replied. "What kind of person doesn't pick up perfectly good pain pills?"

One who is tired and just wants to get home and fall asleep in her own bed, Minerva thought. But aloud she said nothing.

"Anyway," Chad continued, "these things are like gold. *I* might need them, you know."

An old woman standing next to them turned and stared, her beady little eyes growing dessert plate-sized, as though she were amazed to see a self-professed druggie in her midst.

"You know, for legitimate reasons," Chad said to no one in particular.

Minerva sighed.

The line slumped sluggishly forward.

Finally, it was their turn. Chad slapped a wadded ball of paper prescriptions onto the pharmacy counter. The pharmacy aide lifted his head wearily and studied Chad, as though he wanted to get a good look at a person who would molest prescriptions in this manner.

The aide muttered something as he dug through a drawer. Minerva would have sworn it included the word *troglodyte.*

"Date of birth," he said.

Chad looked helplessly at Minerva. She said her date of birth.

"April 8?" the aide said. "Huh, that's the Buddha's birthday, too."

Minerva didn't know quite what to say to that. It was the first time she'd ever heard that.

"There's a big celebration in Asia and everything for it. I have a cousin who's flown out for it. She's an April 8th baby, too. Might be something to consider."

Minerva smiled. "I'll keep that in mind."

"Sounds boring," Chad commented.

The aide scowled and threw a dirty glance at Chad. "Anyway, your total comes to $110.86," he announced.

Chad looked helplessly at Minerva again. As always, he liked to be in charge until it came time to do anything or have any responsibility. He certainly wasn't one to pick up the bill.

Minerva leaned wearily against the pharmacy counter and fished through her purse for her credit card. She handed it to the aide.

It occurred to her the moment that the card left her hands that she had no idea what would happen when he ran it. She was close to her limit, and the medications had cost more than she expected. She had just lost her job. Money was likely to be tight for a while yet, too, until everything got squared away with the accident. It wasn't like she could just go to an ATM and pull out extra cash.

Confirming her suspicions, the card came back declined. "I'm sorry, do you have another card?" the aide said.

Minerva shook her head. "Just the one," she said. "Run it again."

As she made this suggestion, she felt her fingers crossing behind her back. "I'm sure it'll go through the second time."

It was strange. She knew she was lying. She had no reason to suspect the second time would be any different – she was certainly far from sure it would. But as she lied, she felt a strange absence of the normal stress that accompanied a lie.

The lie felt true.

The aide looked at her skeptically but agreed to the request.

Minerva squeezed her middle and index fingers on her right hand even more tightly together, feeling more and more foolish by the second. When was the last time she'd actually crossed her fingers when telling a fib?

And why the heck had she asked him to run the card a *second* time? Wouldn't it be more embarrassing for the card to be declined twice?

"Huh," the aide said. "Went through this time." He smiled. Minerva felt a surge of warmth go through her crossed fingers. The sensation felt satisfying, like a deep stretch. She smiled and uncrossed her fingers.

"Can't remember that ever happening," the aide said. "Card rejected on the first swipe. Approved on the second. Maybe the machine's having a bad day."

"Aren't we all?" Chad grumbled, clearly put out that he wasn't the center of attention.

Not me, Minerva thought, feeling an overwhelming sense of relief. Her card had mysteriously gone through. She'd lived through an ordeal that could have very well killed her. In fact, the doctors had seemed amazed that she'd healed so quickly and already wanted to go home – part of why she'd had to sign so many extra papers to get out.

She stepped out into the open air. An orderly pushing a wheelchair followed her outside, moving in hot pursuit. As he commanded her to sit down in the chair this instant for liability purposes, she felt the sun on her face and whispered a quick "thank you" into the ether for this new life.

Firmly agnostic, she'd never believed in miracles and didn't know exactly where to send the credit for this marked turnaround. But she did know one thing:

She was grateful.

One rule: everyone is willing to give you something—they are ready to give you something—for whatever it is they are hungry for.

-Henry Oberlander, con man

The Origin of Psychic Powers

As with many other scientific communities, the great nature versus nurture debate has raged for years among intuitive taxonomers. Some insist that psychic powers – or lack thereof—are present at birth, wired into the genetic code. However, all attempts thus far to link any form of psychic mutation to DNA have been fruitless.

Others insist that psychic abilities manifest due to environmental factors. Various possibilities have been suggested as to the source. Climatic patterns remain a popular explanation, particularly as North America's Tornado Alley has produced more intuitives than any other region in the world.

However, current lines of research are also investigating the possible role of nutritional and psychosocial factors in the development of psychic powers.

Intuitive endocrinology is another fast-expanding field, created after it was noted that while some intuitives do possess extrasensory powers as infants, the vast majority only reach discernible psychic prowess after puberty. Intuitive endocrinologists are hard at work not only at mapping hormonal changes observed in psychic practitioners versus controls but also in exploring the potential manipulation of hormonal levels to either suppress or potentiate existing psychic powers.

The ultimate grail of these endeavors is the ability to instill psychic powers in a non-psychic control. However, this is believed to be a rather fantastic notion, as likely as the machinations of mad scientists in pulp fiction.

Still, apocryphal reports have emerged of secondary onset psychic powers in previously normal individuals due to extreme physical or psychological trauma.

from Insecta Psychica: Towards an Intuitive Taxonomy by Cloche Macomber

"So I was thinking," Chad said as they got home, "You're going to be laid up for a while, aren't you?"

Minerva nodded as she stepped over a pile of clothes that had amassed in the living room. It seemed as though in her absence Chad had made no effort to throw his clothes in the hamper. Instead, he'd shed them wherever he pleased, much like a snake sheds its skin before slithering away – except instead of ropy lace stockings, he left a trail of slim fit T-shirts and cargo shorts. This ejecta smelled ever so faintly of musky body spray.

"I imagine it'll be a while before I'm back to one hundred percent," she said. She felt so tired already, not only thrust rudely back into her old life but thrust into this additional mess that Chad had left for her while she was laid up. True, he normally didn't pick up after himself, but usually she was left with half a day's worth of Chad's laziness at a time.

Two weeks... well, it looked like an artist's happening gone horribly wrong. She noted grimly that every kitchen cabinet was wide open, and the cupboards were bare. No doubt every dish in the apartment was piled into the sink, shellacked into perverse ceramic layer cakes, glued together by neglected food scraps, the bits that Chad had opted not to eat.

She didn't dare look.

The trash can was overflowing, and while the air didn't smell rotten yet, it did feel stale, and like a hard-grooving baseline, it threatened to deliver gnarly dirty funk at any moment.

"So if you're going to be out of sorts for a while..." Chad began.

You'll hire a maid? Get a buddy to help clean this place up? Minerva found herself hoping. She didn't dare imagine he'd offer to do it himself. That thought was simply preposterous.

"Maybe now's a good time to open our relationship," Chad finished.

It was the last thing she expected to hear him say. Minerva felt a bolt of shock course through her followed by a feeling of unsteadiness. She pushed aside a pile of discarded Chad sweater-skins and sat down on the sole available couch cushion. "Open our relationship?" she said, wading in delicately, although she wanted to scream at Chad's cluelessness about the state of their surroundings.

"We've talked about this, babe," Chad said.

And it was true. They had. Or at least *he* had. Extensively. About how much he'd like to see other women, or as he put it, "Get a chance to sample other flavors."

Minerva had always hated it when he put it that way. Really, really hated it. For some reason, Chad always wanted to compare women to ice cream.

Maybe it's because he only knows how to consume, she thought idly but pushed the thought out of her head.

She hated when he made her bitter. It wasn't what she wanted out of a romantic relationship, to sit there feeling resentful about someone she cared about.

Anyway, just because they'd talked about opening their relationship, it didn't mean they were ready to do it. Chad was selfish enough as it was, with just the two of them more or less monogamous. She knew it was possible that he'd had an affair or two during the time they'd lived together but didn't have any proof, only a sneaking suspicion that it was unlikely for Chad to continuously exercise self-control *of any form* for that long.

Opening up could make things considerably worse. She felt certain that Chad would end up gorging himself on the possibility to see other people. Making a huge mess in the process.

And as with every other mess he left in his wake, Minerva would be the one who'd have to clean it up.

Even if they pursued women together, Minerva was fairly certain that she'd end up doing a lot of the emotional work to attract other women in the first place and then later on to keep any potential lovers from fleeing in the other direction. Because Chad was a handful. A handsome handful. But a handful nonetheless.

And if Chad went off to date other women on his own... ooh boy. Things could get hairy and fast.

It was a dicey proposition in the best of times. And given her current state of physical health, this was certainly *not* the best of times.

"Did we?" Minerva said.

Chad frowned. "Are you telling me you don't remember talking about it?"

"Yeah," Minerva lied, feeling the normal frisson of stress that accompanied dishonesty, a sensation that zigzagged up her spine like a lightning bolt.

"I don't believe that for a second," Chad said. "I've brought it up at least a dozen times. Probably more."

More like three dozen, Minerva thought.

Aloud she said, "Oh, that's right... I remember now." Another lightning bolt shot up her back as she pretended that she'd forgotten. *Liar.*

Chad smiled. "So you're on board?"

As she went to speak, she felt her right index and middle finger crossing again, like they had at the pharmacy counter. *I'm so superstitious today*, she thought. *Who actually crosses their fingers behind their back when they lie? That's something little kids do.*

"Definitely," she said. "I'm a little surprised you were so insistent that I should date other people, but if it's what you want, then I'm willing to explore that."

It was half-meant as a joke to break the tension, but Chad looked confused. Minerva noted that no attendant stressful feeling shot up her spine. In fact, what she said felt true to her when she said it. Not like a joke – but true.

"Yes," Chad said, in response. "It means a lot to me."

Minerva's fingers began to pulse and throb again as they stayed crossed.

"I was surprised you only wanted our relationship open on one side," Minerva said, wondering how far Chad would humor this strange reversal, noting all the while that she felt nothing as she lied. "But that's you, Mr. Monogamy."

"Mr. Monogamy," he replied, nodding his head.

Minerva looked into his eyes and saw a passivity there she had never seen before. Respect for her.

He believed every word she was saying, even though it was ridiculous and a complete break from reality.

How peculiar. Chad's normal reflex was to dismiss what she was saying the moment it came out of her mouth. To invalidate her feelings. And to insist he knew better than her.

He'd never been one to easily accept her words when she told the truth – let alone when she was joking, or telling obvious lies.

Her fingers throbbed again. She uncrossed them.

Incredulity flooded back into Chad's eyes. "Geez, I can't believe you forgot about that."

"So while I'm out of commission, I should start dating other people?" Minerva asked. She wondered how far she could push the joke. Any moment he'd stop playing along. She was sure of it.

But she was wrong. "Duh," Chad replied. He looked uncertain as he said it though.

"And why's that?" Minerva said.

Chad paused and thought for a second. He made faces that reminded Minerva of people doing mental math that's just at the outer limits of their calculative abilities without pen and paper or a calculator.

Looks a little like cognitive dissonance, Minerva thought. It was a concept she'd dealt with a lot in marketing. Cognitive dissonance is what happens when a person holds two or more contradictory, conflicting beliefs in their head at the same time.

In her old line of work as a marketer, they'd leverage cognitive dissonance on occasion to motivate people to buy a product that would eliminate it. Consumers would happily rush towards a product that would resolve the inherent conflict.

That's because cognitive dissonance is generally a stressful situation and something that people find uncomfortable.

Active cognitive dissonance can also make a person look as though they're scrambling to make sense of nonsense that they firmly believe. Or like they're doing math that's too hard for them.

"Because seeing other people will help you heal!" Chad said suddenly.

Apparently, that was the result of his intense calculation. That was how his brain was making sense of the inherent contradiction.

Minerva laughed. "Well, maybe it will," she said. "But if it's alright with you, I'd like to take my time."

"Fine," Chad pouted.

As he did, Minerva felt her fingers curl back into a cross. *I guess this is just something I do now*, she thought. *I cross my fingers before I lie convincingly. So convincingly that I nearly fool myself.*

What was most peculiar to her was that her body seemed to know before her conscious mind that she was about to be dishonest. Her muscles would twitch and spring into action before she registered what was going on. What was giving her away? Minerva wondered.

And where did this strange new physical twitch come from?

"I'm so glad you offered to help clean this place up," she said. Her fingers uncurled. "It's filthy in here, and I really don't have the energy to pick up the mess you left."

Chad stared at her dazed for a moment before replying. "Of course," he said. "No problem."

But the words were odd and stilted coming out of his mouth. It was as though he were uncertainly speaking someone else's lines in a play he didn't know at all. It lacked the conviction of a skilled actor who has been practicing a role and more had the remove of an untrained person who's helping an actor study and reading back the other half of a scene in an effort to help them out.

There was something almost robotic about the way Chad spoke.

She thought for a second that Chad might in fact be mocking her, but then he turned and began to gather his discarded clothing.

She watched with amazement as he threw the laundry in the washing machine. As he returned and set aside clutter to clear surfaces. Dragged out cleaning supplies from the closets.

And she positively gawked as he began to wash the countertops.

Especially since she couldn't remember how many times she'd asked for Chad's help and his response was to shrug his shoulders helplessly and declare he didn't know how to begin.

It would appear he'd been perfectly capable all along. He just didn't want to do it.

And why does he want to now? Minerva found herself asking. It was possible that her brush with death had scared him. Another person might suggest that Chad was grateful she'd survived and wanted to show his appreciation.

But that person didn't know Chad nearly as well as she did.

It just didn't make sense as an explanation.

Her fingers throbbed in a pleasant way that sent a shiver up her back, not a zigzag of stress but one of pleasure. The frisson hit the top of her forehead and traveled downwards across the front of her body, thrumming in her solar plexus. She shuddered. A phantom warmth spread out from her.

Minerva studied her hands. They looked perfectly normal to her, just the same as before. But there was something different about them. Something different about her.

I don't think it's Chad who changed, Minerva thought. *It's me. I've changed.*

He *was* listening to her for the first time she could remember. Chad was normally dismissive, skeptical in the best of times. But not anymore. Even when she was joking or telling bald-faced lies, he treated her words as though she spoke gospel.

He seemed perfectly gullible suddenly.

But maybe that's not it at all, Minerva thought.

Maybe she had become incredibly convincing.

And as soon as she considered it, she felt like it *had* to be true.

See, she thought, it's even easier to convince myself of things than it used to be.

Not knowing quite what it all meant, she smiled broadly as she watched Chad exert Herculean effort to scrub the quarter-inch sheet of mystery residue off their sticky kitchen countertops.

Poor man's gonna need a chisel.

She sighed happily, snuggling into the couch cushions. She closed her eyes and let sleep take her.

Something within her bones knitted together even more tightly, pulling knots taut. Radiated heat hung around her, cocooning her like a blanket.

Retaining Counsel

After Minerva booked the appointment to see the lawyer – or "ambulance chaser" as Chad called him, smirking with such pride that you would think it were actually an original joke he'd come up with himself and not a regurgitated cliché – she had immediately regretted it.

It was far too easy to schedule a consult with the attorney, and she thought this was a terrible sign indeed. Either this lawyer had a hard time getting clients, which pointed at incompetence, or he saw very few and managed to make a good living regardless, which pointed at overpriced services.

She was leaning heavily towards the latter when she showed up at his office and found it to be well appointed and the receptionist, professional.

This is going to cost me an arm and a leg, she thought idly. *I'll need a second personal injury lawyer to go after the one I have once he's done with me.*

It wasn't funny, but she was nervous, and so she laughed aloud at her own thoughts.

The receptionist's eyes raised from whatever she'd been working on. Her expression was smooth and placid, and yet Minerva couldn't help but feel scolded simply by her gaze. It was as though she were being silently reprimanded by her high school librarian.

Mrs. Cohen. The name leapt into her mind forcefully. Cohen the Librarian. At the time, it was peak humor, calling her Cohen the Librarian. While she bore little physical resemblance to Conan the barbarian, there was something just as intimidating about her. She had a bearing that demanded respect. Mrs. Cohen was the type of woman who seemed to have been born a matron. A person cannot be that forbidding and stern without a lifetime of practice.

The receptionist rose from her desk. "Mr. Delvecchio will see you now," she said to Minerva, leading her down a hallway with several offices in it, each marked with a hanging plaque announcing its inhabitant.

She stopped two doors short of the end. "Your six o'clock is here, Mr. Delvecchio," she called around the door to a person who wasn't visible from where Minerva stood.

Whoever sat inside said nothing. The receptionist nodded at Minerva and pushed past her into the hallway, returning to her desk.

Minerva sighed and stepped into the office uncertainly.

Minerva had seen many people in her life who looked perfectly uncomfortable being an adult, even as they did their best to play the part.

Darren Delvecchio, attorney-at-law, was the latest addition to this long string of people who seem to have aged up by default rather than any conscious exertion of will.

True, he was arguably the most handsome example she'd seen. Clean cut, sharply dressed in what appeared to be very expensive clothes. He was, however, clearly quite uncomfortable in them. They were on his body and approximately the right size, but as he moved in them, it looked as though his clothes belonged to someone else.

Something was wrong with his face, too, Minerva realized. Something subtle that was easy to detect but hard to pinpoint. While he had a strong jaw and forehead, his other features were conspicuously boyish, as though he'd never quite grown into his face.

He looked less like a grown man and more like a little boy who had stepped into his father's shoes, perhaps quite literally.

His office, too, seemed a strange fit for him. It was a nice enough room, but it seemed like it was more likely to belong to someone else. The décor was quite modern, she noted, but rather self-consciously modern. It was like the designer had been trying to conform to an unknown rubric, racking up points for each hip motif ventured, instead of trying to create something visually pleasing or an environment that was good for a human being to work in.

"Ms. Cantor, it's so nice to see you up and about again. Please have a seat," Delvecchio said in a refined voice that reminded Minerva of the Mid Atlantic accent that actors spoke with in old movies.

Minerva sat down. "Up and about *again*?" she asked.

"Hmm?" Delvecchio said.

"Well, I heard you visited my hospital room, but..." A waft of the lawyer's aftershave hit her, spirited her way via the magic of office HVAC, no doubt. The fragrance reminded her of a cologne that a high school boyfriend had worn. She struggled to finish her thought.

Thankfully, Delvecchio, like most lawyers, was more than happy to finish her thoughts for her. "But you're wondering if our paths have crossed before?" he asked.

As he said this, his eyes twinkled. *How peculiar,* Minerva thought. *I always thought that was just a silly expression. That stars twinkled and eyes never did. Well, you learn something new every day.*

"The answer to that question," Delvecchio continued, "is yes. I've seen you walking around this area. Your boyfriend—"

"He's not my boyfriend," Minerva said quickly. She wasn't sure why she wanted to be so clear about that, but she felt comfortable in her denial, knowing that Chad wasn't a big fan of the B word anyway.

"Well, your guy friend." Delvecchio began again. "Your guy friend told me you worked across the street in 3519."

Minerva nodded. "I did. At a marketing firm."

"Ah, isn't that lovely?" Delvecchio said. "A fellow liar."

Minerva cocked her head. "What do you mean by that?"

Delvecchio chuckled. "Surely, in your line of work, you must get that from time to time. Marketers aren't renowned for their candor."

Minerva scowled. "Well, no, we aren't. But I resent the implication that I'm a liar."

"I don't see why," Delvecchio replied. "Anyway, coming from a fellow liar, it's a compliment. You do know what they say about lawyers, after all."

"Of course," Minerva said. "People in your profession are also known to finesse the truth."

Delvecchio smiled. "I like that. Sometimes I hear people talk about massaging the truth. That's a little more sensual than I like to go with it. Marketing can involve sex, but it's not exactly sexy, is it? Same with law, really."

Minerva didn't respond. She wasn't sure exactly where he was going with this. Even hearing him say the word "sex" did something to her. Her mind was starting to wander, but she didn't want to get her hopes up. She had Chad's blessing to see other people, but the notion still seemed strange to her. Plus, Delvecchio was a hotshot lawyer with a fancy office – solidly out of her league, not someone who would be into *her*, a recently fired marketing executive in a newly open relationship.

"Anyway, that's the thing people don't understand. Well, people who aren't liars. People who are different than you and me, Minerva. To finesse the truth, or even *massage* it," he said letting his eyes flash in a way that again stirred something in her, "you have to first locate the truth. You must deeply understand the truth in order to grab it and effectively stretch it. You and I, and every other so-called liar out there, are more acquainted with the truth than all these self-professed honest people ever will be."

He smiled. "If you ask me," he said, "I'd trust a liar over one of those 'I'm an open book' people any day of the week."

He leaned backwards in his office chair. "I know you didn't ask me though."

"No, I didn't ask you," Minerva replied. "And I imagine you don't get too many clients with an opening speech like that. It's hardly professional, this form of getting-to-know-you talk."

"I do pretty well," the lawyer responded. "I wouldn't last in a place like this if I didn't."

Minerva considered this. He had a point.

"I don't talk like this to all of my clients. I have a standard spiel that's so comfortable for me that I find myself reciting it in my sleep," he said. "But honestly, Minerva, there's something different about you. I just met you... and I couldn't lie to you. And I don't know why. Because... well, to completely level with you, lying is how I got here in the first place. Every major success I've had has been born of a lie. That's the way it is with most people. It's just that some of them are better at pretending that it's the truth than others. They buy into their own bullshit."

He pulled open a drawer in his desk. Handed her a flask. "Want some?"

Minerva laughed. "Do I really look like I'm in that rough of a shape?"

Delvecchio considered this. "Yeah, you do."

Minerva frowned.

"I mean… you look great. You're beautiful, you know. But it's like something else in you got really damaged. Probably long before the accident," he said.

"You're weird," Minerva said.

"I know," he replied. "You're weird, too. That's why I like you."

Minerva's cheeks flushed at the words *I like you.*

Get a grip on yourself, you're not in middle school. That doesn't mean what you think it means, she scolded herself mentally.

"Tell you what," Minerva replied aloud. "You put that flask away, and let's go grab a drink and talk somewhere else."

The lawyer smiled. "I'd like that," he said. "My treat."

"Okay," Minerva replied. "Just don't go billing it to the client. Can't get me to pick up the tab that way. I'll ask for a breakdown. I'll notice."

He laughed.

She noted with great amusement as they walked to his space in the office parking garage that he drove a red sportscar. Because of course he did. It was another example of something flashy and expensive he thought he should own. The red sportscar was part of his expected costume, not something that truly suited him. It was his father's shoes yet again.

Delvecchio drove her to a bar with amber lights that washed over everything in a soft, flattering way. Sitting under them, he reminded Minerva of how people looked in old photographs, the ones that flowed out of her mother's hope chest with strange names and dates scrawled on the back. Those photographs were always of people who had been dead for ages, who had no one left to mourn them, no one left who would even know who they were, let alone have strong feelings about them. Looking over those photographs always made Minerva desperate to live, really live.

After finishing an old fashioned and a few sips of a second, Minerva felt herself opening up emotionally. Telling him about everything that had led her up to her sudden firing at work. How it had felt to be hit by that truck, in the split-second before she lost consciousness.

What her home life was like. How she felt like the accident had changed her, that she was different now somehow. How she didn't know what she was going to do next to survive, with her job gone and a sense that she had now changed forever, in ways that escaped her.

He outlined a legal strategy for her in the broadest possible terms on a cocktail napkin.

"I thought people only did that in movies," Minerva commented as he began to write it out, fighting the ridges of the pattern imprinted on the napkin that grabbed at his pen.

"That's the funny thing about movies," Delvecchio replied. "People watch them and start to think that's how people actually are. Then before you know it, people are doing things that only happen in movies out there in real life."

Minerva laughed.

"Filmmakers are fellow liars," he added, as he sketched out his plan, "and they're so good at it that the lies they tell eventually become the truth."

"Are they even liars anymore then?" Minerva replied.

He thought about that for a moment, before changing the subject.

"The truck that hit you was a commercial delivery vehicle," Delvecchio explained. "Lucky for you, it's part of a fleet, and a large one, a chain that supplies grocery stores all over the country."

"Why is that lucky?" Minerva asked.

"They have big pockets. And they have lots to lose. You'll likely get a big settlement, no questions asked. I imagine we won't even have to go to court," Delvecchio said.

Minerva felt a wave of relief. Amazingly good news.

"I was thinking, too, after speaking with you about your former workplace, that you might have a case there, too," he continued.

"What kind of case?"

"Wrongful termination. Discrimination. We have a lot of possibilities here," Delvecchio said.

"You think?" Minerva said.

He nodded. "I do. Especially if you have proof that you were an exemplary employee. Proof of discrimination. Anything at all like that."

Minerva thought for a moment. "Yeah. Truth be told, I was a bit of a packrat. I'm glad I came to see you now before Chad got to my records and threw them out. He's been on a huge cleaning kick."

"Chad?" Delvecchio said.

"My not-boyfriend," Minerva said.

He smiled. "That's funny," he said.

"What is?"

"I didn't take him for the neatnik type," Delvecchio said. "If anything, I'd have pegged him for a frat boy who makes a mess and never cleans up after himself."

Minerva laughed. "He used to be that way," she said. "But lately, he's cleaned up his act. Figuratively and literally."

"Huh," he said. "That's not something you see every day."

Minerva had to agree. "No, it's really not."

Delvecchio grinned.

"Anyway, if you want, we can head back to my place after this drink, and I'll show you what I have for evidence," Minerva said.

"Ooooo, is that a 'how about we go back to my place?' Be still my beating heart," Delvecchio flirted.

Minerva blushed. "For evidence," she said, but she was having trouble keeping her composure.

He'd started out their meeting handsome. Under the amber lights and with a little whiskey in her system, she was overwhelmed by him – in the best possible way.

"For evidence," he replied cheekily, raising his glass.

Minerva raised hers in response, and they clinked their glasses together.

When they got back to her apartment, she noted that Chad was nowhere to be found. Probably out with the boys. Good timing, that.

Minerva only made it about halfway to where she kept the evidence, before Delvecchio pulled her to him with strength that surprised her, and they melted into a kiss.

Minerva felt a reflexive pang of guilt. All this time with Chad, she'd never done anything like this.

But it felt so good to kiss Darren Delvecchio. Her body ached. The way Delvecchio kissed her, the way that he touched her, it made her burn all over.

The throbbing she'd felt before in her crossed fingers had spread throughout her entire body.

Oh, what the hell, Minerva thought, as the lawyer's hands tugged at her shirt. *Viva la open relationship!*

Someplace You've Never Been

"So," Delvecchio said later, as he lay wrapped in her blankets, looking awfully comfortable – and even natural – there. "What's your story?"

"What do you mean, my story?" Minerva asked. She scowled.

"Everyone's got a story," Delvecchio said.

"Not me," Minerva said. "What you see is what you get."

"Oh sure," Delvecchio said. "You sprang fully formed from the head of Zeus, for realsies."

"You're familiar with the myth then?" Minerva asked.

"Of course," Delvecchio replied.

He'd gotten it mostly right, she observed. Jupiter was the Roman name for Zeus. Zeus was the Greek version. He should have said Jupiter, since Minerva was the Roman name, and Athena was the Greek. But he was awfully close. Closer than most people ever got.

He got the important part right, the general gist of the myth. According to the Romans, the goddess Minerva wasn't born in a traditional way. Instead, she'd jumped out from the head of Jupiter as a grown woman, clothed in full plate armor. And apparently ready for a fight.

"I imagine your parents wanted you to be independent, naming you like that," Delvecchio said.

"Nah," Minerva replied. "Not at all. Not even a little."

"Where'd you get your name then?" Delvecchio said.

"I was named after the nurse who delivered me," Minerva replied. "Mom liked the way the name sounded. She'd never heard it before. And they'd been expecting a boy, so they didn't have one thought up for me."

"Glance at a nametag in the hospital and get a great idea?" Delvecchio said.

"Something like that," Minerva said. "I don't really know."

"You never asked?" Delvecchio said.

Minerva nodded. "People don't really ask followup questions where I'm from."

"Which is?" Delvecchio said.

"Someplace you've never been," Minerva replied.

"I dunno. I get around," Delvecchio said.

"Apparently," Minerva replied. "With moves like that, I figured you're not a virgin."

He smirked. "That's not what I meant."

"I know."

"I've traveled a lot. You'd be surprised where I've been," Delvecchio said.

Minerva smiled. "I just don't like to talk about it, is all."

"Clearly," Delvecchio said.

"There's not much to talk about. Because there's not much there anymore. Not that there ever was. I grew up in one of those places where there's a lot more land than there are people. And even fewer jobs. To be honest, I barely know where it is anymore. I mean, don't get me wrong... I know. I can point to it on a map. But I haven't been home – if you could call it home – for so long, I probably wouldn't even recognize it anymore," Minerva said.

"I always thought those places don't change much," Delvecchio said.

"Oh, they don't," Minerva said. "Not much and not quickly. There are little things of course. The store that used to be called one thing is called another. The only mall for hundreds of miles went bankrupt. For the most part, it *should* look the same. But the problem is that it doesn't. And that's not because my hometown changed, it's because I did."

"Maybe we could go there together sometime," Delvecchio said.

"To my hometown?" Minerva said. "Don't be crazy."

"I dunno. You could bring me home. Hotshot big city lawyer. Show me off to Mom and Dad." He waggled his eyebrows for emphasis.

Minerva hit him with a pillow. "You wish."

"Parade me around like a prize you won. A conquered captive. The great warrior goddess coming home with a spoil of war."

"Oh please," she said, rolling her eyes.

"And why not?" he said. "I have an advanced degree. A bank account that means I don't want for anything. And all my teeth. So there's that."

"All your teeth?" Minerva said, her voice turning flirtatious.

"All of them," Delvecchio said. "Every last one of them."

Minerva laughed. "You know, Darren," she said. "You're kind of a weird guy. But despite myself, I'm starting to like you."

"I've got you in my clutches now," he said.

She pushed him flat on his back and climbed on top of him. She didn't mean for the gesture to be sexual at first; they were both giggling like maniacs. Instead, it felt like playground bullying, pinning a kid to the pavement in order to prove dominance or extract lunch money from their pockets.

But as she felt his body underneath hers, its rises and contours, she grew aroused, and before she knew it, their bodies had melted together once again.

Afterwards, he fell immediately asleep, spent.

Two times in a single night, Minerva mused, as she listened to the sound of his breath. *It's been an awfully long time since that's happened with anyone.*

She tried to sleep herself, but her mind obstinately refused to turn off.

What is *my story?* She found herself wondering as she lay there next to him in the dark. She didn't think of big questions like that all that often these days, but being questioned by him brought the painful half-forgotten truth to light.

She thought back to her hometown with its one stoplight and trickle of very familiar-looking judgmental strangers. People who had known her since she was in diapers and accordingly still pictured her in them, even as she grew up lithe and beautiful, albeit a bit wicked for their tastes.

A bit too sensual.

A libertine in blue jeans. Flocked by hungry boys, ready to feast upon the lifeforce she emanated without even meaning to.

There were so many of them, so many boys ready to sneak off into an overgrown field or the woods. Ready to grope and kiss.

Ready to unzip their pants.

And each one who mingled with her in woods and fields found Minerva to be quite unusual for a single reason: She actually *liked* these trysts. It was clear in those moments that making out wasn't an act she endured in order to get a bit of attention. A burden she accepted was the price of popularity, of fitting in. Minerva wasn't going to lie there impassively, seeming bored, while her lover grunted and writhed on top of her.

And she didn't need to be convinced to go further, like some other girls these young men had approached. In fact, Minerva often initiated. She enjoyed every minute of it, whatever happened. It felt good, all the clumsy fumbling, the panting.

It felt good enough that she sometimes worried she'd lose her mind because of it. Even when she was a teenager and her lovers were clumsy and selfish, sex was a magical experience. There were moments when she was making out with boys that something primal rose up within her and howled through her entire body at such a velocity and with such a volume that she felt like she knew why she'd been put on this earth.

And when she started sneaking off to the fields and forests with other girls, well, it just got even worse. Women were somehow even more sensual, the act of mingling with them even more sumptuous. Their skin was soft, their bodies pristine and curvy.

Women smelled so damn good.

And even better, she was able to awaken something inside of other women that they normally feared. Not just the same sex desires – although that was certainly a surprise for many of her first female lovers – but a fearless enjoyment of sex.

She never knew exactly why she thrilled other women so much. But Minerva suspected it was because she was more attentive and skilled than the boys who had gratified themselves quickly and without much care or concern for a woman's pleasure.

And she was also an unwitting role model of sorts to her first lovers, young women who clearly didn't let themselves enjoy carnal delights. Most of the women she was close to as a teenager not only had never seen a model of healthy female sexuality; they were also told by adults that such women didn't exist.

Their mothers had told them that a woman who enjoyed herself was faking. That sex outside of marriage and procreation was a form of disrespectful violence that could only lead to ruin.

They told their daughters that sexual pleasure was only for men. A woman endured sex in order to have a bountiful home and family life. There was nothing selfishly gratifying in the act of sex for a woman. She was told that sex was a toll to be paid by women so they could arrive at other desired destinations, the ones they actually wanted to visit, not an important destination itself.

Minerva stood out starkly as an exception to these lessons. To her sex was truth and beauty and light. With a mature lover, one who was secure in their own self, it could also be free of disrespect. It didn't have to be about shame. And with time and patience, she was able to bring her lovers through their shame and into the light with her.

But that was a tough sell where she grew up. That was something people only believed in short bursts, if at all. The lessons she taught her lovers didn't stick as they were swiftly contradicted by everyone other than Minerva. So she found herself largely inhabiting a different reality than everyone else around her. Living a different truth.

She'd left there the first chance she got, Someplace You've Never Been. She had turned her back on the empty landscape and hadn't glanced back even once.

Now, she hadn't exactly vanished. Mom and Dad knew her number, after all. Mom had even called at first. A lot.

But Minerva had done her best to let the answering machine get it, to take her time calling her mother back, to stretch out the times between whenever they spoke, and somewhere along the way, her mom had basically stopped calling.

Maybe she was tired of talking to the answering machine.

Maybe something had happened to her.

Minerva had never checked.

The same with old friends. A few of *them* had even stopped by, taken a bus to check out the Big City. But Minerva had been an unenthusiastic host. Most times she didn't even take any time off work, let alone play tour guide.

Her old friends spent most of their visits bewildered, staring out the window of her apartment, carless, not sure where to go, let alone how to get there.

Those visits, too, predictably were spread further and further apart.

And then one day Minerva woke up and realized she was all alone in the Big City. That she'd bored and evaded others into complete social independence. She was now on her own in Skinner-Watson, a sprawling metroplex the size of a small state.

She had no ties to anything, anyone before she'd gotten here, she realized suddenly.

"I got no strings to hold me down," she mused playfully.

Perhaps she should have felt lonely, more afraid. Perhaps it should have felt more like she was an acrobat flying above a circus floor without a net and that one fall could mean the end of her.

But Minerva's first impression – and the one that stuck – was that she was free. Really, truly free for the first time in her life.

She was a grown woman no longer plagued by her infamy as a small town legend. "The village bicycle." A fount of wasted intelligence. A disappointment. All those old allegations so easily thrown her way back in Someplace You've Never Heard Of.

No, in the Big City, in Skinner-Watson, she was invisible.

In many ways, the whole shift felt like a second birth. A cleaner, more resolute one. One where she was in control.

Maybe her name wasn't such a bad fit, after all. Just like her namesake had sprung fully formed from Jupiter's mouth, Minerva came into her new life able to shape her own destiny.

It was in the Big City that Minerva felt she could finally tell the truth. While a lot of people think of country folk as being more honest, it was in fact growing up in the country that had forced her countless times to lie.

In the country, she hadn't had a lot of freedom. And certainly not a lot of power.

If she wanted things to be different, her only option was to pretend that they were. Sometimes she did that privately, in acceptable vessels. When she was a little girl, she'd write adventure stories in spiralbound notebooks. Ones where it was possible for her heroine to violate the laws of physics – and everyone around the heroine was wise, worthy, and fascinating.

She wrote stories in which people were generally brave, intelligent, and impressive.

Lies, all of it lies.

But comforting ones. Colorful ones. Aspirational reaches towards a world that she hoped desperately would someday be true.

Writing those stories helped her cope with the world around her, which was topographically and demographically often quite flat, featureless, and unimaginative.

She could escape from the blandness and judgement into the vivid refuge of her imagination.

She wasn't quite sure exactly when it happened, but as the years went on, the stories weren't enough anymore. They were colorful enough, but at the end of the day, they were two-dimensional, divorced from reality.

She needed to bring that magic into the real world somehow, that color.

And before she knew it, she heard herself lying to other people in real life.

Lying had been an easy habit to fall into. When you're bisexual, people are always telling you that you're a liar. They tell you that what you are doesn't exist. They say you're making it up, trying to be something you're not, so you learn to lie to them about it, deny what you are, and in doing so, you become the thing they're accusing you of being: A liar.

The lies were small at first. Things that would be easily believed and hard to contradict. Lies that were of no consequence.

She told a teacher she'd eaten cereal for breakfast when she'd had eggs.

And then she told someone her favorite color was purple when in fact she hated it.

As she heard herself telling those first lies, she could hardly believe she was doing it. She knew it was wrong to do so. Her heart rate sped up as stress chemicals hit her bloodstream.

She felt sick to her stomach. Afraid.

And yet, it was a rush. Particularly as people believed her. And nothing bad happened.

Lies took the place that more proper fiction had, and she felt better.

At first anyway.

As time went on, the little lies weren't doing it anymore. So she upped the ante. She destroyed her cousin's toys and blamed it on someone else.

Told her parents that she'd done her homework when she hadn't – and didn't plan on ever doing it.

Ate ingredients her mother had set aside to cook dinner and denied any involvement when asked.

She was a good liar and did a pretty good job not getting caught in the short term.

Eventually, though, it would become clear that she hadn't told the truth. Witnesses would emerge that contradicted her version of things. Witnesses she hadn't accounted for.

Her homework was never done. Eventually, her report card came in.

Not only that, but she simply started to do it too much. She told a few too many lies. And the sheer quantity all by itself was too much.

The people around her stopped believing her, even before the evidence of her deception had time to catch up to her.

No matter, Minerva resolved. Perhaps she should have taken this as a sign to stop lying, but she didn't. Instead, she found fresh trust to break. She made new friends. Met new people. And cooked up even larger lies to tell them.

She told them her mother wasn't her real mother. Instead, she said, she was a love child from an affair that her father had had with her mother's sister, a brilliant woman with a drug problem who lived out of state.

Her "mother," she said, was in fact her aunt. But it was a well-guarded family secret, her parentage. Her parents had worked hard to reconcile, so because the affair had been deeply hurtful – and particularly because it had happened with a family member—they did their best to minimize the shame, the public damage. And the way they did this was by lying about what really happened.

Even if it meant she never got a chance to really know her real mother.

She told them that she'd had a different name when she was born. Morganna. Witchy and romantic.

But she'd been renamed Minerva when she'd been taken in and assimilated by the family, who all the while acted as though nothing was amiss.

They had their reputations to consider, you see.

None of her new friends batted an eyelash. Perhaps they'd been watching too many soap operas. Or perhaps she was just *that* good at lying.

Or perhaps, Minerva had found herself thinking on more than one occasion, *people trust you until you give them a reason not to.*

It might have been fine if that were the last big lie she ever told in her life. But it wasn't.

Minerva felt herself spinning out of control. What had started as simple embroidery around the edges of her actual life turned into a complete rewriting of herself, her history, her entire makeup.

She told others she hadn't always lived in the middle of nowhere. Her life had once been amazing, colorful, accomplished. She'd moved from state to state when she was much younger, before things had changed with her father's job, and she and the rest of the family had been forced to put down roots.

This was all a phase and probably a short one, living in the most flyover state she could think of.

She was a prodigy. She'd won awards. A special girl.

Her true mother would be back for her. It was only a matter of time.

She wasn't wrong about everything. Not everything she said was a lie. She was a very special girl; she just didn't realize it. And she was destined for an interesting and unique life, although it would turn out nothing like she ever planned.

That part felt like a lie but was actually true.

Minerva knew that "thou shalt not lie" wasn't one of the Ten Commandments, but everyone acted like it should be. There *was* a dishonesty-related Commandment: "Thou shalt not bear false witness against thy neighbor," but that had to do more with perjury. Regardless, lay people didn't seem to make much of a distinction: A lie was a lie was a lie, whether it was told in a casual setting – or whether it was all dressed up in trial day digs.

Lying was a sin, regardless of context, the adults around her told her – again and again. And yet, their actions painted a different picture. She found that she was just as easily punished for speaking an inconvenient truth in the wrong context as she was for telling a minor falsehood.

There were times when she told the right lies – the face-saving ones for powerful people – that she was even rewarded.

Besides, her tendency to stretch the truth wasn't born out of some grand moral failing. If things had only been slightly different, she probably would never have started lying in the first place.

Minerva was like a lot of other bright kids who grew up in Podunk towns, ambitious but trapped, and like those other kids, she coped with it any way that she could. She told herself – and everyone around her – lies until she could escape. Lies that brought a brighter richer world to life, even if it wasn't solid, even if it wasn't really there, and even if it dissipated the moment that someone else challenged her.

The moment she could leave, she left.

Sometimes even now there were moments when she'd realize she still had some persistent strands of hick clinging stubbornly to her ribs. Moments when she'd realize that she'd burst through ceilings she was told didn't exist by everyone who wanted to be safe no matter the opportunity cost and gave up on intelligent risks.

At times like those, her bones thrummed with it. It was a better feeling than drugs, being right about taking the risks that others wouldn't.

The lying, sure. But also leaving the very first moment that she could get out of there.

As she watched Darren pull away from the curb in front of her apartment building in his sleek black sportscar after their night together, she felt a pang of regret. She had meant to tell Darren the complete truth. It would be a first, being completely honest with a lover. Over the years, she had tried so many times to be truthful, but there would inevitably be a moment when fear would creep in and answer questions for her. And those answers that fear provided were far from the truth.

She had felt at first that this time would be different. That she would be able to speak the plain and honest truth – despite all of Darren's fantastical talk celebrating liars and lying.

But it hadn't turned out that way, had it? She had found herself telling little white lies, feeling foolish as the first two fingers on her right hand curled up like a snake trying to keep itself warm in marginal weather.

Each time she had lied, they pulsed, a pulse which felt good… if unsettling.

It turned out that Darren wasn't one of those guys who waited three days to call you. The phone rang the very next day.

"Hey kiddo, you got a minute?" Darren said when Minerva picked up.

"For you?" Minerva said. "I have more than a minute. What's up?"

"Well," Darren said and hesitated. That was unlike him. The Darren she knew was confident, flippant. A little smug, even. This guy had doubts. Oh boy.

"I had a look over all the evidence you gave me back at your place," Darren said, "and I'm sorry, Minerva, but... I don't think you have a wrongful termination case."

"What do you mean I don't have a case?" Minerva snapped.

"I looked over the correspondence you printed out. Paid special attention to your notes, and Minerva, even giving you the benefit of several doubts, I just don't see discrimination here. And neither will a judge."

Minerva rolled her eyes. "But I *was* discriminated against!"

"I believe you," Darren said. "There's no proof of it, that's all. Nothing that would convince a judge. It'd be a waste of time for us to pursue a case like that."

"Okay," Minerva said, frustrated, "so discrimination is off the table. But I was clearly an exemplary employee. That much is obvious from the performance reviews I sent you, right?"

"No, Minerva," Darren said. "I mean... maybe you were..."

"Maybe?" Minerva said, her tone rising.

"I mean, you probably were," Darren corrected himself, sensing he was in great social peril, "but the documentation you provided me paints a different picture."

"How do you figure?"

"Your performance reviews were marginal. You were on a performance improvement plan for years. Your attendance record was deplorable," Darren said.

"You take that back!"

Darren swallowed hard. "I'm not saying that's what I believe, Minerva. I'm just saying that's what the evidence shows. And that it's what a judge would see."

Minerva frowned. "Alright, fine," she said in a tone that underscored that it was not fine at all. "I think that's bullshit, but I guess my opinion doesn't matter."

Darren wisely did not say anything.

"What does it mean, Darren? Where do we go from here?" Minerva prompted him.

"Well, that's the good news. The trucking company agreed to the settlement. And it's a huge number." He told Minerva the figure.

She had to brace herself to keep from passing out. It was an enormous sum. More than she'd ever need.

"So it doesn't really matter, Minerva. You don't need the other case. You're set for life," Darren said.

"Well, I was a good employee," Minerva insisted.

"I believe you," Darren said.

"Good," Minerva replied. But it didn't feel good to her. Nor did it feel good when Darren invited himself over to her place to celebrate her good fortune. She said yes and did her best to enjoy the evening, but while being with Darren felt right, something else felt terribly wrong.

She tried to push the foreboding out of her head and focus on the positive turn her life seemed to be taking, for in the days following the accident she realized she was even freer than before, than when she'd first landed in the big city.

Now she wasn't even chained down by her job. She had something she had never thought possible – financial freedom.

Perhaps I'll write, she thought. Follow that childhood passion of hers to tell stories.

She sat for days in the fancy new ergonomic chair paid for by the settlement with the trucking company, a settlement that comfortably padded her bank account and took care of her basic bills in perpetuity.

But the words never came.

On the other hand, all that gazing out the window and waiting for inspiration to strike afforded her an opportunity to make another new acquaintance – and through that acquaintance, she would make many more.

Max Meteo and Skinner Makes

Later, looking back, Minerva would have an awfully hard time pinpointing the exact moment she first met Max Meteo. She ran into him so many times over and over again. Not surprising since he lived in the apartment downstairs, and she had been spending hours gazing out her window desperately trying to think of something to write.

And frankly, Max seemed to have an awful lot of free time himself for an adult who could afford to live on his own.

Because as best as Minerva could tell, Max had no roommate. And he didn't seem to work a normal nine to five. She never saw him dressed up and leaving for work at the normal times. Instead, he spent a lot of time in his apartment, occasionally drifting outside to the park or the coffeeshop.

Max was a short man with a solid rectangular build. He had shoulder length strawberry blond hair and green eyes.

The most striking thing about Max Meteo was that he was always smiling. Always. And in a way that didn't seem forced.

"Do you think that guy's on drugs?" Chad had asked her.

"What makes you say that?" Minerva had replied.

"No one's that happy without a little help," Chad said.

"I dunno," Minerva had said. "He takes awfully good care of his hair."

"What's that have to do with anything?" Chad had asked.

"I've never known a long-haired guy on a ton of drugs whose hair wasn't a disaster," Minerva had said.

"How many long-haired guys on drugs have you known?" Chad had asked.

Minerva hadn't answered that. She wasn't in the mood to enlighten Chad about the parade of snarly-maned stoner Jesuses she'd met over the years before they'd gotten together.

Instead, she kept running into Max and wondering about him.

She couldn't recall the first time they'd crossed paths. Nor could she recall the first time she realized he lived downstairs.

But she'd remember the day she met him properly for a very long time.

"What kind of café runs out of *coffee*?" Minerva asked.

The barista shrugged helplessly.

"Hey, it's no big deal," a man's voice said from behind her.

Minerva spun around to face her long-haired neighbor. "What do you mean it's no big deal?"

"It's just a miscalculation, running out of something. Shipping logistics are complicated. Someone must have made a mistake somewhere. Forgot to carry a one or something. For all you know, there's a big rig lying on its side in Omaha that's full of coffee beans," he said.

"I don't see your point," Minerva said.

"It's not a moral failing to run out of coffee. Even for a coffeeshop," he said.

"I didn't say it was. That's not what I meant," Minerva protested. She knew she was just disappointed and suffering from caffeine withdrawal. It wasn't like she was yelling at the barista or being super rude. She was just annoyed at the situation. Who was this guy to lecture her on trucking routes of all things?

"Do you want anything else?" the cashier asked.

"No," Minerva said. But in her guilt, she shoved a five-dollar bill into the tip jar as she spun around and headed for the exit.

He pursued her. "Hey, I didn't mean anything," he said.

"Whatever," Minerva replied.

"No, really," he said. "I'm sorry if it came off as a lecture. My grandma says I do that a lot. That I'm a born lecturer." He screwed up his face and said in a higher, quavering voice, "Max Meteo, who died and made you head professor? The only BS you ever got was in bullshit."

Minerva laughed in spite of herself. "Nice to meet you, Max Meteo," she said, extending her hand.

"Ooh fancy, fancy, we're a couple of businesspeople," Max said. He shook her hand. "Nice to meet you..."

"Minerva Cantor," she offered.

"You have nice hands, Minerva," Max said. "Wait... Minerva, like the goddess?"

"She's named after me, actually," Minerva said. It was an old joke, one she'd told thousands of times, so she had stopped finding it funny a long time ago. Max laughed at it though because it was the first time he'd heard it.

"You know... If you need caffeine, I have an espresso machine at my place."

"Is it that obvious?" Minerva asked.

"Written all over your face," Max said. "Please send caffeine." He paused, before adding, "Seriously, come get some coffee. I swear it's not a come-on. Just one neighbor helping another."

"Well..." Minerva said.

"Think of that poor trucker who went off the road in Iowa," Max said.

"I thought it was in Omaha," Minerva replied.

"You got me," Max said, still smiling.

"Okay," Minerva said.

They walked to their apartment building. Minerva noted that his place had an identical layout to her own, although he'd put his couch in a different location, which made all the difference as far as living room flow.

His walls were also conspicuously bare. He hadn't made any effort to decorate.

He'd been telling the truth about the espresso machine though. It was a monstrous appliance, completely dominating the kitchen counter.

"Wow," Minerva said.

"Nice, huh?" Max asked.

She nodded. "It does kind of make me wonder why someone with a machine like this would bother going to the coffeeshop as often as you do."

"Ah," he said, as he began to make their drinks, "I work at home. If I didn't make excuses to go outside, I never would."

"That doesn't sound so bad," Minerva said.

"Not at first," Max replied. "But you do get a little crazy. You turn into one of those House People."

"House People?" Minerva asked.

"Oh, I'm sure you've seen them," Max said. "Those folks who don't know how to function in public anymore. Who have lost all their people skills. House People."

She nodded.

The coffee was delicious. She sat with him at his small kitchen table as they drank it. Outside the open window, a bird sang.

"What kind of last name is Meteo anyway?" Minerva asked.

"I take it you haven't played *Final Fantasy II*," Max replied.

Minerva stared at him blankly. "Is that one of those dirty board games for couples?"

Max's normal smile cracked into a deeper one, like sunlight drying a patch of mud. "No," he said. "It's on Super Nintendo."

"Ah," Minerva said. "Video games."

"But of course," Max said. "I take it you haven't played much."

Minerva shook her head. "I always thought they seemed interesting, but my parents said they'd rot my brain. And my money was always somewhere else, spoken for."

"Well, today's your lucky day then," Max said.

He led her into the bedroom, sat down on the bed, patted the space next to him. Minerva sat down tentatively.

He turned on the game system. Minerva watched as the title screen came up. *FINAL FANTASY II*. The T in the title was a sword. The opening theme began to play as a series of harp arpeggios. Then the orchestra came in on top of it, blasting powerful chords, the voicings shining over the arpeggios.

"It's beautiful," she said.

Max nodded. He began a new game, and she watched rapt as the plot unfolded.

They stayed up all night playing and well into the next day. There was a save function, so they didn't have to pull this marathon. But Minerva had a hard time stopping. She wanted to see the ending. She wanted to know what would happen to the characters. And if they'd be able to save the world.

Max was happy to indulge her.

She brewed them Americanos in the wee hours of the morning, wearing one of his old shirts, happy to slink out of her bra and get comfortable.

Max's face ached from smiling. He'd never dated a woman who didn't gripe at him about his video game playing. And now here was one chilling in his apartment who was eager to get through a game.

Not that they were dating, but she was wearing his shirt. And that was a promising start.

They took turns over the 20 hours it took for them to beat the game, swapping when one of them needed to go to the bathroom. Whoever wasn't playing cooked food, brought in drinks.

It was fluid and continuous.

And when the game was done, Minerva set down the controller and smiled at Max. With one hand, she pushed him back onto the pillows and climbed on top of him.

Skinner Makes was at the bottom of a particularly harrowing hill. The building was a dingy gray and not quite rectangular, reminding Minerva of a refrigerator she'd seen at the scratch and dent appliance shop. On all four sides of its parking lot, the building was flanked by an intricate latticework of railroad tracks.

This meant that getting there on time was tricky. Invariably, you would land there too early or late. Never exactly when you intended to show up.

The trains did what the trains did. Trying to figure it out ahead of time was akin to solving one of those needlessly complex word problems: "If the train to Bosque leaves at 8:05 going 70 miles an hour, and the train from Partridge leaves at 9:10 going 55 miles an hour, when will they pass each other?"

Minerva had gotten quite enough of that in school, so she and Max did as he'd suggested: They always left early, planning for a worst-case scenario in which they would get stuck behind every single possible train. After all, it did happen sometimes.

Typically, this meant they had some time to kill, which was more than alright with Minerva. Max was a fantastic conversationalist.

"Welcome to geek church," he'd said expansively the first time they'd walked through the doors.

A short man bent over a jewelry station raised his head and nodded at Max in recognition. As they exchanged pleasantries, Minerva noted that this jeweler had a deep cowboy drawl. This was not at all what she'd expected him to sound like before he opened his mouth. Nothing about him screamed cowboy. He wasn't wearing a 10-gallon hat or rawhide boots. Instead he had on a black T-shirt with a Dungeons & Dragons logo and a pair of rumpled jeans that were so long that they covered his shoes and looked as though he'd probably walk on the cuffs if he didn't try hard not to.

Do all cowboys ride horses? Minerva found herself thinking. *Or do some of them ride dragons?*

"You'll see lots of different types of people at geek church," Max said to her.

Minerva laughed, but she'd later think that he had a point. "Oh, geek church? Who's the geek pastor then?"

"Depends on what the sermon is," he'd replied. "They teach classes here, and we all take turns being teacher once in a while."

"Even you?" she asked him.

"Even me," he replied, smirking.

Skinner Makes was a private club, volunteer run, volunteer driven. A community center whose members focused on making. "Making what?" Minerva asked Max.

"Anything you can think of, really," he answered. "All sorts of things."

And as Minerva explored the space, she saw that he was right. The club was composed of a variety of smaller groups that met. Instructors gave classes.

Members collaborated on larger projects.

"So, what do you think?" Max asked.

"I'm not sure what to think," Minerva said. And it was true. There was a lot to see here. Potentially a lot to do. And that was half the problem. "There's so much here that it's overwhelming."

"Overwhelming?" Max frowned. "I'm not sure if that's a good thing or a bad thing."

"This is a good place," Minerva replied. "Of that I'm sure."

"You don't sound sure."

Minerva thought about that for a few seconds. Finally, she said, "I just don't know how I fit in here."

"These are welcoming people," Max reassured her.

Minerva nodded. "They seem it."

"They're not pulling mean kid shit on you. Don't worry."

"That's not what I'm worried about," Minerva said. "They seem like accepting people."

"Then what is it then?"

"I don't feel like I fit in here," Minerva said.

Max frowned. "So, you're excluding *yourself*?"

"Max," Minerva said. "Don't be like that. I'm just trying to be honest here."

"That's what people always say when they're doing something shitty but looking for absolution. 'I'm just being honest.' Well congratulations, you're just being honest. Like honest wins you a fucking medal. You can be honest and shitty."

"I know that," Minerva said. "It isn't that I don't *want* to fit in. I do."

Max frowned. "That doesn't make any sense."

"Well, I don't make any sense," Minerva replied. "I don't make *anything* for that matter. And that's what I'm talking about. Your friends, all of you... you're special. You build things. Invent stuff. You're creative. You change the definition of what's possible."

He smiled. "Thank you."

"I can't remember the last time I made anything."

"No?" he said. "Didn't you make anything for your old job?"

"I made people think a certain way. Feel a certain thing. But nothing concrete. Nothing like what you do here."

"You didn't make up charts or storyboards or presentations or anything like that?" Max said.

"That doesn't count," Minerva said. "That's not the same thing."

"Sure it is," Max replied. "Maybe it's not art or tech. At least not the way those things are usually defined. But you're taking an idea, planning it, and translating it to another form. It's all the same thing."

"No, it's not," Minerva said. "There's a world of difference between working in the realm of ideas and working in tangible form."

Max shook his head. "It's still all about planning. Sure, the final execution can look a little different depending on the medium you're using. Maybe you're whipping out a saw, a chisel, or paint at the end of everything. But you don't get there without the careful planning, no matter what kind of project you're working on. Masterful planning needs nothing more than competent execution. And anyone can learn competent execution with enough dedication and patience. Trust me."

Minerva considered this. "It's a little hard to believe right now. But you've never led me astray before."

Max smiled.

"I'll keep an open mind."

"You're good like that," Max said.

She kept coming with Max to Skinner Makes. Bopping around as he socialized with people she was only just meeting. As they bandied project terms back and forth. And as she felt hopelessly lost in their discussion but didn't dare to ask any questions lest she reveal her relative ignorance.

She stood there, listening intently, hoping that like an immersion course in a foreign language that simply being around makers would bestow her with knowledge.

But somehow she couldn't seem to get the grammar right.

And then on her third visit to the space, that all changed.

It's funny, given how much effort some folks expend trying to assert their individuality, but deep down inside, in processes that are largely unknown and unseen to us but are always at work, another truth reins: We want to be in sync, with our environments and with each other.

When we become close to other people, entrainment kicks in. By the act of simply coming together, parties will often find themselves slightly changed and mysteriously coordinated without a lot of conscious effort.

In some cases, this entrainment never happens. There's just too much distance, too much interference. Other times the process is much easier, happens more quickly, more naturally.

Minerva had found that this was usually the case when she'd meet people that she felt like she met before, even though she hadn't, because they seemed familiar somehow. When this happened, she was always consciously aware that this was false recognition but still felt that unconscious pull anyway.

When it came to the unconscious mind, the primal midbrain structures, it was almost as though there were a second steering wheel and brake, duplicated controls that an unseen driving instructor could command at any moment, overriding what the conscious mind had planned.

Perhaps this was intended to prevent accidents, but what had been installed in a primitive world often caused just as many accidents when deployed in a complex psychosocial world.

Minerva's driving instructor made a sharp sudden move on the third time she visited the space for a beginner ceramics course, turning her towards someone. That sense of false recognition set in, and something within her said, "This person is someone who will become close to you. You are meeting someone important."

Before Minerva stood a lady with thick black curls tucked underneath a fuzzy knitted rainbow cap. Her heart-shaped face ended in a strong chin. Her eyes were large and brown. Staring directly into them was intense, even though they were shielded behind a pair of large rose-gold framed glasses.

Her body was so curvy that even her curves seemed to have curves. She had enormous breasts that jutted out in front of her, displacing her arms to her sides.

Although Minerva took note of her and found herself smiling reflexively at this woman, the eyes that stared back at her did so blankly. The expression in them implied an accompanying shrug regardless of the woman's current posture.

Come to think of it, Minerva noted, there was something profoundly non-committal about this woman and her energy. It was as though she were the human embodiment of a shrug.

"Take a seat," the walking shrug said. "Plenty of room at the workbench."

So, Minerva did. "Rosie," the woman said. "Rosie Drake." She extended her hand towards Minerva. Minerva reached forward to grab it and shake. Rosie froze, staring at Minerva's hand, with a horrified expression that looked as though she saw something crawling on it.

Minerva glanced down at her hand, wondering why Rosie looked positively afraid of it. Was it dirty? Bleeding?

No, it looked as it always did.

"Oh," Rosie said, backing away slowly. She walked away from the workbench into a closet that stood against the wall. "I need clay for the class."

Minerva retracted her hand, wondering at what had just happened. Perhaps Rosie was absent minded.

Other students began to shuffle in. Minerva noted that they shook hands with Rosie and introduced themselves without any visible reaction from her. Everyone exchanged names. Minerva tried her hardest to commit them to memory, but they kept being pushed from her mind by the awkward interaction she'd had with Rosie Drake.

"I'll be your instructor today," Rosie said. "Welcome to Ceramics 101."

Oh, Minerva thought. *She's the teacher. Of course I'd rub the* teacher *the wrong way on my first day of class. Lovely.*

Feeling resigned, Minerva pulled out a sheet of paper to take notes.

She noted with great disappointment that today's class was more basic than she'd expected it to be. They weren't making anything. Instead, Rosie was providing a quickstart guide on how to be a good citizen of the workshop. And, Minerva noted with alarm, today's class was nothing that even required clay.

Rosie had lied to her. She didn't need clay for class, after all. It was always jarring when someone lied to her, but even more so now. Being lied to felt like something that belonged to another part of her life.

And it was in that moment that Minerva realized that no one had lied to her since her accident.

Not that she had picked up on anyway.

And yet here was this woman. This eccentric artist. Lying to her for basically no reason. With Minerva believing every word until real life evidence came in to contradict her claims.

"Ceramics is a risky business," Rosie explained. "There are multiple points at which the whole process can go off the rails. Where whatever creation you dreamt up will break away from you and become something else."

"It can crack in the first firing, the bisque firing, where the clay hardens into a form of stone because it dried unevenly or you didn't properly reinforce your joins. Or you can glaze it and find after that second firing that it doesn't turn the color you had envisioned. Perhaps the kiln is having a bad day and doesn't reach the temperature it should. Or maybe it burns too hot. Maybe your glazes were mixed wrong. Or maybe you painted the damn thing wrong when you put on the glaze."

"This happens even more when you're a beginner, but no one is safe. Ceramics always has an element of risk built in. It's a bit like gambling. You put something into the kiln and have to wait to see what comes out."

"If you need complete control over the process, there are two paths you can take: One, quit pottery. Or two, make multiples of everything you want to turn out a certain way. Because they're willful, just like living things, just like children."

A classmate interjected. "Pots are like children?" The class laughed nervously.

"Children are just like pots," Rosie said. "If you want at least one to turn out the way you planned, you'd better make extra."

Maybe that's the reason her relationship with her parents was so strained, Minerva thought suddenly. She was an only child, and they really did seem like they set forth having a kid with a specific goal in mind. Some way they expected her to turn out. She had been planned, and when that happened, all their parenting eggs were put in one alarmingly adventurous and rebellious basket.

They had dreamed of one thing coming out of the kiln, and something vastly different was what had emerged after the firing.

It made a lot of sense. Minerva strained to listen to the class instruction as the weight of the epiphany descended upon her.

I don't care if Rosie's lied to me, Minerva thought suddenly. *I like this woman.*

Fingers Crossed

It wasn't quite right. No, not quite right.

Minerva stared at her own hands. She took measurements, sketched them out on paper. She worked the clay with her fingers, staring at the anatomical diagram as she went.

It would be better to consult her hands, she thought as she worked. Unfortunately, those hands were busy striving to make a copy of themselves.

The center of the palm itself gave her no trouble. There laid an intransigent plane of bone, not quite sheer as a cliff face, but approaching that. It was the matrix of muscles over it that was fussy. The knuckles. The lines in her skin.

She did her best to copy her diagram, and yet something was wrong.

Sighing, she took some water and wet the parts of the clay that were beginning to harden, reworking them. Instead of consulting her diagram, she tried holding the incipient hand sculpture in her other hand at intervals and comparing it to her real one.

She did her best to cradle the clay gently as she did, making sure she didn't inadvertently crush her delicate sculpture or turn it back into the lump she'd started with. The fingerprints she left were fine, she reminded herself. The glaze would cover most of it. And if she were really concerned, she could remove them with a sponge while it was still pliable or sandpaper once her sculpture dried to leather hardness or beyond.

Slowly, she realized how to fix her proportions so they looked right, and she reworked the clay.

It took a few hours, all told, but at the end of it, she had a remarkably lifelike sculpture of her right hand with the index and middle fingers crossed. Slipping and scoring as she went, she added a base onto the sculpture, copying the contours of the first few inches of her wrist as she did so.

She turned over the sculpture and made five venting holes with a chopstick in the bottom of this clay wrist spacing them out evenly like the five-face of a six-sided die, in order to ensure even drying and provide a place for steam to escape in the kiln. Nothing was guaranteed of course, but this step would make it less likely that the piece would explode.

"It came out wonderfully," Rosie observed.

Minerva swiveled quickly in her seat. When had her instructor entered the studio? She'd been so focused that she hadn't heard Rosie come in.

"So, which is it?" Rosie asked.

"Which...?" Minerva said.

"Well, with crossed fingers, it's either about lying or good luck," Rosie said.

"Who says it can't be both?" Minerva asked.

"Not me," Rosie said.

Minerva smiled. She bent over to do some detail work. While the focal point of her sculpture – the index and middle fingers – looked perfect, the pinkie still wasn't quite up to her standards.

"I wonder what it is that you feel guilty about," Rosie said.

"What?" Minerva said.

"That's what I see whenever I look at you," Rosie said. "Guilt. Like you've done something terrible you feel bad about. Or like you're about to."

Minerva laughed. "Then I guess you're not that good at reading people. Because I feel fine." But something within her faltered. She did her best to conceal it.

"Ah, my mistake," Rosie said. "Except I don't make mistakes."

"Everyone makes mistakes," Minerva said.

"Well, my mistakes are different. They have a way of becoming the way things should have been. And I get the feeling you know what I mean."

Minerva set down her clay sculpting tools while she struggled to think of something to say, some way to attack a silence that was becoming more uncomfortable and unbearable by the moment.

Rosie laughed suddenly, breaking the tension. "Since we're both artists and all," she said.

Minerva smiled. "You think I'm an artist?"

Rosie nodded. "You're very gifted. I've never seen anyone become proficient with clay this fast, and I've been teaching for a very long time. Sure, I've seen beginners who can work the wheel and throw off a series of passable cups or bowls. But a sculpture this structurally sound and with this level of detail... never. I've never seen such a thing in my entire teaching career."

Minerva beamed, soaking in the high praise.

"It's a shame, really," Rosie said.

"A shame?" Minerva asked.

"Yeah," Rosie said. "With students as gifted as you are, there's not really much for me to do as a teacher. Mostly my role is to just be here and support you. Maybe accelerate your independent learning by introducing you to resources you would have stumbled onto on your own eventually. But the talent itself and the development of that talent, that will be your achievement. Not something I can take credit for."

"I don't know," Minerva said. "You've been quite helpful in teaching me about the properties of clay and the studio rules."

Rosie waved her hand in the air dismissively. "Nothing a decent pamphlet on the subject or a posted sign couldn't have done for you."

"Well," Minerva said, "don't sell yourself so short. I'm sure there will be things that come up that you can teach me."

Rosie frowned. "Mm," she said. Rosie was worried about this student but didn't elaborate further. How could she explain to this student how her instructor's mind worked? That she often found she was right about what, who, where, how, and why – but wrong about *when*.

How could she explain that the right answers often came to her at the wrong time? And that the future would come to pass to match a present feeling but only after the intervening time had wreaked havoc on everyone involved.

No, there were no explanations for this. There was no way to explain a mind like hers. Rosie barely understood it herself, and she'd been forced to endure its quirks for an entire lifetime.

So, she didn't explain this. And she didn't tell Minerva the thing she longed to tell her the most: "Creation is truth"

Because she had a feeling – a strong one – that life would be teaching Minerva that lesson before too long anyway.

And as a teacher of such a gifted student, it was not her lot in life to teach such lessons explicitly but to support a student through them as the lessons came and found her.

Darren Makes

"Where is this place anyway?" Darren asked.

"Hm?" Minerva said. He was talking to her through her back as he held her, and as that sound reverberated through her torso, it was quite difficult to understand what he'd said from what little reached her ears.

Darren had that habit, especially following sex, while they were cuddling. He would press her to him, and only when his face was flush up against her skin would he become talkative. At moments like these, she felt like a reed in a woodwind instrument, a vessel to carry sound, not a proper conversational partner.

"Skinner Makes," Darren said, pulling a bit away from her skin and raising his voice. "What exactly do you do there?"

Minerva smiled, rolled over, and faced him. While she had been reluctant at first to go when Max explained it to her – and reluctant still indeed even after going there a few times – the club had quickly become a passion. Clay was a big part of this, yes. But there was also something positively intoxicating about being in the company of so many people who saw possibilities where others didn't. It was wonderful to be around people who did more than sit and consume. Makers.

"Anything we want, really," Minerva said. "And that's the whole beauty of it." She inventoried the various pursuits of her fellow makers.

Darren listened patiently, quietly. When she had finished, he asked, "Are they open to people starting up new groups there?"

"Of course," Minerva replied. "That's the whole spirit of the organization. Most of what's there started organically, with a member spontaneously deciding it was something they wanted to do and then others joining them."

She paused for a few moments. "Were you thinking of starting something?" she asked.

Darren nodded.

"Something to do with law?" she asked.

"Kind of," Darren said, nodding. And then he shook his head. "And also, kind of not."

Minerva frowned. "You need to explain that."

"Okay," Darren said. "Promise not to laugh."

Minerva stopped for a moment. It was so easy to agree to a request like that, she'd found over the years, and most of the time she could honor it. But you never really did know what someone would say next – in general and especially so when it came to Darren, who as she had grown to know him better had more moods and facets to him than she would have guessed on first glance. Some sides of him resonated so perfectly with her and her values, and others were strange and hollow. She had been glad to know him over the past few months. The way they fit together physically was absolute perfection. But if she'd been forced in a traditional scenario to be with him as her one and only, she wasn't sure if they would have worked as a couple. While so much of their bond was harmonious, eerily perfect, there were more rough edges than she normally would have expected to see with someone who made her feel so good in general.

But then again, Chad was even worse in that respect, and in all respects, really. When pressed, she had a hard time thinking of one way that she connected perfectly with Chad, especially before she went into the hospital. At least in the intervening time since then, he'd become more considerate, handier, more actively useful. Still, they had very little in common. And before she'd met Darren and Max, she'd managed to get along with Chad's companionship well enough.

It was funny how once she had more men in her life that her standards had raised. She found it strange that even a relationship that was a vast improvement over what she'd had before suddenly stuck out as having its limitations. Still good. Lovely. Something that she was grateful for.

But, Minerva noted, you couldn't create a single perfect relationship out of a mess of imperfect ones. It just didn't work that way. You had to accept that most relationships would be imperfect in some way, shape, or form – it was all a matter of degree—and then choose your response to that.

And that, Minerva thought, was where the tricky bit came in.

The whole situation reminded her powerfully of a principle called the paradox of choice. It had been something important to keep in mind in her career as a marketer. Basically, people like to have options. It makes them feel free, in control. But at a certain point, too many options would backfire and make them less happy. No matter what they eventually chose, it was all too easy to fall into patterns where they second guessed the choice they made.

Was it the absolute best? Could they have been even happier with something else? It was hard to stop asking these questions and be confident in what you'd ultimately chosen.

Sometimes less really was more.

Of course, when it came to marketing, you were talking about choosing between six flavors of jam versus 24. Not her current situation, with three boyfriends instead of one.

Still, she reflected, there was probably something there. Something she should keep an eye on if she ever found herself in two dozen relationships at the same time.

One never knew.

Minerva realized Darren was staring at her. "Huh?" she said.

"I said 'promise not to laugh,'" he said.

Minerva bit her lip. "I'll be kind," she replied tactfully. Her fingers stayed uncrossed. It was true, a promise she could keep. She had a hard time not laughing at something that struck her as funny or absurd, but she knew she could never *maliciously* laugh at Darren. And that was what was important. It was what he seemed to mean.

"I'd like to start a club for liars," he said. "But I don't know if anybody would join if I called it that, so I think I'll start up an acting class. Acting and lying are so close, if you really think about it."

Minerva felt a laugh threatening to bubble up from within her. Not a malicious one, no. But a surprised one. A nervous one. "Of course that's what you're doing," she said.

"You said you wouldn't laugh," Darren said.

"And I'm not," Minerva replied. Because it was true.

"But you think it's a dumb idea," Darren said.

"I'm not saying that," Minerva said, "but I'm not sure exactly how it would work. I'm having a hard time picturing what it would look like. That doesn't mean it's dumb or a bad idea. It just means that I don't get it."

"Whatever," Darren said, turning away from her.

"Darren," she said, with as much softness as she could muster.

He didn't respond.

She stroked his bare back. He pointedly shrank away from her.

She lay there silently beside him. It was funny how even people who were good at asking for things didn't ask for what they actually needed. Instead, they'd ask for something neighboring, something that seemed like less to ask of other people, instead of what they actually wanted.

Take Darren's case. He'd asked her not to laugh at him – and she'd managed to honor this. But what he really wanted from her was for her to respect his idea, for her to think it was a good one. And that was an entirely different request than what he'd voiced – that she not laugh.

It was only after she'd failed to give him what he really wanted, after she witnessed how suddenly hurt he'd become, that she understood what he should have asked her. And as he lay next to her in bed, she combed her mind for a way to give that to him that wouldn't feel artificial or forced for either of them.

This was, as always, a tall order. It required a difficult social calculus in every instance. There was usually a path forward, Minerva noted, but that path could easily become covered by other distracting factors, like ego, pride, defensiveness. You know, everything that made a person human.

She crossed her fingers behind her back. "You should start the group," she said. "I'm sure it'll grow into something very successful. It'll be very popular."

Her fingers ached and throbbed, swelling momentarily to nearly twice their normal size before relaxing, shrinking, and uncrossing.

Darren turned back towards her, smiling. "That means a lot to me to hear you say that, Minerva," he said.

She smiled back but felt guilty somehow. Darren seemed entirely unaware of the lie, so she was tasked with carrying it for both of them.

It's hard sometimes, she thought idly as Darren kissed her, *being such a convincing liar.*

As Minerva had expected, Darren received quite a warm welcome from the rest of Skinner Makes when he accompanied her and Max to tour the facilities. She noted that Darren was quite analytical in his approach. He had a lot more questions than she had on her first visit there. He wanted to know about how they managed the logistics. How were rooms apportioned for groups? How did they advertise events? Who oversaw managing their finances, paying for rent and supplies?

And of course, how would a person go about starting up a new club if they were so inclined?

As Minerva went to answer all of Darren's questions, she was interrupted by several other members who had begun to accompany the three of them as they walked around the space. More and more people dropped what they were doing to follow them. And all of them seemed to be vying for Darren's attention – treating him as though he were a quiz show host who would at any minute award them a bevy of cash and fabulous prizes.

This is strange, Minerva thought. Her own introduction had been far less heralded. Of course Max had done his best to give her a tour, just as he was doing for Darren now, but outside of Max, no one had given her a second look. Instead, the present members had kept their distance. Perhaps they'd been deeply engrossed in their current projects, or maybe the truth was that they were skittish introverts, who preferred to watch new people, much like a wary housecat will often eye their human's friends when they first start coming over.

In any case, Darren's introduction was quite different than hers. Minerva fought a bubble of jealous indignation that rose in her chest. The early days and even weeks at Skinner Makes had been quite awkward for her. She felt like she'd had to work hard to engage with others at the organization and over time to earn their trust.

And now here Darren was, being treated like a visiting dignitary instead of a potentially suspicious outsider.

Annoying.

And then another thought occurred to her: Maybe Darren's warm reception wasn't about Darren at all. Maybe it was about *her* and the fact that she *had* worked so hard to build trust with members. That was a comforting thought, a flattering one.

In any case, members accompanied them throughout the space.

And at the end of the tour, Darren could barely get out the words, "So I was thinking about starting a group," before he was interrupted by several members saying, "Sign me up." "I'll be there." "I'm down."

"Beautiful Liars?" Max said, as he hung the new schedule.

Minerva shrugged. "I don't know what to tell you. I tried to tell Darren this was a weird idea."

"It is," Max replied. "But it's strangely popular. It's full already."

Minerva frowned. "I just have a bad feeling about this, Max. I have a hard time explaining it, but I do."

"Aw," Max said. "One of the members has been running a philosophy discussion night for years, so acting classes don't seem all that farfetched. I'm sure it'll be alright."

"I'm not," Minerva said.

"I've seen members start up a lot of weird groups here over the years, and you know... most of them don't meet anymore. And that's that. I figure Darren will have some interest here. Folks will meet. And then they'll get to figure out whether they think it's a good thing or not." He frowned. "Beautiful Liars, though. What a name for a group. That's like something out of a soap opera."

"To be fair," Minerva said, "Darren's like something out of a soap opera."

Max nodded. "An old one. Back when they were actually selling soap on the commercial breaks."

"In the times when no one left home without a hat," Minerva said, smiling.

"In fact, when Darren enters rooms, the colors not only drain from him but also from his surroundings. He turns everything into a black and white world. That's how stuck in the past that man is," Max said. "And how maddeningly concrete."

Minerva laughed. "Concrete?" she said. "Yeah, when it suits him anyway. And when it doesn't, there's no shortage of shades of gray for him to dabble in."

"He's crazy-making, Darren Delvecchio," Max said. "And I'm not just saying that because he hogs my woman."

"Awww," Minerva said, feeling a twinge of guilt.

"You're worth it, though," Max said. "I can't imagine having you all to myself. That would be a kind of crime against the world, bogarting your company."

Minerva smiled.

"Darren on the other hand," Max said, "that guy would hog you in a heartbeat."

Minerva laughed.

"He'd try to patent you if he could. Make it so nobody else could even say your name," Max said.

"You're probably right," Minerva said. "Luckily, those have never been the terms of our relationship. He walked into this with Chad already there. He knew what he was getting into."

"And he still wanted in," Max said.

Minerva nodded.

"That should tell you something about yourself, Minerva," Max said.

"Whatever," she said, blushing. She tried to hide behind her hand.

"Seriously," Max said, "I know you discount yourself. Constantly. Some of the time aloud. And then I strike it down with a mighty blow." He mimed attacking an invisible enemy with a giant sword and then watching the corpse crumple to the ground.

Minerva rolled her eyes at the spectacle.

"But I also know you do it silently, in your own head. Where people can't argue with you," Max said.

"How did you get to know so much?" Minerva asked.

"It's elementary, my dear Watson," Max said.

Minerva scoffed at the cheesiness.

"It's like speeding," Max said.

"Speeding?"

Max nodded. "By the time a person gets a speeding ticket, even if they claim, 'honestly, I never do this,' and say it's the first time they've ever driven that fast, they've likely gone way too fast for a very long time. So if I'm challenged by how much you doubt yourself *aloud*, it's gotta be a right mess up there in your head."

"Good detective work," Minerva said.

Max smiled at her.

"So, Sherlock," Minerva said, "what should we do about Darren and the Beautiful Liars?"

"It's simple, really," Max said.

"Yeah?"

"We go to a meeting," Max said, "and we take it from there."

Minerva cringed as she watched Max struggle to impersonate a tree. True, he was standing stock still. He had that part right. But something about his posture wasn't quite... leafy enough.

No. She caught herself and shook her head violently. That was a completely mad thought. How was a human being supposed to stand leafily?

Perhaps if he stood.... stalk still.

Oh no. That was terrible.

Acting classes brought on this kind of madness. Perhaps that was the whole point, she reflected. You lost your sanity, and then you were an empty vessel, just waiting to have a fictional personality poured into you.

Or, she thought, longing to be back in the pottery workshop where she felt comfortable and knew what to do, maybe you were more like a featureless lump of clay, wedged, ready to be molded into whatever the occasion required.

It was so odd that we exalted actors these days, she reflected, as she took a stab at imitating a magnolia tree while Max watched her, a pensive finger curled under his chin. Once upon a time, actors had been looked upon as scoundrels, the lowest of the low. And now here people were paying exorbitant salaries to them and striving to be just like them. "Stars, they're just like us!"

But then again, professional athletes, too, were heralded, and once upon a time, gladiators had been slaves. And they, too, were half-worshipped and highly compensated.

It was an inescapable madness of these times, she supposed. But she didn't like it one bit.

During their first break, she sat with Max and danced around the topic gently. Once that failed and he didn't get the hint, she quickly trod on the topic with full force. "Max, I don't think I'm cut out for this acting stuff," she confessed.

"Phew," he said. "I'm glad I'm not the only one."

"It's a bit silly, isn't it?" she said.

"Definitely. Although..."

"Although?" Minerva said.

"Maybe acting is the kind of thing that takes a while to really grasp. To really grok, y'know."

"I see you're doing Heinlein speak again."

Max smiled. "Well, I am a stranger in a strange land. Always."

Minerva had enjoyed *Stranger in a Strange Land*, the Heinlein book of the same name that Max had lent her, even if some of it hadn't aged well. There was a lot of sexism that probably made sense in the sixties but as a nineties woman made her violently twitch. But aside from that, it was an interesting read. A Martian came to Earth, clashed with Terran culture, and ultimately transformed it.

Two specific concepts from the book had been on her mind since then. One was "grok." She'd heard it in passing in everyday use, as the book had successfully popularized it. When most people used it, grok seemed to mean to understand something intuitively, implicitly rather than explicitly. Or in other words, to "get it" in a way that perhaps defied description.

In the original context of Heinlein's book, she saw that it was a Martian concept that didn't translate neatly into Earthling terms. In Martian, "grok" meant something more, something more figurative and universal. Fittingly, "grok" could only be grokked and not really *understood* as we understand understanding to be.

The other concept that had intrigued her had been the concept of "water brothers." While the term itself was gendered language, water brothers could be of any gender. In the Martian custom, sharing a glass of water with someone wasn't something done lightly. Instead, the act forged a deep, profound bond with someone. Partly this was because water was scarce on Mars and therefore it was a bigger sacrifice to share it with someone else.

Still, this idea follows the Martian to Earth, where he proceeds to share water in a world of plenty and still finds great significance in the act and becomes profoundly partnered with several people.

"What are you thinking about?" Max asked her suddenly.

"Water brothers," Minerva responded truthfully.

"Ah, you were thinking about me then," he said, smiling.

She smiled back at him. The two of them, water brothers? That was a nice thought.

"Just promise me that when we get back to your place, you'll make us lattes," Minerva said to him.

"Lattes?" Max said, frowning.

"Yeah," Minerva replied.

"And how would I do that?" Max said.

Minerva studied his face. "Umm... with your espresso machine. The giant one that takes up half your kitchen," she replied. "Stop being weird."

Max shook his head. "I've never had an espresso machine," he said.

But that was how we got together in the first place, Minerva thought, a sudden feeling of alarm coursing through her. *You took me back to your apartment and we made fancy drinks.*

Max didn't seem to be joking. Could it be that she was remembering things wrong? But why would she remember something like that if it hadn't happened?

None of it made sense. It made her feel a little crazy.

She was trying to think of a way to tell Max all of this, when Darren called the class back together, interrupting her train of thought.

A woman in the back of class raised her hand suddenly, and Darren called on her. Before now, Minerva had barely noticed her, but in this moment, she focused her attention on this woman. The best word for her, Minerva decided, was incredibly average. She was average height. Her body hinted at perhaps a slightly athletic build but not conspicuously so and largely hidden beneath an oversized grey-blue sweater worn over a pair of entirely unprepossessing pressed khaki pants. She had ruler-straight sandy brown hair with a banged fringe and hazel eyes.

Perhaps a slight tan, Minerva noted. Not a glamorous tan, to be sure, nothing that was reminiscent of *Baywatch* and its siren beach goddesses, but a color that served to make her hair and face almost blend together, as though her face were trying to hide from her hair – or vice versa.

Her facial features themselves were symmetrical and well formed, but there was nothing flashy about them and certainly nothing sultry. She had quite an unremarkable chin and nose. Nothing about her really stuck out.

Yes, Minerva noted, this woman was pleasant looking but average, almost as though she had been artificially generated off a number set, as a combination of every available mean.

Visibly screwing up her courage, this human statistical mean spoke. "I know you said that we're here to learn acting and that this class isn't about lying *per se*, but…" Her voice trailed off.

Darren waited for her to finish.

"When I signed up for this, I really only saw the name of the group, and I gotta say I got my hopes up," she finished.

"And why's that?" he asked.

"Hm?"

"Why did you get your hopes up when you saw the name? What were you hoping to get out of this class?"

The woman looked embarrassed. She looked down at her feet.

"I wanted to get a few things off my chest," she said.

"Ah," Darren said, "you were hoping for a confessional?'

"Not a confessional exactly... more like..." she started

Darren waited.

"More like a support group," she finished.

"Well," Darren said, "that's the nice thing about Skinner Makes, isn't it? We get to choose our own destiny here. We get to take our groups any direction we want them to go." He thought for a moment.

"But I thought this was an *acting class*," another student complained.

"I don't see why it can't be both," Darren said suddenly.

"Both what?" the dissenting student asked.

"An acting class and a support group," Darren said. He had started out uncertain about the whole premise, but as he spoke, it seemed as though he were convincing himself more and more that it was a good idea.

At his direction, the class set up a ring of chairs.

Minerva groaned. This felt like groupwork, the scourge of her school days.

Darren shot her a stern look and persisted in organizing the sharing circle.

"Okay," he said, turning his attention back to the painfully average woman. "Why don't we start with you? What's your name? Tell us a little about yourself."

She blushed. "Hi everyone," she said, waving.

Minerva tensed the muscles in her legs, waited a few moments, and then relaxed them. It was a stress response she'd had her whole life, squeezing her muscles instead of exploding in a more obvious way. *What the heck am I doing here?* She asked herself.

She glanced over at Max, but he didn't seem to be in similar dire straits. Instead, he was leaning forward in his chair, looking intently at the woman who was speaking.

"My name is Regina Withers," the statistical mean said. "I... uh... I'm a journalist." As she said this, Regina's eyes darted around. The way her expression changed reminded Minerva of a person who has just told a whopper of a lie and is monitoring her audience to see if anyone will catch her in the act.

Of course Minerva also knew this didn't necessarily mean active deception. She had seen the same behavior in people who aren't lying consciously but instead don't believe in themselves, so everything truthful they say about themselves, especially when positive, feels like a lie to them.

I wonder which one it is, Minerva thought idly. *Dishonesty or a lack of self-confidence.*

"A journalist!" Darren said. "Who do you write for?"

There was an uncomfortable pause as Regina froze. She wasn't used to being asked followup questions about herself, or anyone noticing her at all, really. "Well, whoever will have me," she said nervously. "I'm technically freelance, although you may have seen some of my work in the *Skinner Morning News*. Or the

Watson Herald. At the moment, I'm covering a lot of city council meetings, but if I work really hard, maybe I'll get to do more than that."

"Like what?" Darren said.

"What sorts of things do I want to cover? Is that what you mean?" Regina asked.

Darren nodded.

Regina thought for a moment. "I don't know quite what exactly. Just something important. I'd like to be there when something important happens. And be the person who tells the world about it, y'know? Capture the big events that rivet the world. Not just be someone who's stuck with reporting routine meetings. I'd like to be the person who's there when something big and historical happens. Something that never would have seen the light of day if not for me."

What you really mean is that you want to be famous, Minerva thought.

"And..." Regina continued, "Well, someday it'd be nice to be on television."

Her suspicions confirmed, Minerva rolled her eyes.

"But not to be famous," Regina added defensively.

Yeah right.

"But to make a difference!" Regina finished hopefully.

A difference with your name on it, Minerva added mentally, unimpressed.

"*You* know what I mean, don't you?" Regina said.

Minerva realized suddenly that Regina was talking to her. She forced herself to sit up a little straighter in her chair. "Me?" Minerva said.

Regina nodded. "You seem like someone who wants to make a difference."

"Why do you say that?" Minerva asked.

"I don't know," Regina said. "It just hit me. I don't know why."

"Well, it's not true," Minerva said.

"No?"

"I mean… no. No, I don't have some burning need to make a difference," Minerva said. "And I don't really want to be famous."

"There," Regina said, and as she did her entire demeanor changed, "That right there is why I think we need a support group. It's way too easy to lie to yourself."

"I'm not lying to myself," Minerva muttered. She noted as she said this that her fingers stayed room temperature and uncrossed.

"I think I'm a bad mother," a familiar voice said. Minerva turned and saw that it was Rosie Drake, the pottery instructor. Others from the group responded as Rosie talked through her issues, revealed the secrets she'd been too scared up until this point to speak aloud.

One by one, the confessions flew out of the attendees. "I don't think I'm good enough for Minerva," Max said.

"Of course you are," she responded to Max, but her classmates shushed her.

"Don't invalidate the poor man," someone else scolded her.

Minerva felt violently ill. But her classmates continued to open up, pour their hearts out, and offer support to one another.

It was a never-ending flood of catharsis. An hour later, a group of woodcarvers needed to use the room, so Darren broke up the meeting but reluctantly.

And just like that, the session was over, without Minerva having to impersonate another tree.

But as she gathered up her things, she thought idly that she'd rather imitate an entire forest than go through that sharing circle again.

She was one of the last people to leave the room. Regina Withers lingered behind, speaking to everyone she could, smiling in a way that looked wrong on her face.

Even Darren had left, and it was just Regina and Minerva standing together in the room.

"That was a good session today," Regina said.

Minerva didn't respond.

"People had a lot on their minds," Regina explained, answering a question Minerva wasn't asking, at least not with words. "It was good for them to unload it."

Minerva shrugged.

"I hope I'll see you at the next meeting," Regina said.

Minerva shrugged again.

The woodcarvers filtered in, carrying blocks of wood and knives with them. They began to set up tables and arrange their equipment.

Regina stared at Minerva a moment longer. Regina looked at the woodcarvers and headed for the door. As Minerva watched Regina walk away, it suddenly dawned on her that despite saying she wanted to get a few things off her chest that Regina hadn't revealed any actual secrets of her own during the session.

As Minerva walked out of the classroom, it hit her: *I think she was there to get other people to open up in front of her.*

The reason why remained to be seen.

"So what do you think of Regina?" Minerva asked Darren when she finally had an opportunity to see him alone.

"You mean the blackmailer?" Darren said

Minerva's mouth hung open.

"Surely you saw it too?" Darren said.

"Well," Minerva said truthfully, "I felt like something was off about her. But now that you mention blackmail, the pieces certainly fit."

Darren nodded. "She gave up nothing but did so vulnerably. It's easy to confuse that for vulnerability. And that makes people want to spill their secrets."

"Sometimes," Minerva said, "the way you talk scares me."

"If you're going to defend against this stuff, it's important to know how blackmailers operate," he replied.

"Still," Minerva said, "it makes me glad you're on my side."

Darren smiled.

"If you were my enemy, you could easily destroy me," Minerva said.

Darren's smile fell. "Don't say things like that," he said.

"Would you prefer I lied?" Minerva asked.

"Always," Darren said.

"I wonder if it's her first time," Minerva said.

"Regina?"

Minerva nodded. "My gut says no, that she's blackmailed people before."

"Why do you say that?" Darren asked.

Minerva shrugged. "Just a feeling I get."

Darren thought about this. "I bet she had a stooge," he said.

"A stooge?"

Darren nodded. "A plant in the class. Someone else who knew what she was up to and helped her get the ball rolling."

"Clever," Minerva said.

"She struck me that way," Darren said. "The stooge would be whoever spilled the beans first."

Minerva thought back to the class. "Rosie," Minerva said. "Of course."

"Of course?"

"The first time I ever met Rosie she lied to me. About something small. But still, it was obvious. And also… unnecessary. She had no reason to lie to me. There was nothing at stake. And yet she did," Minerva said.

"Sounds like an abhorrent person," Darren said.

"That's the strangest part," Minerva said. "I still like her."

"Even though she lied to your face when she didn't have to?"

Minerva nodded. "It confuses me, too, if I'm being honest."

Darren thought about this for a second. "It reminds me of you."

Minerva scowled. "And what's that supposed to mean?"

Darren paused and gathered his thoughts. He wanted to make sure he said what he meant, because he had the feeling that he'd only have one chance to say it. Minerva was in danger of becoming too defensive to really listen to what he had to say. If he said the wrong thing, it'd be over.

"Well," Darren said, "sometimes you say things to me, and while they don't exactly seem true at first, I want to believe them – and I want to believe you – so much that I find myself questioning my own disbelief. It's like…" He searched for more words. "It's like your truth is more important than anyone else's. To you and to me."

"That's the silliest thing I've ever heard," Minerva said, but she found herself guiltily rubbing her right index and middle finger with her left hand.

"Anyway," Darren said.

"No anyway," Minerva persisted. "Why does that remind you of what I said about Rosie?"

"It's not the same exactly. It's just that I can understand having that experience, feeling as though someone has blatantly lied to you but not holding it against them. And in your case, I even came around to your point of view," he finished.

Well, there, Minerva thought. *So that's what it feels like on the other end of… whatever the hell's going on with me.*

At that moment, she considered coming clean. Just coming right out and telling Darren about the whole sorry mess, no matter how incredible the confession might sound. She considered telling him about the way her fingers throbbed and crossed when she said things that were untrue, the way that lying no longer was stressful and had begun to feel identical to speaking the truth and in some ways more powerful.

But just as she was mustering up the courage to do so, Darren derailed her train of thought.

"So," he said. "I think Rosie's our in."

"Our in?" Minerva asked.

"Our way of figuring out exactly what Miss Regina Withers is up to," Darren replied.

Minerva nodded. "On it."

It's often quite easy to agree to things; it's another matter to actually do them. No matter how many times Minerva experienced this duality, she still found herself walking into that same trap over and over.

"On it," she'd said to Darren so quickly, volunteering to shake down Rosie about… what exactly? What was really going on with Regina?

It was, like many things, easier said than done.

And as Minerva approached Rosie Drake for the first time with an agenda that wasn't pottery related, she felt profoundly silly. It seemed to her as though she were stepping into her first day as a private detective without a lick of training, formal or informal.

Still, there was something about Rosie that felt so familiar.

False recognition, her conscious mind said.

But that false recognition set the rest of her mind at ease.

Anyway, Rosie was seated on a stool, bent over the potter's wheel, and it was hard to be intimidated by someone in such a vulnerable position.

"Hey Rosie," Minerva said.

Rosie nodded in acknowledgement of the greeting, hardly taking her eyes off the spinning mass of clay before her.

"What are you making?" Minerva asked.

"Whatever the wheel decides," Rosie replied.

"Reminds me of game shows," Minerva said. "C'mon, c'mon, no whammies."

"Hm," Rosie grunted. She dipped her hands into a container of water before her. "You have to keep the clay wet when you're on the wheel. It takes a lot more water than you'd expect," she explained, answering a question Minerva wasn't asking.

Minerva watched Rosie guide the clay as the wheel spun. "It takes a lot of pressure to get it centered," Rosie continued. "You feel a bit like you're fighting an unseen enemy. Or at least I always did."

"I always feel that way. Doesn't take a wheel," Minerva said, hoping for a laugh.

She didn't get one.

"Once it's centered though, it takes quite a bit less pressure to open and stretch," Rosie said. "You have to get out of that initial brutish mode. Stop wrestling and start coaxing. That switchover is what gets a lot of people. Most people want to work in one mode and just stay there. They want to have to do one thing, be one thing. In actuality, we're more dual than that." Rosie smiled at the centered clay as she opened the middle. "Especially potters."

"That's going to be a really cool shape," Minerva said, as she watched Rosie coax the clay into position.

"Why are you so afraid of the wheel?" Rosie asked.

Am I afraid of the wheel? Minerva asked herself. "I'm not afraid of the wheel," she said aloud. She tried to cross her fingers, but she couldn't.

"Then why haven't you used it yet?" Rosie said.

"I just haven't gotten around to it," Minerva said.

Rosie took her foot off the pedal. The clay stopped spinning. "Well, if that's the case," she said, pointing her clay-caked hands to the set-up beside her, "that wheel's open. You're welcome to join me."

"I don't know what I'm doing," Minerva said.

"You're just scared of the wheel," Rosie said.

"I told you I wasn't," Minerva said.

"And you were lying," Rosie said.

A jolt of fear rose from Minerva's stomach into her head. It had been months since anyone had challenged anything she'd said. How could this woman see through her new authoritative front? Why wasn't she convinced the way the others were?

"It's fine by the way," Rosie said. "I don't judge. I'm not always honest myself. It doesn't mean anything."

"Yeah, right," Minerva said.

"Not to me anyway," Rosie clarified. She restarted the wheel and continued to work on the clay's form.

Minerva watched the piece spin. What an odd woman, Minerva thought. Was she somehow immune to betrayal? Minerva wondered. Did deception not hurt her? Was she that disconnected from others and trust? Did she not long for comfort, stability... and truth?

Because the importance of honesty had been a constant lesson for Minerva her entire life. Sometimes it came from the words of other people, who scolded her for being dishonest. "You liar!" The accusation meant to wound, to discourage, to sear shame into her – and it had worked.

There were even times when she'd simply said things that were inaccurate, and others had attached ill intent to it. She'd been called a liar for saying things that were false that she had thought were true.

And on the other side of things, she had been lied to. She knew what betrayal felt like. She'd felt the pain and confusion that came from realizing, suddenly, that what someone had assured you to be true absolutely wasn't. And instead, you'd been living in a different reality, one that didn't actually exist, because of what you'd been told.

All of it had been important education – that the truth mattered.

Honesty was a messy business, she'd learned, but always an important one.

And yet, she couldn't help herself sometimes. It was that tiny second driver, the unconscious mind, taking hold of the wheel and steering her off course. Lies would sometimes escape from her before she even realized she was speaking them. Lies to protect others, lies to protect herself.

But that didn't make it okay. And that didn't make the truth unimportant.

"You're okay with people lying to you?" Minerva asked Rosie.

"Well, I have to be," Rosie explained. "Because that's what they do."

"Not everyone lies," Minerva said.

"The biggest lies of all," Rosie said, "are the ones we tell ourselves." She cut what was now a vase from the bat with a length of wire. "That's why I like making things," Rosie said. "Physical objects don't care about your self-stories, your bullshit. You don't lie a vase into being. You have to make it. Words are sophistry, self-delusion. Creation is truth."

It was at just that moment that Regina Withers walked into the studio. Without making eye contact, Rosie said, "Hey Gina."

"Rosie, that's creepy," Regina said.

"Creepy?"

"How did you know it was me?" Regina asked.

"It's the way you walk," Rosie said. "Or really, the way you glide into rooms. Like you're on roller skates. You make less noise than other people. Just enough to announce your presence but not enough so that you sound... human."

"I'm telling you," Regina said, turning to Minerva, "Rosie isn't that friend you go to when you're feeling bad about yourself. She's not the one to pump up your ego."

Minerva nodded.

"It isn't that she tries to be mean," Regina explained, as though Rosie weren't sitting right there. "It's that she just doesn't care how she comes off."

"And you say I'm *not* the person you want to pump up your ego," Rosie said.

Regina laughed. "She's not a bitch," Regina explained to Minerva. "She's just seen enough things that she's over it all."

What must that be like, Minerva wondered, to have seen enough that things no longer really affected you? It was an attractive prospect on one hand, because arguably you'd never feel that sting, that harsh bite of reality, at moments of misfortune. But then again, could you really enjoy anything? Or would you be condemned to numbness, anhedonia?

"I'm not over everything," Rosie said. "I'm just over you." Harsh words, but she was smiling.

"No, you're not," Regina replied. "I can see right through you."

Rosie and Regina looked at each other, traded a strange glance. What was that about? Minerva wondered. A private joke between old friends probably.

She felt suddenly uncomfortable, out of place, as though she'd ventured somewhere she didn't belong. No one likes to be a third wheel, Minerva thought, even when on an espionage mission.

Regina turned to her at that moment. "I could use a drink. What do you think, Minerva? Want to go out and grab one with us?"

Maybe it wasn't so bad, Minerva thought. Maybe she could be one of the girls. "Sure," she said. "I could go for something with an umbrella sticking out of it."

Regina grinned. "I know just the place."

Forgot to Feed Them

Rosie and Regina took Minerva to a tiki bar. It was dark inside, not a spacious place, but filled to its meager capacity. Rosie seemed quite surprised that they didn't have to wait and smiled as the hostess led them to the last available table, so Minerva suspected it was always this hopping. A good sign.

The décor was lowbrow and busy, as though someone had flung an unfortunate garage sale haul up onto the walls. Dusty tiki masks loomed over them. Leis festooned the ceiling trim. Strangely lifelike parrot decorations perched throughout the place. As they chatted at their table, Minerva half-expected the birds to swoop down and contribute to the conversation.

Inexplicably, several pink plastic lawn flamingos were hung around the bar as well. The waiters all wore flowered shirts.

If there was music playing, Minerva couldn't hear it. The other diners made a din simply through the number of conversations that were ongoing at one time in such a small place.

They had to repeat their drink orders multiple times to the harried waitress who eventually came over to check on them. She seemed stretched to her limit but plastered on a rote customer service smile.

"Got it," she shouted, repeating their orders back perfectly, having managed to finally understand them through the racket.

Minerva ordered a fruity drink that came served in a skull, a concoction that by golly had not just one – but *two* – drink umbrellas poking out it.

Regina's drink was antifreeze blue and served in a coconut. Rosie's cocktail was promptly set on fire once it arrived.

Their appetizer platter featured fire as well. This fire was fueled by a scoop of pink Sterno in a small black crucible that resembled a cup made of cooled lava. This setup would have looked perfectly at home in, say, a pupu platter, but looked a little odd surrounded by an assortment of more standard bar fare, in this case chicken wings, meatballs, and cheeseburger sliders.

Rosie and Regina were unfazed by this, however. They roasted the wings and fork-speared meatballs in the tiny flame.

"I don't know if doing this actually makes it taste any different," Regina admitted, "but it's more fun this way."

As Regina said this, Rosie turned to her and openly admired her face.

They had an intense interpersonal chemistry between them that struck Minerva as odd. *If I didn't know any better, I'd say I'm on a date,* she thought.

She pushed down these strange thoughts and attacked her drink. It was quite good, sweet but not cloyingly so. The flavors were so well balanced that she would have sworn there was no alcohol in it.

Probably isn't a lot, she thought. That was how bars made their money, after all, on the markup of the alcohol. Put less in the drinks than normal, while still making them tasty, and then you'd clear even more than usual. It was a handy little racket, she had to admit.

After a few minutes of drinking, however, she realized she had been mistaken. This was a deceptively strong drink. She was only halfway through her first drink, and she knew at once that she was already unfit for driving anytime soon.

A dopey grin crept onto her face.

Rosie noticed. "Good drinks, yeah?" she said.

Minerva nodded. "Very." She noticed that both of her companions were quickly downing theirs as well.

They were also now holding hands. As Minerva watched, she realized that her initial instincts had been correct.

"So how long have you two been a couple?" Minerva asked.

"A couple of what?" Rosie said clumsily.

"Rosie, it's okay," Regina said. "Two years next week."

Minerva smiled. "You seem really happy together," she said.

"It's been wonderful," Regina said.

Rosie remained silent.

"She doesn't like public displays of affection," Regina explained.

"They aren't safe," Rosie said.

"So what?" Regina said. "Who cares about safe? Who builds their life around being safe?"

"A lot of people actually," Rosie countered. "There are entire industries set up to meet that need. Insurance, food inspection, whoever makes bike helmets."

"Whoever makes bike helmets?" Regina said. She laughed. "Honestly, Rosie."

Rosie rolled her eyes.

"I suppose I should rephrase the question. Who *worth knowing* builds their life around being safe?" Regina asked.

Neither Minerva nor Rosie said anything in response.

"Exactly," Regina said.

"I know it's hard for you to understand," Rosie began tentatively.

Regina took on the classic guarded posture of a person who feels as though they are being underestimated.

"Things were different 20 years ago, when I first was out dating and had to deal with my own sexuality in a practical sense," Rosie continued. "It was even more dangerous to be open about who you were when you weren't straight." She lowered her eyes. "I honestly never thought I'd marry anyone, let alone a man. Always thought I was a small doses person. It felt like winning the lottery to find someone."

"Twenty years ago, I was in kindergarten," Regina admitted. "I need another drink." She was having a hard time getting the waitress to come over to their table, despite a rather elaborate system of hand signals that reminded Minerva of semaphore.

Regina gave up trying to flag down the waitress and said, "I met Rosie when I first got to Skinner. A chance meeting actually. I was fresh out of college, didn't know a soul in the city, and needed a job. Rosie had just gotten divorced and needed someone to watch her three youngest kids while she went to night school. My landlord was an old friend of hers, and when I told him I hadn't found work yet and couldn't pay the rent, he introduced us, made the whole thing happen."

"That's when you became... the nanny?" Minerva asked, in the exact cadence of the popular sitcom theme, throwing in jazz hands for good measure.

"Exactly like that show, yes. Well, not exactly. Rosie's not so posh as Maxwell Sheffield. Her ex did give her a good monetary settlement in the divorce though, which is how she could afford to pay me in the first place. But nothing too crazy. And I suppose I don't have hair as big as Fran Drescher's," Regina said.

"Or a laugh like hers," Minerva said.

"Thank God," Rosie said.

Regina smiled. "But yeah... Funny how it all turned out. I really liked Rosie, felt very connected to her. It's hard to explain. To be honest, it's hard for me to get close to people, but with her it was so easy. It just happened. I wasn't expecting that. Before I knew it, I'd fallen in love."

Minerva smiled.

"My poor landlord," Regina said. "He set me up so he could get steady rent, and I ended up moving in with Rosie, and he had to re-advertise the place. He was good about it though. He saw what Rosie went through in her marriage. It's something no one should be subjected to."

Minerva didn't want to ask.

The waitress approached their table finally. "One more for everyone!" Regina ordered expansively.

Rosie raised her eyebrows. "Are you sure that's a good idea?"

Regina shrugged. "You only live once."

The waitress asked which drinks they'd like.

"Surprise us," Regina said. "Your choice."

The waitress nodded.

The next round of drinks was a giant fish tank that had been filled with a combination of various alcohols and mixers that rendered it a queasy green. Gelatin candy fish littered the waters, floating belly up.

"Forgot to Feed Them," the waitress announced. "It's only one drink, but it's meant for four people, so I think it works as another round."

Regina's eyes grew huge as she regarded the tank. "It's perfect," she said.

The waitress placed three extra-long bendy straws into the tank before walking away.

The more Minerva sipped on her straw, the more she felt as though she understood what the candy fish felt like. She was floating somewhere, too, oriented in the wrong direction but powerless to stop it with her brain half-pickled. What few inhibitions she had left melted away, and she found herself blurting out the first thing that came to mind.

Later, she would have the hardest time recalling what she said, the questions she asked and what Regina and Rosie answered. In fact, most of the evening collapsed in on itself, melted into unrecognizable shapes. There was enough alcohol in her system that she lost conscious control of herself.

There was a cab ride, not to Minerva's place, but to somewhere else. Minerva could remember a large blue couch that practically swallowed her when she lay down on it, feeling as though her body was too heavy and the room was moving too fast.

It was a large room she found herself in – a combination living room, dining room, and kitchen. Open layout. There was even a fireplace, although Minerva couldn't fathom why. It wasn't like winters got cold enough down here to warrant one. There was occasionally a freak day or two when temperatures would dip over the winter, a cold snap with snow every five years or so. But that was it. Skinner didn't have real winters – certainly not like what she was used to growing up.

But a lot of the fancier apartments in Skinner inexplicably had fireplaces. It was a standard "luxury" offering. That and the open layout were very in vogue in the Skinner high-income housing boom. A fireplace and open layout were easy ways to demonstrate to tenants that they were going to experience modern living at its finest.

In the next room, there was a bed. The idea of crashing onto a bed and falling into oblivion was quite an enticing prospect, but Minerva knew in her current state that she couldn't quite make it there. It was a noisy bedroom, too, she thought, as the world spun above her. The living room ceiling fan was certainly off, but now it rotated artificially, taking the rest of the world with it.

Soft moans were coming from the bedroom. Kisses. Susurrations. Bodies whispering across sheets as they moved across the blankets and across each other.

It sounded... delicious. Minerva wanted to be part of whatever was going on in there. She gathered her strength and rose from the massive couch, staggering towards the bedroom. Looking inside, she could see Regina's and Rosie's nude forms, wrapped in one another and bedsheets in a complicated matrix, their bodies pressed together. Regina was kissing Rosie's shoulder with a lazily open trailing mouth. Rosie's eyes were squeezed shut.

Sensing Minerva's presence, they snapped to alertness as both of their heads turned in her direction.

Minerva felt her lying fingers throbbing in time with other parts of her body. "I'm part of this," she said. She squeezed her right middle and index finger together. Bolstered by the alcohol, she didn't bother to put her hand behind her back, didn't try to conceal the gesture.

The familiar energy surged through her crossed fingers. But outside of her, nothing happened. Nothing had seemed to change. A moment later, she felt a wall of energy coming towards her, hitting her face with great force as though someone had slapped her.

"No, you're not," Rosie said.

"Get the hell out of here," Regina said.

Minerva's fingers instantly went numb. Confused, she backed out of the bedroom and closed the door.

Shuffling back to the couch, she contemplated calling home, getting one of her boyfriends to come pick her up.

But it was impossible.

She didn't know where she was of course, although she supposed that could be rectified by stepping outside, looking at the number on the building she was in, finding a street sign. She was drunk and exhausted, so it would be more difficult than normal, but it could be done.

No, the bigger obstacle was her own shame. How could she explain any of it?

Darren would understand the girls' night out, since it had been part of her mission to find out exactly what Regina's story was, but would he understand how much she'd had to drink? He wasn't exactly a vision of temperance himself and certainly enjoyed his booze, but Minerva had found that even heavy drinkers could have pronounced double standards when it came to how they felt about how much other people drank.

In some ways the evening had been a great success. Minerva had discovered plenty about Regina Withers that she didn't know before. On the other hand, however, she was far from confirming her suspicion that Withers was a blackmailer.

The moaning started again in the adjacent room. Even through the door, Minerva could hear it. It was fainter now, but her mind amplified the sound and supplied an accompanying visual.

Minerva grabbed a throw blanket and crawled under it. The moaning continued, tantalizing. Sleep was elusive. Her imagination was too engaged. At first she stewed, feeling miserable and rejected.

But as the sounds continued to come from the bedroom, her fingers crept lower to the familiar spot. This touch was automatic, really, an old impulse, and it introduced an additional element that helped her sensory imagination along. The tension within her built –swelling and rocking. Everything in her tensed as she crested on the top of an incomprehensible wave, one that felt as powerful as it felt precarious. Before too long, the wave crashed on the shore, and she choked holding back a scream that threatened to erupt from her, not wanting to disturb her friends in the next room, who by the sound of it had just felt a large wave or two break themselves.

Minerva awoke to the sound of butter sizzling in a pan. Rosie stood in front of the stove. Her hair was a mess, a rat's nest of snarls, but her face looked relaxed and happy – particularly given how much they'd all had to drink the night before.

Rosie was wearing a puffy blue terry cloth robe that looked to be several sizes too large for her. The belt was cinched tight, securing the unwieldy garment in place.

"Over easy okay?" Rosie asked Minerva.

"Perfect," Minerva responded. As she did so, she winced. The sound of her own voice hurt her head. Lovely.

Minerva surveyed the room quickly. "Where's Regina?" she asked.

"Still sleeping," Rosie answered. She walked over to Minerva holding a small dessert plate in her hand.

The plate held a fried egg on a piece of wheat toast. Over easy.

"Here," Rosie said. "You should get something in your system."

"That obvious, is it?" Minerva asked.

Rosie nodded. "It's okay though. It was your first time swimming in the fish tank." She grinned. "I've done enough laps to have learned my lesson."

Rosie plowed into a less colorful meal she'd made for herself. To Minerva it looked like a bowl of plain oatmeal. Gruel of some sort.

Rosie and Minerva ate in silence. When Minerva had finished her meal, Rosie took the plate and stacked her empty bowl on top of it. She walked over to the dishwasher.

"I'm warning you," Rosie said sternly. "Don't you dare try what you tried last night again."

"What do you mean?" Minerva said.

"You know exactly what I mean," Rosie said, glaring. "Take it from me – because I know *exactly* what I'm talking about – manipulating other people never ends well."

Minerva felt a frisson of fear.

"It's easy for you," Rosie said. "It's easy for me, too. But just because you *can* do something, it doesn't mean that you should."

"I just… I just wanted to be part of it."

"I know," Rosie said. "But we didn't want you to be part of it, and you can't just cross your fingers and barge your way into it. That's not the way a friend is supposed to act. That's not something a good person does. That makes you something else. It makes you a consent violator."

Minerva didn't know what to say. There are times in life when someone says something that fills you with such shame that you desperately don't want it to be true – and yet part of you knows that it is, and you also know that you can't go back and undo what you've done, and all that's left for you is to move forward and try not to make the same mistake again.

When that happens, sometimes an apology can help build a way forward with someone else. But there are other times when an apology will sound more like excuses to the person you've giving it to and will do more harm than good.

Minerva wasn't sure which of these situations she was in. Rosie didn't seem like the forgiving type, so perhaps it was better to move on and hope that time would come in and start easing down the intensity.

In the meantime, Minerva did what she could. "It won't happen again," she said. "I promise."

"Good," Rosie said. "Now gather up your stuff. I'm bringing you home."

"Walk of shaaaaaame," Darren crowed as Minerva walked through the door.

"Oh, are we acting like Chad now?" she challenged him.

"That was pretty delicate for Chad," Darren said.

"You both know I'm right here, don't you?" Chad piped up.

"Did you hear something?" Minerva teased.

"Not a thing," Darren replied.

In the far corner, Max put his hand over his mouth to stifle a laugh. The gesture was so pronounced. Where had she seen it before? It reminded her of the overly dramatic ways that mascots moved when they were in their costumes. A dog mascot probably.

No, she thought suddenly. Not a mascot. A character from one of Max's video games. It was the dog from *Duck Hunt*, the one who popped up after you missed a shot mocking you with barely concealed laughter.

Come to think of it, Minerva thought, Max had a lot in common with that little dog, and she'd never seen them in the same place at one time, had she?

Her lips curled into a smile at the idea of this conspiracy. Maybe there was something to it. After all, the real Max had gotten up and walked over to her and was now standing directly in front of her in a way that reminded Minerva of how a dog will greet its owner when the owner arrives home from work.

"What are you smiling about?" Max asked.

"It's a long story," Minerva said truthfully.

"The good ones usually are," Max said.

While none of her boyfriends were making a big fuss out of the fact that she was out all night, Minerva could tell by glancing around the room just how much her absence had troubled them. All three of them looked disheveled and sleep deprived, as though they'd been sitting up all night waiting. The living room told a similar story. It appeared that they'd been camped out, trying a variety of strategies to keep themselves awake for her return. A dizzying array of video game cartridges and systems were pulled out along with all three controllers. Half-eaten bags of corn chips and empty green two-liter bottles of soda were stashed all around the room.

"What?" Darren said defensively, as Minerva studied the room. "We had a slumber party. It's a free country."

"Did we do something wrong?" Max asked.

Minerva shook her head. "No," she said. "I feel like I did. I should have told you I was going to be out, that I wasn't coming home."

"Why didn't you?" Darren asked.

"I didn't know anybody would miss me," Minerva said. And it was the truth. Although she'd been living with Chad for quite a while now, he'd never seemed to miss her exactly. True, she hadn't been out much on her own. In fact, she couldn't remember the last time she'd pulled an all-nighter like this. But she hadn't been staying home out of a sense of obligation, and she certainly hadn't thought Chad would miss her. They'd lived like bachelors before the last couple of months. More like buddies than like a family. They shared space. Sometimes they ate together. But they had never really synced up, found a stable orbit that they swung through together. It had been more erratic, more sporadic.

We'd never entrained, Minerva thought.

This was completely different. Even Chad looked like he hadn't been to sleep and as though he were happy she'd returned.

"Don't take this the wrong way," Chad said. "But you look like shit."

Well, that cracked the illusion wide open, didn't it?

Darren swooped to the rescue. "What he means to say is," Darren began, throwing a stern look at Chad, "that you should probably grab a nap. You look like you had a lot of fun last night."

Max smirked at both of them. "Come on," he said to Minerva. "I'll tuck you in."

Minerva nodded. As she left to follow Max to the bedroom, she could have sworn she caught envious looks coming from both Darren and Chad.

Well, she thought to herself. *That was something new.*

That had been the most curious and unconventional aspect of their admittedly curious and unconventional living situation: The fact that none of her boyfriends really seemed to suffer from any jealousy.

It was idyllic, really. Before living with three men, she'd entertained the fleeting fantasy of having more than one partner at a time, but even in those imaginings, she'd never let herself conceive of a harmonious domestic situation like the one she was in. Before it happened to her, it seemed impossible.

Actually, she thought, as Max pulled the covers up over her body and tucked them practically beneath her chin, now that it was happening to her, it still seemed impossible.

"Nighty night," Max said, before giving her a little wave and closing the bedroom door.

She closed her eyes and rolled over onto her side. It was like living in a dream, the situation she now found herself in.

She felt a lump in her throat. Why then, she wondered, was she not completely satisfied?

Why didn't she feel happy?

What more could she possibly want?

She pondered this as sleep took her.

Dream Invasions

Minerva started suddenly and peered down at her body. Her body was wrapped in bedsheets. But they were blindingly white.

This was strange because she didn't own white sheets. Too easily stained and difficult to get completely pristine again, even with the aid of bleach. Because of this, all the sets she put on her bed were a royal blue.

The sheets were wrong. That was her first clue that something was off. And then she noticed she wasn't in bed.

She was sitting on the ground. The dirt ground.

As she glanced back at the white sheets, she realized she wasn't actually wrapped up in bedsheets, as she initially thought she was. No, she was wearing a white cloth that looked an awful lot like a bedsheet. It was slung around only one shoulder, the left one.

Her right shoulder was bare.

The white cloth hung down nearly to her feet.

It dawned on her. She was wearing a toga. Of course.

Something else was wrong, too. Minerva noticed suddenly that her breasts were gone. Her chest was flat. She even had chest hair. How curious.

On either side of her were two women. One was a woman with frizzy blond hair. She wore bright lipstick and heavy eyeliner that made her eyes seem to recede into her head. Despite her newness, she smiled with keen familiarity at Minerva. The other woman Minerva was certain she had seen before. It was Rosie Drake.

Both women smiled at her with blistering heat emanating from behind their eyes. Their hands disappeared under the toga, moving, fumbling, until Minerva felt them both stroking her...

Her penis.

I have a penis? Minerva thought. Her penis responded in the affirmative, throbbing as both women paid attention to it.

This was a kind of madness, Minerva observed. She felt overwhelmed by sensation. Controlled by pleasure in a way that she hadn't been in a very long time, if ever.

Her penis propelled her body forward as hands became mouths and mouths turned to other forms of lovemaking. They mounted her in turn. Over and over again. Rising and falling.

Afterwards, Minerva would not have been able to tell what exactly happened, in what order, and with whom. But her strange new body ached with a glowing exhaustion.

She realized guiltily she didn't even know the blond woman's name, only that she had spectacular curves and her eyeliner and mascara had run from exertion, making her look quite ghoulish while afterglowing.

In that moment, Minerva bristled. Of course. It was Regina. Why had she not realized who it was at first? Had the frizzy blond hair thrown her off, or had Regina's face changed during the sexual encounter?

Everything seemed quite a bit fuzzier than normal. The sky was changing color in a disconcerting and unpredictable manner. It reminded Minerva of the way light moves in time lapse photography, with shadows being thrown haphazardly across the landscape at breathtaking speed.

Had Regina's identity moved as well? Or had she simply not noticed it?

Rosie smiled at Minerva as she collapsed beside her. "You're quite a man," she observed.

"I guess I am," Minerva replied. "Not sure how I got so lucky."

"To the victor go the spoils," Rosie explained.

It wasn't much of an explanation, but Minerva wasn't about to go asking a bunch of questions. No need to spoil the moment by interrogating it.

And she didn't have to. Regina dressed and left them. Rosie chatted easily about where they were, their circumstances, what would likely come next.

As Minerva listened, it became evident that she was a warrior. And both women and their sexual favors were prizes she'd won via valor.

Minerva woke from the early morning nap, drenched in sweat and deeply sexually frustrated. Rosie and Regina were off limits. She knew that, but apparently her subconscious didn't.

It was funny, she mused, how an entire world of possibility had unfolded before her because of this strange new power. What had previously been fantastic was well within her reach, and yet, she was fixated upon what she couldn't have.

Infuriating, really. She'd always found herself looking down on people who were like that, who seemed unable to enjoy what they had and were instead obsessed with what they didn't.

She'd sworn she'd never be that way. When she was longing for more, she told herself that she'd be different. When her circumstances improved, she would appreciate the upward mobility, savor it. She wouldn't be one of those people who let a taste of power corrupt them, turn them insatiable, make them less satisfied. But now here she was, doing the same thing herself, what she promised herself she'd never do.

It was a humbling position to be in. The attendant depression that followed sadly made her long even more for what she couldn't have, clutching for something new to cope.

"Someone has a crush," Darren teased her after she reported back to him on her evening with Regina and Rosie and what had transpired.

"Stop it," she said.

This didn't deter Darren. If anything, he took requests to cease a behavior as a challenge, typically assumed she was kidding.

"Minerva and Rosie up in a tree, K-I-S-S-I-N-G."

"Darren," Minerva said. "Just don't."

"What?" he said. "It's nothing to be ashamed of. And I don't blame you, really. There's something…different about her. Something that reminds me of you. It makes sense to me that you'd be attracted to her."

"Well, she doesn't like me back, so it doesn't matter," Minerva said.

"Can't win em all," Darren said.

"I know."

"Look on the bright side," Darren said. "At least you're not alone. You've got plenty of company." After a beat, he added, "Including present company."

"I know," Minerva said.

"You know," Darren said, leaning in and speaking the words directly onto the nape of her neck. "You know. Is there anything you don't know?" He brushed her earlobe with his lips before he pulled away.

Minerva considered this. "Apparently how to deal with rejection," she said.

Darren laughed.

Darren had a point. She did have plenty of company between Darren, Max, and Chad – even if Chad did leave a lot to be desired. He'd turned into a good housekeeper in the last few months, but little else had changed.

He still had a way of saying things that hurt her feelings. She rarely bothered making love with him anymore, since he was so much more selfish in bed than Max or Darren.

She had begun to wonder what she'd ever seen in him.

I don't know if I saw much in him, she thought, *or if I didn't see that there was anything else more suitable out there.*

Darren and Max had changed all of that.

She continued to run into Rosie at Skinner Makes and become bitterly disappointed with herself every time she felt her stomach drop in response. This was ridiculous. Why was she so hung up on Rosie? She had plenty of other companionship, financial freedom, and a new creative outlet in pottery.

Perhaps, Minerva thought, *there's still something missing. But that doesn't mean it's only something Rosie can give me.*

She continued to attend Darren's Beautiful Liars meetings, making a concerted effort to make new friends there. She also pushed herself to talk to strangers around Skinner Makes, as awkward as it was.

Most of the members were men. And it was not hard to become close to them. Most of them were introverted and uneasy around her, which told her they weren't used to a lot of female attention, but with a little persistence – and the aid of crossed fingers – she found it quite easy to break down their walls.

Just as before, she found herself going a bit far with it, and before she knew it, she'd bedded about half of the makers that frequented Skinner Makes. She was honest about her situation – that she was already seeing Darren, Max, and Chad – that in fact all three men were squeezed into her apartment, taking turns sleeping on the couch and the living room floor – and in spite of this, each new man seemed to want to not only be her lover but also move in with her.

"But there's nowhere for you to sleep!" Minerva said.

One enterprising conquest named Tom had the solution. "I'll build you a house." He procured a plot of land and got to work.

And so it began, the largest group project Skinner Makes had ever attempted: A new home for Minerva and her many boyfriends.

Tom was a construction engineer who was used to designing large-scale projects, so a single-family home was well within his purview. He drew up the plans quickly and doled out assignments to her other boyfriends. Minerva watched in wonder as her boyfriends organized themselves and cooperated to accomplish the task.

Twenty days later, her new home was finished, standing on land she didn't have to pay for. No more apartment life for her. There was a beautiful master bedroom for her of course – and anyone else she wanted to join her for the night – and plenty of other space for her boyfriends to sleep. Tom had the foresight to construct the other bedrooms in a barracks style that made it easy to fit many bunkbeds into the space.

"It should easily accommodate us now," Tom had said, "and there's room for more." He indicated the possible need for further future expansions had also guided his selection of the lot.

Her lovers took care of moving everything into the house – they hauled in Minerva's possessions and all their own without troubling her. *This might just be the hottest fantasy of all*, she noted, realizing she'd moved to a house of her own and had managed to avoid packing, lifting, or unpacking while doing so. She was a bit troubled, however, to note when she moved through the house that Max had been telling the truth, as much as it conflicted with her memory – there was no espresso machine. He hadn't moved one in with him anyway.

Still, Minerva regarded the new home in awe. This wasn't simply a house; it had the makings of a compound. One that had materialized rather seamlessly, manifested simply through her desires. Curious, really, as until recently the universe didn't seem to care at all about what she wanted. *Is this how Cinderella felt when her pumpkin turned into a coach?* She wondered.

And yet… the dreams persisted. Nearly every night, she would find herself transforming physically into the same form, losing her breasts and gaining a penis, and carousing with Regina and Rosie at the same time.

She wasn't always a warrior claiming them as trophies, wearing the gladiatorial costume of a frat boy. The setting changed countless times. There were different costumes. The action took place in a variety of different locations.

In one dream, Minerva took them both on a beach at sunset while a group of curious tourists stood by and watched, their mouths frozen open in shock, snapping pictures of the three lovers with cameras that hung around their necks. Upon waking, Minerva found herself wondering where someone would get a roll of film like that developed exactly and found herself laughing at the thought.

In another dream, she screwed Regina and Rosie while hanging off the side of a building, attached to a precarious snarl of climbing ropes. As she climaxed, her tether came loose, and she plummeted many stories down. Thankfully, she woke up before she hit the ground and felt the impact.

Not everything changed, however, from dream to dream. It was always Regina and Rosie, and Minerva always found her body transformed in the exact same way.

Every time she awoke, she found herself wanting more.

It seemed obscene to be this sexually frustrated given the circumstances. Her sex life was an embarrassment of riches. She wasn't going through a drought by any stretch of the imagination. In fact, she'd been naughtier than she'd been in a long time.

She walked around practically every day feeling like she had a dirty secret, one that made her entire body glow. Before the past few months, she'd never had sex with more than one person in a single day. Now that was old news. It wasn't at all uncommon for her to be intimate with three or four of her boyfriends in a single day. For the most part, this was one on one, and they stole their opportunities when they could, but sometimes a few of them would cooperate, and she'd find herself enmeshed in a cage of hands, mouths, legs, and cruces.

Even one on one, however, it was all a blur. One man in the shower, another at night to go to sleep, and yet another encounter in the morning.

Was it truly random? Were they simply seizing opportunity? Or were they coordinating the order somehow among themselves?

It seemed almost random but not quite. Plus, she noted, so far there had been no arguments over her. Not as far as she knew anyway. If they were fighting over her, they kept those conversations far away from her, where she couldn't hear them. And as far as she could tell, none of her boyfriends seemed to be in relationships with one another, or anyone else outside of the house.

True, it would have been possible for them to sneak off and see a lover when she was preoccupied – which was most of the time lately – but she didn't feel like that was happening. They seemed strangely devoted to her.

"Max Meteo, reporting in from your personal man harem," Max said, as Minerva ate breakfast together with him one morning.

It was just the two of them, Minerva's idea, because she had started to miss him. If whatever system they were using to divide intimate time with her were under her control, she would have given Max two or three shares in the schedule. But it wasn't, so this was the best she could do, finding stolen moments when they could be together unexpectedly.

It meant cutting into her precious alone time, but to her thinking, it was more than worth it. Where a lot of other people took energy for Minerva to be around, Max had a way of refilling her energy whenever she spent time with him. He relaxed her, and she hadn't been able to find that with anyone else.

"Man harem?" Minerva said, bristling.

Max smirked. "You have to have a sense of humor about these things. Anyway, it must be pretty great having your own man harem."

"Actually, it's not," Minerva said.

"Oh?"

"Well, it has its moments," Minerva said.

Max smiled. "I can think of a few myself." His eyebrows punctuated the thought.

"It doesn't seem quite right though, Max," Minerva said.

"What do you mean?'

"Here I am, I have everything I'd ever want. I'm financially stable. I live in a beautiful house. I have a… gaggle of boyfriends." Minerva frowned. "You know, it's hard to talk about any of this without making my life sound ridiculous."

"That's why I go with 'man harem,'" Max said. "Just go for it. Lean into the ridiculousness."

"It doesn't feel real," Minerva said.

"It doesn't?"

Minerva shook her head. "It feels... conditional. Provisional."

"You mean, you're worried that we're going to up and leave you?" Max said.

"No," Minerva said. "I mean... I'm worried it's not actually happening. That I'll wake up one morning and it will have never happened. It doesn't feel real. It feels like a fantasy... and not a well-thought out one either. It feels like something you think about when you're trying to get off. A fantasy you keep adding details to, embellishing it more and more, trying to get that shock out of yourself, that one rush of chaos that brings you over the edge. Sometimes if you're not careful enough, you'll think of something distracting that'll bring you away from the edge. Something confusing or gross. And before you know it, the entire fantasy is gone, and you're just a sad sweaty naked person who can't get off."

"That's a very interesting theory," Max said. "The solipsism angle."

"Solipsism?"

"The philosophical idea that the self is the only thing that exists, that your mind is the only real thing in this world, and that the rest of us are just figments of your imagination. However sexy any given figment might be." Max smiled. "Just to be clear, I will happily accept a trophy that says World's Sexiest Figment on it. Store that idea away for the holidays."

"Noted," Minerva said, laughing.

"But there's just one hiccup in your theory," Max said.

"What's that?"

"I know my own mind. I have my own reality," Max said. "So I know you're full of it. And for all I know, *you're* a figment of *my* imagination."

"True," Minerva said, "but it would be pretty easy for the figments of my imagination to just *say* that."

"This is why I hate solipsism," Max said. "It turns into an impasse. No one knows anything, and no one can ever know anything. I'd say the whole thing's an armed standoff or a hostage situation, but that's giving it too much credit and too much entertainment value. Solipsism is a yawn fest."

"I guess," Minerva said. "I'm just having a hard time reconciling the past few months. So many things just don't make any sense. It makes me feel like I'm going crazy."

"You?" Max said. He thought about it for a moment, before shaking his head. "No, you are stone cold sane." He reached out and grabbed her hand before adding, "Now the rest of the world? It is crazy. And that's where you run into trouble."

Minerva laughed but found herself wondering if there could be truth to that. Was it possible for the world to go mad? Not in the colloquial sense, not what people normally mean when they say such a thing, that people have strayed too far from traditionalism and there will be significant societal tension as a result.

No, a more literal kind of madness.

"Maybe it's the opposite of solipsism, really," Minerva said.

"And that would be?"

"Maybe the world has its own agenda. Maybe it's the only thing that's truly real, and we're the illusions." She took a long sip of her coffee as she considered this, noting that Max had made it up to perfection with generous cream and only the faintest whisper of sugar.

"This is really good coffee," she said.

"Thanks," Max said. "It's an Americano actually. I went out and got an espresso machine. Seemed like a good idea once you brought it up."

Minerva shivered, as she took another sip of coffee. Even though it had been pleasantly warm moments before, it felt icy to her suddenly. "Maybe the mad world is sick of us and is trying to shake us off its back," she said to Max.

"By getting much-needed mental help?" Max prompted.

Minerva shrugged. "Sure." She took another sip of her coffee. "If the world's gone mad, there's no telling what it might do, right?"

"Including get help?" Max asked, smiling broadly. Clearly, he was amused by this idea.

"Including get help," Minerva affirmed, nodding her head.

"You know, Minerva," Max said. "That's one thing I've always liked about you."

"What's that?"

"You believe so powerfully in the power of recidivism – in reform – that you project it on to inanimate objects, even in hypothetical analogies."

Minerva shrugged. "You gotta believe in something, right?'

He smiled at her. "Indeed."

Finally, one night Minerva had a break from the typical pattern of her dreams. Rosie was there like usual, although fully clothed this time, but Regina was nowhere to be found.

Minerva noted with great surprise that her dream body was her normal everyday one and not the form she had become accustomed to assuming in dreams.

"This has to stop," Rosie hissed at her, pushing Minerva away. "And this has to stop now."

As Minerva stumbled back from the dream push, she awoke in her own bed. It was only a dream of course... but then why did she feel so ashamed?

Minerva was pulling up at Skinner Makes before she was fully cognizant of what was happening. She'd driven there on autopilot, barely registering what she was doing.

Even as she stopped the car and climbed out, walking up to the building entrance, she didn't feel as though she were moving voluntarily. Instead, she felt more like she was being pulled there by someone else, and she was left to simply observe what was happening.

She'd seen nature documentaries about instinctual animal responses. There was the migration of birds of course as well as the organized way that honeybees swarmed together. But it didn't end there. Many animal species seemed to have a predisposition towards complicated emotional patterns like grief and empathy buried deep within the brain, even without the benefit of language as humans knew it.

She felt what she was doing at that same level. There was no questioning it or planning it. There was nothing volitional about what she was doing. It was just happening, like a reflexive response.

And because of this, she wasn't quite sure exactly where she was going, not until she stood in the pottery studio before Rosie Drake.

Rosie looked up and nodded at her. There was no surprise on her face. Minerva knew that Rosie had been expecting her.

"I mean it," Rosie said firmly. "It has to stop."

Minerva shook her head, feigning confusion. "I don't know what you're talking about."

Rosie scowled. "Of course you do. Don't try to bullshit me."

Minerva bit the inside of her cheek, not sure what to say. How did Rosie know? She hadn't told anyone about the dreams. Not Darren. Or even Max. They knew that she was jonesing for Regina and Rosie of course, but she had told no one about the dreams, barely able to make sense of them herself. It had particularly confused her how her own body had transformed in them and how much she'd liked that transformation, something she never really thought about when she was awake.

"You need to stay the hell out of my dreams," Rosie said.

Minerva cocked her head. "How could I…?" she began, not sure how to even finish the question.

"Invade my dreams?" Rosie finished.

Minerva nodded.

"You're so in denial," Rosie said.

"Denial?"

Rosie rolled her eyes. "I can't believe I have to explain this."

"Explain what?"

Rosie let out a deep sigh and took a couple of slow, deep breaths.

"What?" Minerva prompted.

"You're not like other people, Minerva. Surely you've noticed. You can do things other people can't. When you lie, people believe you even if it doesn't make any sense. And you're never found out, are you? Because the truth comes in and backs you up. The way things are changes whenever you open your mouth," Rosie said.

Minerva didn't reply to this. She suddenly felt very naked.

"You can do it when you're asleep, too," Rosie continued. "You can shape your own dreams, yes, but you can also shape other people's dreams – and participate in shared dreams. Or, in my own case, you can invade dreams." She shook her head. "You can but you shouldn't. And I'm telling you I need you to stop."

"How do you know all of this?" Minerva asked. "How do you know about me?"

"I know what you are," Rosie said, "because I am what you are."

"You are?" Minerva asked.

Rosie nodded. "And I am more."

Truthshapers

Some intuitive forms are yet to be definitively confirmed and instead have been calculated and theorized to exist due to currently unexplained phenomena. The last century has brought tremendous change to our world. Some even say that things are changing so rapidly that even the rate of change itself has accelerated. This was first written off as a product of technological innovation and ingenuity – but as the phenomenon persists, some have looked to other places for an explanation.

A number of disruptions in the fabric of reality point towards a theoretical psychic subtype: The truthshaper.

As proposed, a truthshaper would not only be able to lie convincingly and have their deceptions believed – but provided a given truthshaper were powerful enough, they would even be able to reshape reality itself to match any lies that they tell.

While these powers could have many potential positive applications, for example, ridding humanity of various ills with a quick word, an unscrupulous truthshaper could wreak great havoc if they had destructive aims, or even if they used their powers carelessly.

This is because there is only so far you can bend the truth before you start to strain reality, and the consequences of doing so can be catastrophic.

Analyzing the last few decades of inexorable change, some experts in the field of Reality Momentum believe this is precisely what has taken place.

from Insecta Psychica: Towards an Intuitive Taxonomy by Cloche Macomber

"You're more?" Minerva said.

Rosie nodded. "We are both truthshapers," she said. "Now, I'm not as powerful a truthshaper as you are, but I am also a precog."

"A precog?" Minerva asked.

"A precognitionist," Rosie said. "I can see the future."

Minerva's eyes widened. "So you know what's going to happen?"

"Well, sorta," Rosie said. "I see *possible* futures anyway. But it's often more than I want to see."

Minerva nodded. Suddenly, Rosie's apathy made a lot more sense to her. How would she feel, Minerva wondered, if she was always contending with what would happen next? Would it make it impossible to stay in the moment?

"It's how I know that Regina's going to leave me," Rosie said, her tone level.

"But Regina adores you!" Minerva protested.

"For now," Rosie replied. "When her career takes off, she's going to have to make a choice. Does she stay with me and risk being blackmailed by anyone who figures out we're together and sees a big payoff in threatening someone famous? Or does she end it with me?"

Rosie frowned. "It will be an easy choice for her. I'm something unexpected that happened to her. Becoming famous is her real dream. True love never was. Especially not finding true love with a divorced mother 20 years her senior."

"Couldn't you just reshape reality so she wouldn't leave you?" Minerva asked.

Rosie nodded. "Of course I could. But I won't."

Minerva studied her face, looking for an explanation.

"Every time I'm with her, it's bittersweet," Rosie continued. "Because I love her so much, but I'm always acutely aware of when I'll lose her and how. It makes it hard to stay in the present and to stay happy."

"I don't understand," Minerva said. "It would only take one lie."

"I could lie," Rosie admitted. "But if I lied, I'd know. I'd know that's why she stayed with me. None of it would be real. And I would know. Everything that followed would be a lie."

"Or the new truth," Minerva offered.

Rosie shook her head. "I had a dear friend when I was younger, my first lover actually. She was into the occult when we were in middle school. Bought every book she could think of, studying strange esoteric philosophies. Spellbooks, she had so many spellbooks."

Rosie smiled at the memory and got lost in it for a few seconds. Minerva waited while she found her way back.

"Anyway," Rosie continued, "there were love spells in practically every one of those books. Those were her favorites, the ones she labored over the most. As far as I know, she never met with any success. But she tried so hard to get those spells to work. And all the while, I'd watch her, just not understanding, never really understanding why she wanted to cast a spell to get someone to fall in love with her. And not just because someone already was… because I was." Rosie sighed at this, before continuing, "But I also couldn't understand because I couldn't imagine living a happily ever after with someone I'd cast a love spell on. My picture of love always involved someone wanting me of their own accord. Someone *choosing* me. Not forcing someone to adore me by any means, even mystical. If they didn't freely choose me, then I wasn't really their heart's desire, so was it really love? Or was it a kind of magical slavery?"

Minerva nodded slowly. An uncomfortable feeling crept up in her as she considered the events of the past few months, thought about her boyfriends and how they seemed to adore her. It had never occurred to her before to question their affection, but as Rosie spoke, she found herself doing just that.

Perhaps that was why things had started to not feel real. Perhaps they weren't. It was an unsettling thought.

"So yes," Rosie said, "I suppose if I wanted to throw caution to the wind and say to hell with the natural order of things, then I could turn Regina into my love slave by bending the truth. But Minerva, it's not for me. There are times when losing someone is better than keeping them by the wrong means."

Rosie forced herself to smile. The expression looked awkward on her face, but she was trying. "I'll stay with what I have. It's more than some people ever get."

"I won't do it again," Minerva said. Her fingers crawled into position, attempting to flex and to cross as the words were leaving her mouth. But they stopped just short of forming an X. She couldn't quite manage it, not with Rosie.

Rosie glared at her. "You're doing it again right now," she said sternly.

"I'll try to stop," Minerva rephrased. This time her fingers stayed straight and separate.

"I guess I'll have to settle for that," Rosie replied, but once Minerva had left the pottery studio and she was alone, Rosie shook her head in disbelief.

The woman was an addict. There was no helping her. Rosie made a mental note to ask her employer for psychic wards, something that would keep Minerva out. This rogue truthshaper wouldn't change her ways, not on her own.

Asking for the wards would surely set off a chain of events Rosie wasn't quite prepared for, but she couldn't see any other option. It was the only way.

Change and Death

Truthtellers beget liars and liars beget truthtellers. Parents produce children that are shuffles of themselves, and those children in turn produce children that are further shuffles.

At some point, a truthteller will emerge in this pattern of chaos, a statistical inevitability, a byproduct of probability, of shuffling and reshuffling. However, truthtellers are never around for very long. The truth is not static, and even when it finally emerges, it is quickly reshuffled again into what will almost certainly be another lie, whether beautiful or ugly.

-Darren Delvecchio, Beautiful Liars International

Minerva awoke with a phone receiver in her hand, many yards away from where she'd been sleeping. She was already standing on her feet when her brain finally woke up, listening to her aunt's voice.

It had been several days since she'd dreamt, finding it suddenly impossible to dream of Rosie and Regina – or anything else for that matter.

At first, she thought the phone conversation might be a dream, because the words the caller were speaking weren't making any sense.

"I'm sorry, Minerva, but your father has passed away."

She had trouble making out what was said next, as her knees gave way. She sat on the floor, still holding the phone in her shaking hand, as the person on it continued to speak words that made no sense to her. They were about funeral arrangements.

"You should come home, Minerva," her aunt said. "Right away."

Minerva still said nothing in response. Instead, she made a wounded noise, as a wail escaped from her that frightened her. She felt spasms rack her body. Pain. Incredible pain.

She had always expected to be sad when one of her parents eventually died. But instead, it *hurt*. That was all she felt. Pain.

Incredible pain.

"I just thought you should know. I was worried no one would tell you. That you'd be forgotten," her aunt continued. "Minerva? Are you there?"

"Yeah," she choked out.

"Come home," her aunt said.

And then the call was over. Minerva wasn't sure if she'd hung up or if her aunt had. Or possibly the call had simply disconnected on its own, whether through a telephone company blip or because the universe had simply had enough of the call.

It was possible, she thought bleakly. There was so much she didn't know. She was being confronted with that more and more with each passing day.

After the call was over, and the spasms of pain broke for a few moments, the questions flooded her mind: How had he died? When? Had he suffered? Gone peacefully? Would there have been time to say goodbye had she not been so pointedly avoiding talking to her parents?

She resented her own questions instantly. First of all, she wasn't sure who to even ask. Or if she were in the shape to. Calling her mother after such a long time would have been a herculean task to begin with, an epic apology tour stop, but under these conditions... unthinkable.

She could barely choke anything out to her aunt, a relatively neutral third party, during the call. The idea of calling *her* back and asking questions… well, it was also an overwhelming proposition.

And complicating things was the fact that she wasn't sure if she even *wanted* to know the answers to those questions. Even though her brain was intent on asking them, it couldn't be trusted. Not in general and certainly not at a time like this. Her brain didn't always direct her towards what was good for her.

As she sat on the floor, she heard several pairs of footsteps.

She heard Max's voice calling out to her, from atop the staircase. "Minerva, you okay? Is everything alright?"

She didn't want to deal with him. Didn't want anyone's pity. And Minerva had always found that when tragedy struck, telling people what awful thing had happened was arguably more stressful than coping with it in silence.

"It's fine, Max," she lied, as her fingers crossed behind her back, quickly assuming their familiar shape. "Everything is fine. That was a wrong number. Go back to bed."

"Okay," Max said.

She could hear him whispering, "C'mon guys… false alarm, off to bed." She imagined the line of her concerned boyfriends trailing down the hallway, elbowing each other out of the way, and grinned.

What a strange life she had.

As she listened to them shuffle off, her fingers began to hurt. She was now used to them aching whenever she fibbed, but this wasn't an ache.

It was red hot searing pain. She wanted to scream but strained against the reaction, not wanting to alarm her housemates.

As she struggled against the impulse, the pain grew worse. Stars swam in her eyes. Everything went black.

When she awoke, it was still dark.

How long have I been out? She wondered.

"Ah, your eyes are open," said an unfamiliar voice.

A strange man sat in her armchair. He was holding a paintbrush in his hand, a tiny red plastic paintbrush like they use in elementary school art classes. Next to him was a set of plastic paint pots in every color, attached to one another by a strip of clear connective material.

A partially finished painting was before him. It appeared to be a lion. The unpainted portion of the canvas was divided into discrete bubbles, each marked by a number.

"What are you doing in my living room?" Minerva asked him.

"I am painting by numbers," the man responded.

Minerva sighed. "That's not what I meant," she said.

"You shouldn't say things you don't mean then," the man replied.

Minerva groaned. "I mean..." she thought for a moment. "Who are you?"

The man smiled. "That's a better question. A bit grand for my tastes. Philosophical. I've spent a long time wondering the same thing, you know. There's always what people *think* I am. My reputation. My legacy. And then there's who I am when I'm alone in my own thoughts. They're not always the same thing, you know. Which would you like to hear about?"

Minerva frowned. "We could start with your name," she said.

The man considered this. "Names are pretty arbitrary, if you ask me."

"Well, I didn't."

"Well, you're asking me a lot of stuff. Figured that might be next," he said.

Minerva held back another groan.

"My name? Well, an awful lot of people call me Change," he said.

"An awful lot of people? Like who?" Minerva asked.

"My name is Change," Change said.

"Who are these people?"

"Change," Change said. "C-H-A-N-G-E. Not Chance. Sometimes people call me 'Chance,' which I guess if they have to get it wrong is pretty much as close as you can get without getting it right, you know."

"Your parents must have been sadists," Minerva said.

"Because of my name?" Change asked.

"I mean, that's a start," Minerva replied. "Also there's clearly something seriously wrong with you."

"Is there?" Change asked.

"Yes."

"What's that?" Change asked. "What's seriously wrong with me?"

"Everything," Minerva said.

"That could be true," Change said. "Or everything else could be wrong, and I could be the only thing that's actually right."

"Unlikely," Minerva countered.

"We've always had a strained relationship, you and I," Change said.

"What are you talking about?" Minerva said.

"You've forgotten about me, haven't you?" Change said.

"We've never met before," Minerva said. "There's nothing to forget!"

"Are you so sure about that?" Change challenged her.

She looked more carefully at him. Did she recognize him? No, not really. Although there was a little something around the eyes that looked familiar… even though she couldn't quite place it.

"You're crazy making," she said.

"Sometimes," he replied.

Minerva studied the painting before him. "Why is the lion's nose blue?"

"Because I felt like painting it blue," Change replied.

"But you're supposed to follow the numbers. That's the whole point of a kit like this," Minerva said.

Change sighed. "I know. That's why I got it. I crave stability."

"So why not follow the numbers?" Minerva asked.

"I try," Change said. "I do. I just… can't help myself. I keep switching it up."

Or changing it, Minerva thought. But she couldn't bring herself to say such a terrible pun aloud.

"What are you doing here?" she said instead.

"Ah," Change said. "That's a good question." He smiled.

Minerva didn't like the look of his smile. It seemed very unnatural, very forced. "Please don't do that," she said.

"What? Smile?" Change asked.

"Yes."

"Why not?" Change said. "I read somewhere that smiling is good for you if you're depressed. Tricks your body into thinking you're happier than you are."

"Are you depressed?" Minerva asked.

"Of course I am," Change said. "Because I pay attention."

Minerva didn't have an answer to that.

"I'm here to deliver a message," Change said.

"A message?"

"You're in danger," Change said. "You need to stop telling such awful lies."

"Lies?" Minerva asked.

"Don't play dumb with me. There are those of us who know what you're doing. Who feel the repercussions every time you cross those nasty fingers of yours."

Minerva had a sudden urge to hide her hands.

"You can't hide from us," Change said. "You've been very bad."

"What do you mean?" Minerva said. She was tempted to deny it, but she knew that would be lying, and the last thing she wanted to do was risk lying in front of this demented being, whoever the heck he really was.

"We saw you dipping in and out of dreams like they're your personal harems. We see you building an actual harem. And we heard you lie about your father."

Minerva frowned. "That was nothing. I just wanted Max to leave me alone. I didn't want to explain."

"There are consequences to big lies like that, Minerva. Maybe not for normal people, but definitely for people like you."

"People like me?" Minerva said.

Change nodded. "Truthshapers."

"Truth what?" Minerva laughed.

Change rolled his eyes. "Oh, this is the absolute worst. This is the shittiest gig. I should have never taken this job."

"What are you talking about?"

"It's hard enough being an enforcer when I'm dealing with someone who actually knows what's going on. But trying to enforce when the person you're dealing with is absolutely clueless... it's enough to make you want to off yourself."

"Well, that's a little dramatic," Minerva said.

"Sometimes I'm like that, too. Sometimes I'm dramatic," Change said, but mostly to himself, even though Minerva was still there. She noted that was perhaps Change's most aggravating habit. He seemed to like to consult with himself as though she weren't actually there.

"Anyway," he said, "it's one thing to lie about your own personal circumstances. It's another when it affects other people. It's different when you're invading people's dreams. And forget about lies about life and death." Change scratched his chin and in doing so transferred a bit of blue paint there. "Minerva, what were you thinking?"

"I told you," Minerva said. "I just wanted to get Max off my back."

"You did a lot more than that," Change said.

"What do you mean?" Minerva asked.

"You know what? Forget this. Forget this gig," Change said. He got up and gathered his painting supplies. "You'll have to find out on your own."

"Find out what?" Minerva said.

Change left without another word.

She watched him walk down her driveway and down the street. She watched him until he vanished from sight.

"Find out what?" Minerva asked again, this time to an empty room.

Returning to Someplace You've Never Been

Strict parents create great liars.

-Darren Delvecchio, Beautiful Liars International

"You know, Minerva," her mother said, "I'd always hoped you'd find someone special to spend your life with, but…"

She stopped midsentence and considered Minerva's entourage, who were just climbing into their cars and forming a motorcade bound for a nearby hotel. Minerva felt embarrassed. She suddenly wished they had just gone directly there instead of stopping by her parents' house first.

Not your parents' *house, your* mother's *house*, she corrected herself sharply. Little mental changes like that were going to be hard to get used to. The past tense verbs were hard enough, but there were countless other rewrites to be made like the fact that calling it her "parents' house" no longer made sense that were going to hit her even harder. Might as well get used to it.

Perhaps she should have come alone. Or brought just one boyfriend, maybe Darren or Max. They both seemed like they'd make a good impression on her mother. More importantly, she could have acted like either one of them were her only boyfriend. It would have been simpler that way.

But the thought hadn't occurred to her until after she pulled up in front of her mother's home, a tiny ranch house that seemed even smaller on the giant plot of land that surrounded it. Minerva had been moving in a daze ever since she left her house back in Skinner. She was having trouble thinking ahead, anticipating such obvious problems.

The logistical nightmare that bringing all her boyfriends with her posed became immediately evident during the brief introductions in the front yard. The entryway of her mother's house simply didn't have enough room for all her suitors to stand. Neither did any other room in the rest of the house, really.

"I always assumed you'd stop at one person," her mother finished.

Minerva shrugged. "Guess I lucked out."

"Luck is finding one good man," her mother said. "This looks more like some kind of criminal enterprise."

Minerva felt uneasy, as though someone were watching her. She turned to look behind her. A bare tree towered over them. In its branches sat a long-tailed grackle. His yellow eyes were indeed staring in Minerva's direction. His feathers gleamed in the sun, reflecting its rays like an oil slick.

This struck Minerva as very strange. She couldn't remember the last time she'd seen a long-tailed grackle north of Wichita.

"Are you alright?" her mother prompted her.

"I'm fine," Minerva said, turning to face her mother. "I was just looking at that bird."

"What bird?" her mother said.

Minerva turned back around to point out the grackle in the tree, only to find when she did that he was gone. "Oh," she said. "I guess he flew away."

"Or you've been driving too long. Have you slept? You're not on drugs, are you? That's not why all those men are with you, is it?"

"Oh sure," Minerva said, her voice dripping with sarcasm. "I'm running a drug smuggling ring."

"You never know," her mother said. "I saw a story on *Dateline* about that."

"Smuggling?"

Her mother nodded. "*Dateline* covers all sorts of things, you know. Smuggling. Human trafficking." She leaned forward and whispered conspiratorially, "Polygamists."

Minerva laughed. "Makes sense. They air what'll get them ratings. There are just certain things folks can't look away from."

"Are you sure you're not in a cult?" Minerva's mother asked.

Minerva laughed again. "Yes, Mom, I'm sure. I'm not in a cult," Minerva said as her mother led her into the front entryway.

"From where I'm sitting, it doesn't look like she's joined a cult. But maybe she's started one," a familiar voice called out from their tiny kitchen.

"Nanny!" Minerva called to her grandma.

"One and the same," her grandma responded. "Anyway, if you are part of a cult, it looks like one I'd like to be part of, too."

Minerva smiled.

"I'd probably do really well, too. That's the nice thing about being tight with the leader. It gives you an in." Her grandmother squeezed her with a tight hug.

Of all the people Minerva had turned her back on when she'd moved to Skinner, her grandmother had been the one who pained her the most to leave. True to form, however, Nanny June had been the only one who hadn't pursued her. Who hadn't tried to cling to their past relationship. Her grandmother had been the one who had let her go. And somehow, although they'd never exchanged a single word about it, Minerva knew that her grandmother would understand her decision to leave and accept her motivations to set off for somewhere far away and not keep in touch.

Her grandmother had been an adventurer, too, an explorer. Someone who stuck out from a lot of the other small town folks.

True, her path had been different than Minerva's. She'd been widowed fairly young while her four children were still in diapers. Because of this, her path was set for her. Her quest would be to find the adventures hidden in the everyday, tethered in place by responsibility that limited her freedom.

Perhaps it had been a blessing. Once her children were grown and had children of their own – like Minerva – her grandmother had stayed in the area. No need to travel for adventures. Everywhere her grandmother went, adventure dutifully followed.

A lot of people can survive when they must. But few learn to enjoy it as well as her grandmother had. That was what made her special.

As much as Minerva strained to see that same spirit within her mother, the positivity and the joy, she couldn't. It hadn't been handed down to her mother, unlike her grandmother's striking bone structure and intense eyes.

"I'm surprised to hear you say that, mother," Minerva's mom said.

"And why is that?" Nanny June said. "I can appreciate a good-looking man just as well as anyone else."

"It's just… you've been single ever since Dad died. And that was a very long time ago."

"Well," Minerva's grandmother said, considering this, "that's true. But I think I could make allowances for a love slave or two."

"Nanny," Minerva laughed, "they're not my love slaves."

"Could have fooled me," her grandmother said.

"Anyway," her mother said, "I'm not quite sure what to think anymore. Nothing's right. Everything's upside down. Your father's gone. You're here acting like nothing has changed, like you can just waltz back in here and pretend like you only just left. And with a love train in tow. It's Opposite Day apparently, and I didn't get the memo."

Minerva didn't reply to this because she didn't know quite what to say. She couldn't figure out if she should comfort her mom – and she wasn't sure what she'd say to do that. Or perhaps she should be defending herself, her life, and her decisions. She couldn't think of how to do that either. So, she kept silent.

"I never thought someone like you would be able to find someone normal to be with," her mother continued. "Let alone... however many boyfriends you have."

"Gee, thanks, Mom," Minerva said.

"Well, you know how it is, how life goes. It isn't fair, but the pretty ones get first choice, and the rest of us, we get the scraps," her mother said.

"Minerva's a beautiful girl," her grandmother interjected.

"Mom, you don't have to be nice," her mother said.

Her grandmother winced.

"I know what you mean, Mom," Minerva said, as her grandmother turned sad eyes on her. Because she did understand what her mother meant. And she agreed. She wasn't hideous, not even unattractive, but she wasn't about to get discovered off the street to sign a modelling contract or star in a major motion picture. She looked nice enough. Trustworthy. Like the kind of person you'd ask to watch your stuff for a minute while you go to the bathroom.

But beautiful? No, that was a stretch. To Minerva's eyes, her own face looked like what you'd end up with if you tried to draw a beautiful woman, but you weren't very good at it, and the proportions kind of got messed up. All the components were there, but when put together, they didn't quite have the effect the artist had wanted.

She had the kind of face that was less than the sum of its parts.

And definitely not a face that could launch a thousand ships Helen of Troy style. Let alone start a small cult, simply by being so splendid.

The trouble with her mother, Minerva realized, and the trouble with most people for that matter is that they couldn't conceive of women having any kind of power that wasn't tied to their physical appearance.

It just didn't compute when a woman who wasn't exquisitely beautiful managed to meet with success.

It might as well be, for all intents and purposes, Opposite Day.

"Yes, Opposite Day," her mother said, and Minerva realized with a start that she had been talking aloud. She also had no idea for how long and exactly what she'd said, which was terrifying.

"Welcome to Opposite Day then," her grandmother added. "Maybe I should bake a cake or something. I wonder what kind of cake you bake for Opposite Day."

"Maybe an upside-down cake?" Minerva suggested.

"No more cake," her mother replied. "People keep trying to feed me. I can't tell you how many pans of lasagna they've brought. What is it about death and food?"

"I think people want to do something to help, and they don't know what else to do," her grandmother said.

"It's annoying," her mother replied.

"I know," her grandmother said. "Everything's going to be annoying for a while. There's no getting around it."

The phone rang. Minerva's mother rose to answer it, and her grandmother gestured for her to sit down. "I'll get that. You sit tight."

She walked over, picked up the receiver. "Yes? Yes, this is her mother actually." She cupped the receiver with one hand.

"Funeral home," she hissed to Minerva and her mother.

"Mmhmm," she said into the receiver. "Mmhmm."

And then, after a pause, "What do you mean you *lost* him?"

The voice on the other end of the phone suddenly rose in volume to the point where Minerva could hear it comfortably even from across the room. The pace was quick, the tone defensive.

"Forget it, forget it. I'll have to call you back later," her grandmother said, before slamming down the phone.

Minerva and her mother looked at her expectantly.

"Well?" her mother said.

"They've lost David."

"What?!" her mother said.

"The body. It never showed up," her grandmother said.

"Well, it's not just gonna show up on its own," her mother said.

"I don't know what to tell you," her grandmother said. "I'm just the messenger."

"This is bullshit," her mother said.

Minerva noted this with great alarm, since her mother never, ever swore.

"Get your stuff together, we're going down to the funeral home this instant to figure out what the hell is going on."

Believe it or not, bodies aren't exactly well guarded. It's not something many people know, but a lot of times, there's more security involved when the delivery driver drops pizza off on your doorstep.

In that case at least, they want to see your credit card and have you sign a receipt.

When it comes to getting a body from the hospital, basically all you have to do is show up and act like you're supposed to pick it up.

This is what the funeral director assumed had happened to David Cantor.

He explained this as calmly as he could to the widow, Shelly Cantor.

"That's the most ridiculous thing I've ever heard," she replied.

He didn't have a defense. It didn't make a whole lot of sense, and it was a fool's errand to argue otherwise.

Still, who would think someone would steal a body?

He'd been working for 35 years as a mortician, and this was the first time he'd ever had it happen. He would be shocked if it happened again.

There had been nothing formal in his training to tell him how to handle this situation. No set of guidelines for what you do when a body.... disappears.

"Your mother's going to have a rough road yet," her grandmother said as she and Minerva sat in the kitchen together at the small table. Her mother had stormed off to the bedroom after they came back from the funeral home, leaving them alone.

"Oh?"

Her grandmother nodded. "Take it from me, kid. The minute they haul off the body, someone else hauls in the bills." She sighed, and Minerva could hear an incredible weight behind that sigh. The sigh carried a sadness from somewhere removed in time. "They don't tell you about that, really. How much paperwork you have to do when someone dies. How many weird letters you get. The bills. Even when you're supposedly covered. It's expensive to die. And it's expensive to fight dying, too."

"The hospital?"

She nodded. "The hospital, the outpatient visits. Even hospice. You don't get much of a choice. No matter if you live or you die, you pay." She paused. "Well, someone pays. Someone has to pay eventually." She screwed up her face. "It really is the worst way to spend your money."

Minerva reached out and held her grandmother's hand.

"You are such a wonderful granddaughter," she said.

"It's what you deserve," Minerva replied, and her grandmother's face bloomed into an absurdly bright smile.

Her grandmother's expression suddenly darkened. "I worry about it, you know."

"About?" Minerva asked.

"The bill I'll leave. Who will have to pay it. It's such a mess. You come into the world owing people, and you go out just the same way. I'd rather be even Steven for once in my life."

"Nanny," Minerva said.

"Hm?"

"You're more than even. When it comes to you, the world comes out ahead every time. I'm lucky to have known someone like you."

"Oh, don't tell your mother that, she'll have you picking up the bill when I croak," her grandmother said.

Minerva laughed.

"Anyway, I think maybe that's the way it works," Nanny said.

"The way what works?"

"I think that's what grandmothers do," Nanny said. "Your mother is there to nitpick, criticize, and diminish you down to a small point. And then she grows up, mellows out, maybe goes through the change... and she realizes it just doesn't matter anymore. Of course, this happens just in time for her to be a complete angel to *your* children. Meanwhile, she was a complete nightmare to you."

"Are you saying you got on Mom's case?" Minerva asked.

"I plead the fifth!" her grandmother said.

"That only works in court," Minerva said. "This isn't *Law & Order.*"

"*Law & Order* isn't really court either," Nanny said.

"You know what I mean," Minerva said.

"Well, how about this for a defense?" Minerva's grandmother said. "A lady never tells."

"In that case, I don't know what I am, but I've never been a lady."

It was her grandmother's turn to laugh. "Ah, I've taught you well," she said, reaching out and rubbing Minerva's back with one wrinkled hand. "My understudy."

An Unwelcome Visitor and a Welcome One

When she first heard the rapping on the door, Minerva thought the noise was part of her dream. In fact, it had been. In her dream, the first one in quite some time, she was still at home at the house in Skinner, with her boyfriends, and someone had come to her door. Instead of answering the door, she had dropped to the floor and crawled away from the line of sight that a person could use to peer in through her front windows.

She let the visitor knock and knock.

"Why not just answer the door?" a shirtless dream Chad called to her from the stairwell.

"Shh," Minerva had answered. "Go back upstairs," she hissed.

He'd thrown his hands in the air. "You're so weird," he'd said, still louder than she'd ideally want, but she felt relief hit her as he'd turned around and walked back up the stairs.

Several sets of eyeballs peered down after him. Her other boyfriends. Of course. Chad had been the only one bold enough, brash enough to saunter down into a delicate situation. Now, seeing how badly that had gone off, the rest of her boyfriends knew better than to stumble down into the fray.

The knocks persisted. Grew louder.

What was she afraid of? That this person would sell her something? Evangelize?

Pretend to need to use her phone because their car had broken down and then stab her the moment her back was turned?

That last one was an old fear. She'd had a series of vivid dreams where a stranger had done just that, knocked on her door asking to use the phone and killed her when she let them in. She'd been having that precise nightmare since childhood.

Maybe this is a nightmare, too, she thought.

However, as she thought that, the dream world faded from her, and she realized she was lying on the foldout couch bed in the basement of her mother's house. It was a fully functional apartment, with a separate door from the main dwelling. After Minerva moved away so many years ago, her parents converted her former subterranean bedroom into a rental unit.

Normally, it was occupied, but the former renter had cleared out a few months ago, and they hadn't found someone yet to replace them.

Still half-stuck in her dream, Minerva expected to find at least one of her boyfriends lying beside her, but no such luck. She was alone. She remembered suddenly that they were sleeping a quarter mile away at a local hotel, in adjoining hotel rooms. There hadn't been enough room for all of them to sleep in the basement apartment with her. When they couldn't decide amongst themselves, Minerva had snapped and said that no one could, that they should all stay at the hotel.

Sitting in the darkness in an empty bed with a strange rapping on the door to the outside, she suddenly regretted that decision.

Just as in her dream, her instinct was to freeze, to let the rapping continue and hope it would go away.

But as it continued, she began to worry that it would wake her mother and grandmother, who were sleeping upstairs in the main house.

Exhaling deeply a few times in order to curtail the panic that filled her, she rose and walked the stairs that led up to the door.

When she looked through the peephole, she thought at first that she must still be dreaming. The lighting was terrible on this side of the house, and it was quite dark, but if she didn't know any better, she'd think the person standing outside of her door and knocking so furiously was her father.

Perhaps this is one of those *grandpa dreams*, she thought. When her paternal grandfather had passed away, he'd visited her in dreams for months and even years. They would have conversations about anything and everything. Minerva had never been a particularly religious person and didn't believe in traditional notions of heaven and hell. She also didn't believe in ghosts. She did believe, however, that dreams were where our subconscious mind worked out its problems and achieved whatever closure it was craving. Real life could be awfully withholding when it came to closure, so the dream mind had plenty to work on – and it did so gladly.

Another grandpa dream, Minerva thought, as she twisted open the door.

Strangely, she felt the cold air leaking in through the edges in the outer door. The figure outside placed its hands on the glass, and Minerva flicked on the internal light switch. As she did, she noticed something quite disturbing.

It was her father, she was sure now, but there was something wrong with him. His face was the wrong color, lacking its normal rosy hue. In truth, it had been a little rosier than a normal man's face once upon a time – her father had enjoyed good Scotch and bad jokes, about equally.

The face of the man before her had all the familiar features of her father's face, but his skin was Crayola white and translucent, so that the veins in his face were quite visible. There was also something wrong with his eyes, Minerva noted. Her father had always had eyes that belied an active mind, a person who was always thinking, planning, or yes, even scheming, and yet the eyes that regarded her now were lifeless and still.

She felt torn in that moment. Part of her wanted to slam the door, lock it tight, and hide for as long as it took for this to all be over.

Another part of her wanted to open the door and let her father in, find out exactly what was going on.

Her inquisitive half won out.

She opened the outer door, and as she did, a second larger blast of cold air hit her and chilled her. Very curious for a dream. She couldn't recall a time when she felt cold in a dream before.

Her father pushed his way past her and shambled over to an armchair. He sat down onto the cushions without saying a word.

"It's good to see you, too," Minerva said.

The dead eyes looked up at her. There was little of her father in them, Minerva realized. Was this really her father? This visitor resembled him, to be sure, but not completely. He didn't move like her father, wasn't acting like him. It was as though some other creature were wearing her father's body as a costume.

The visitor grumbled for several seconds. It sounded a bit like speech but not quite. There were no words that she could make out, no purpose. It was more like noises you would make to mock someone else when you were angry with them.

Or, Minerva realized, it was like zombies talk in movies. The noises that they make other than the plaintive appeal for "braaaaaaains." That was a hideous thought.

Equally hideous was the fetid smell emanating from her father. Decomposition. The odor filled the room, a smell so putrid and thick that Minerva felt as though she might vomit.

As she pondered what to do about this incredible situation, Minerva heard another rapping on the outer glass door. This second one was much more delicate than the first. She walked over to the door and looked out. Her mother was standing there, wrapped in a bathrobe. Minerva cracked the door ever so slightly, hoping that the stench wouldn't be too obvious.

"Everything okay?" her mother asked.

"Why do you ask?" Minerva said, dodging the question, hoping that her mother would simply go away. She was becoming more and more certain by the minute that this wasn't a dream. Minerva wasn't sure exactly what she should do about this strange visitor, but she knew that whatever she did, she wanted to keep her mother out of it. That woman had enough to deal with, working through her grief, trying to figure out what to do with the rest of her life now that the center of her former life had passed away.

The last thing she needed was to deal with a zombie.

"I heard someone knocking on your door. I just wanted to make sure everything was fine. It is, isn't it?" her mother said.

Minerva's fingers crossed behind her back, aching powerfully as she spoke. "Of course it is. Everything's fine. Not sure what that noise was, but there's no one else here."

"Oh good," her mother said. "Do you mind if I come in?"

Minerva wasn't sure what to say. As she considered the question, her mother assumed her answer was a yes and pushed her way past her.

Must be something about our family, Minerva thought. *We have a way of forcing our way into rooms when we aren't invited in.*

She noted as she turned around that her father was no longer in the chair. For that matter, the putrescence was gone. The basement apartment smelled as it had before – like the lilac air fresheners that were scattered throughout it.

Her mother walked over to the chair where her father – or whatever had been impersonating her father – had been sitting moments before. She sat down.

"I couldn't sleep anyway," her mother said. "It's weird without him there, without him next to me in the bed."

"I'll bet it is," Minerva said. It had been strange for her to spend the night alone, after all, and she hadn't been sleeping next to the same person for 40 years, like her mother had.

"You talk just like him sometimes. The things that you say. Your expressions, your mannerisms," her mother said.

Minerva thought again of the strangle grumbling sounds the visitor had made.

"I never thought it'd be that way, when we had you, when we found out that I was having a little girl. I thought you'd be just like me." She smiled. "But you've always been more like him."

Minerva smiled back. "He was a good man." She walked towards the kitchenette. "You want some tea?"

Her mother nodded. "Tea would be great."

They talked while she made the tea and well after. It felt strange to sip tea while perched on the edge of a fold-out bed, but Minerva hung on every word of their conversation. They'd never really talked before, Minerva realized. Not like this. It had always been surface level chats. While Minerva found herself drawn to deep topics no matter how ugly or challenging, her mother was always more content to stay on the surface of things. Her mother preferred to spend her time where she was comfortable, where she was emotionally safe.

But tonight Shelly Cantor was brave, lacking a filter.

"I didn't know what I was getting into," her mother admitted. "I didn't know the first thing about what being a mother was actually like."

"Oh?" Minerva said.

"Yeah," her mother said. "It seemed so much simpler before I actually had you. I thought being a mother meant that you made someone who loved you unconditionally, who you could mold into whatever you wanted them to be." She looked down at her hands uncomfortably. "I was immature. I was looking for a child who'd act like a golden retriever, following my every order, adoring me. I didn't realize I was bringing a human being into the world, someone who would grow into an adult with their own wants and needs."

"I wonder how many people do that," Minerva said.

"What?"

"I wonder how many people have a baby when what they really should do is adopt a dog."

Her mother laughed. "Probably happens a lot more often than folks will admit." She shook her head. "I shouldn't be telling you things like this."

"Why not?" Minerva asked.

"Because I don't want you to feel like you weren't wanted. You were. We wanted to have a child so bad," her mother said.

"Oh, I know," Minerva said. "I was wanted… just not in a way that was realistic."

"He talked about you all the time, you know," her mother said. "Even though we didn't talk to you all that much, he liked to tell his friends that you were out there, having adventures in the big city."

Minerva felt a tight knot of guilt. She wished suddenly that she had answered her mother's calls, that she had come back and visited her father, before it had been too late.

Well, there was nothing to be done about that now. Nothing more left to do than drink tea and deal with whatever the future held.

The sun was starting to come up. The colors in the room had grown strange, as they had always done when Minerva slept down here as a kid. When she was little, she had awoken in the early morning hours swearing that a UFO or something must be parked right outside, so strange the room looked at dawn.

"Well," her mother said, setting down her mostly empty mug, "I'm going up to the big house. Going to try to grab a few hours of sleep so I won't be *completely* useless."

"Good idea," Minerva replied.

Her mother walked to the door. "Your father would be proud of you," her mother said, before she stepped outside.

A few moments later, Minerva walked to the door and peered outside. She felt superstitious checking, but it had been a strange night, and she thought she'd make sure that there was nothing lurking outside ready to rap on her door again.

That was when she saw it. A long-tailed grackle. He was sitting in a tree just outside her window and appeared to be looking in. She didn't know how she knew exactly, but she felt certain it was the same bird she'd seen earlier right when she'd first arrived. He was closer now than before.

His sharp yellow eyes were trained on her as before, but from the shorter distance, she noticed something else: There was something familiar about them. A little something quite familiar around the eyes.

It wasn't quite human, not quite bird. She opened the door and stepped outside to get a closer look, but the bird flapped his wings, thrust into the air, and flew away.

"Did you find what you were looking for, Change?" she called to the darkness, feeling more than a little foolish.

There was no response.

The Return of the Body

It turned out to be a very good thing that Minerva and her mother grabbed those few hours of sleep.

There was a lot of commotion in the house bright and early that morning. The funeral home called to announce that they had finally "found" her father's body. That it had been there when the director arrived to open the building.

They still weren't sure what had happened to it, only that there had apparently been some sort of mix up at the morgue.

But all was right again. The funeral could proceed as scheduled.

"Right on time," Minerva's mother said. "I was this close to telling everyone I knew and ruining their business."

As Minerva prepared for her father's funeral, she noted that everything seemed a little out of phase. Death had a way of doing that, she noted. Of making real life seem like a dream.

Later she would not remember showering or changing into her funereal clothes, a smart black dress with a ruffled collar paired with a suit coat, a pair of black nylons, and chic but sensible low-heeled black pumps.

Her recollection of the day would later start with the memory of staring at her own legs as she sat in a car with her mother. Her uncle was at the wheel.

The door would open shortly afterwards, as they reached the funeral home.

She would at first be glad for what she had chosen to wear while in a daze, noting she looked quite elegant but had kept her options open, wearing shoes that were formal but also suitable for traversing the graveyard at the interment. Spikier heels might have risked tearing up the lawn and ticking off her relatives in the short term and riling some innocent groundskeeper down the line.

However, as she strode into the visitation, she immediately felt out of place. Her cousins stood in their work boots and jeans. Shooting a quick glance around, many of her relatives weren't even wearing black. Instead, the most common choice seemed to be black and red check gingham paired with denim.

"Well, aren't we fancy?" a waiting cousin teased, wrapping her in a hug. He smiled at her from underneath a baseball cap, which he wore backwards, with the tabs facing outward.

A thin layer of muck seemed to cling to him. And yet Minerva was the one who felt embarrassed.

Minerva shrugged, not sure what to say to him. She didn't consider herself fancy.

"I guess they do things a little different down in the big city, don't they?" he joked.

"I guess," Minerva said.

She did her best to blend into the crowd, but she didn't have a lot of options. Removing her jacket still left her looking rather formal and drew more attention than she'd like due to sexiness, since her cleavage was now fully exposed.

She suddenly regretted not bringing another pair of shoes. The pumps that had looked sensible before now looked like over-the-top glamor.

But as Minerva looked again to her mother, she realized it didn't really matter what she was wearing. She realized that being overdressed was a trivial concern in the grand scheme of things. Her mother was clearly struggling to walk, kept tottering as though her knees were going to give out any time she had to move. She needed help to stand, especially when she got to the casket and peered in at her late husband.

Minerva looked around for her grandmother but couldn't spot her. Well, that was alright. Nanny June could join them when she got here. It wasn't like Minerva and her mother were hard to find. They were at the front of everything today, playing the role of Grieving Immediate Family.

Her aunt caught Minerva's shoulder. "Everything happens for a reason, dear," she said to Minerva.

Minerva suppressed a groan. She'd always hated that saying. "Everything happens for a reason." It was meant to soothe, but provided little comfort.

Of course everything happened for a reason – but that didn't mean that everything happened for a good reason. And having a reason didn't mean that the reality was any easier to deal with.

No. To hell with "everything happens for a reason." Everything that happens has a lesson. That was what was truly important, knowing what that lesson was and getting the most out of an experience — not trying to understand why horrible things happened. Who cared why they happened? They happened. The question was what happened next? And that's where the lesson came in.

As Minerva wound her way to their seats at the front of the room, she had to stop several times to receive condolences and hugs from other family members. She tried her best to be gracious but found she was already sick of people's pity. This did not bode well. It was too early to feel that way.

Minerva made her way up to view the body, feeling unsteady. As she stood at the side of her father's coffin, she noted that he didn't look as though he were dead but merely sleeping. This was the mortician's craft, after all, transforming the unsettling and foreign face of death into something more palatable, more compatible with our memories of life. A mortician was a kind of interpreter. They translated a confusing message into one we could better understand, even if something were lost in that translation.

Minerva realized, however, if she really strained that she could see the face of her father as he had visited her in the dead of night. She could discern the profoundly unhuman visage that lie under the skillfully applied mask.

Once she saw it, she found it difficult to unsee. She tried to focus on her father's heavily made up face in peaceful repose, but the memory kept leaping into her head unbidden, superimposing itself upon what she was seeing.

She turned away from the casket.

She felt angry. Angry at how much her parents had built themselves up when she was a little kid. How they had made her feel like she was defective and inferior to them as a person.

Angry at how they had acted like minor gods. And angry at herself for believing them.

When it came to life and death, what really mattered, they erred just as obviously as anyone else would have. Her father had waited too long to go into hospice and too long to say goodbye.

Even though her father had been ill for quite some time, no one had told her, and her mother hadn't made any funeral arrangements until the moment he passed. Minerva had a feeling that her mother had been in denial about his illness and was now in denial about his death. It would be a long while yet before her mother would realize he was gone for good and never coming back. It would hit her weeks or months later on some night that was a bit too quiet, once all the sympathetic people had left with their long parade of "sorry for your loss" casseroles and offers of "if there's anything I can do."

It would all happen too late.

As Minerva contemplated this, she felt the anger burn her veins. Her parents were fallible just like she was, just like anyone else. They'd just made her think otherwise.

It was the Big Lie. And it was completely infuriating.

She would later not remember the eulogy at all. Most of the day would be gone from her memory, not erased exactly, but absent – as though it failed to encode in the first place. There was something unreachable about her on the day of her father's funeral, something that made it so that most of what she saw and heard just didn't connect with her.

She'd have brief flashes of memory. The scene in the graveyard would remain like a still shot. Again, she stood out in the crowd, feeling like an extravagant black-plumed bird in her funeral getup, surrounded by folks in the country attire of hard work and harder play. They wore clothes that were meant to be dirtied, strained, and challenged.

She felt like she was wearing wrapping paper at a time when it would have been better to wear armor. That was what her namesake wore, after all. The goddess sprang to life in a suit of armor.

And she wouldn't speak to her mother until they were back at the house for the evening, dropped off there by her uncle, who left immediately after helping them bring in an astonishing number of lidded casseroles.

"Well, you won't starve," her uncle had joked, before wishing them a good night.

"Can you help me with these?" her mother asked her, gesturing to the army of dishes.

"Sure," Minerva said. She walked over to the refrigerator, opened the door, and peered inside. "I think I can fit just about all of them if I shift some things around."

"Okay," her mother said.

Minerva crouched before the fridge as her mother handed her each casserole in turn. It was rough going at first, like solving an unfamiliar style of puzzle, but as she worked each successive dish in, it began to become more natural.

When all was said and done, there was a single casserole dish that wouldn't fit. A pan of lasagna.

"Guess I know what we're having for dinner," her mother said.

It only took a few minutes to serve it up onto plates, and they sat down for dinner, or at least for the ritual of dinner. Minerva realized she wasn't actually all that hungry. She looked across the table to find that her mother was sitting there idly poking her slice of lasagna with a fork but not doing anything that could be called eating.

"Is grandma okay?" Minerva asked.

Her mother frowned. "Minerva, please, don't."

"What?" Minerva said. "I looked everywhere today and didn't see her. I expected her to be sitting up with us."

"Are you feeling okay?" her mother said.

"Yeah," Minerva said. "Why?"

"Sweetie, your grandmother has been dead for years," her mother said.

Minerva's head suddenly felt much too heavy for her. "Oh," she said, feeling ill. For a second, a vision flashed into her mind, of chatting with her grandmother the night before. But as she focused on it, it faded from her visual imagination. It felt more like a dream than a memory.

Maybe her mother was right. It had been a long day. She was probably exhausted. And her memory wasn't really that good anyway, especially not lately.

When Minerva met up with her cavalcade of boyfriends the next morning to make the long drive home to Skinner, she was glad that no one asked any questions.

Russ Minot and the Biggest Lie in 254 Counties

It was the weather's fault, Russ Minot reflected. That was the whole reason he'd gotten here. The entire reason he'd managed to claw his way up out of a life that many of the other people around him would never escape.

He couldn't bear to be controlled by the weather. Couldn't stand to be fenced in by something so arbitrary.

He'd grown up seeing the farmers do everything right and still have nothing to show for it.

One year there'd be too much rain. The next there would be too little.

And no matter what happened year to year, everyone else was in the same situation right there with you, with all your competition laboring under the same capricious sky.

Farming was no better than gambling, really, and arguably worse. Because at least you didn't stand at a craps table for months before walking away with nothing like a farmer did when entire fields of crops withered.

The gamble that the farmers took made Russ think of an entire casino crowded with hundreds of people making the same exact bet, waiting for months, and then walking away empty handed while some unseen enriched banker chafed his hands red raw, rubbing them together, celebrating bankrupting everyone.

Russ had learned early on that it was better to devote your time and energies to something less controlled by luck. Farming was hard work and took a lot of effort, but effort only went so far. It wasn't like effort beyond what the work required at baseline could take you to an exceptional place.

The extra work couldn't make it rain more or rain less. Extra work couldn't make the winds calm down. It couldn't keep storms from rioting.

Russ knew early on that farming wasn't for him. The kind of profession Russ had always wanted was one where he could work hard, harder than anyone else, and one day find himself in an exceptional place because of the extra labor he'd kicked in.

He wasn't sure exactly what that would look like when he was a little kid. Whether it would unfold in the incomprehensibly brown but fertile expanses of his home state – or whether it would take him around the world without the expectation that he'd ever come back.

As it would turn out, Russ would have been safe with either bet. Later, he would look back and laugh at that, how he'd originally framed it in terms of "or," not knowing that his own destiny would turn out to be "and." Here and away. The country and the city.

And everything in between.

No "or" about it.

"Or" was for a different sort of person. For a person who prioritized. Who was satisfied with only taking part of it.

This was not Russ Minot.

He wanted it all.

That alone wasn't all that unusual. There were plenty of ambitious people out there, especially in the hungry country where he grew up. People wanted to get ahead. And they would probably always want to get even farther ahead, no matter how elevated their position became.

The difference between them and Russ Minot was simple: They were willing to do just about anything to get it.

Russ Minot, he had limits.

And paradoxically, those limits that should have held him back, didn't. It was those limits that drove other people to respect him and want to do him favors. An extra hand here and there. To elevate him.

Out of pity.

To help "poor Russ Minot," the naïve Boy Scout who actually thought hard work would get him somewhere. Who honestly thought that he could afford to cater to his principles in one of the poorest areas of the country.

So, they threw him crumbs. And crumbs. And even more crumbs.

Each person who paid pity on him thought they were the first and the only person to help him. But Russ knew different. And he didn't say a damned thing about it. He took the honest help and didn't let on that there were plenty of folks who had helped him out.

And he pushed himself to work even harder, even with all that charity from others. He saved every penny that he earned and every penny he was given, reinvested it in himself, and stayed poor and shabby looking.

He didn't let on to others that he was getting anywhere.

No, that would become known much later and suddenly. The pauper would rise and create a company seemingly out of nowhere. A man who lived with his young wife in an unfurnished apartment sustaining himself on the lowest rungs of Depression food—Hoover stew and lard sandwiches—would hire a staff of polished young professionals to work for him one day. Lease an expansion office space. Revolutionize technology.

Just as everyone else was counting him out.

Some of those who helped him in his earlier years would be angry later. They'd be spiteful when they discovered that Russ had made good.

One would accost him on a crowded street. "Russ, it's me. It's your old neighbor."

Russ greeted him warmly. But a warm exchange was not what the neighbor had in mind.

"You old bastard," the neighbor said. "You weren't poor at all. Why didn't you refuse our help?"

Russ thought about this as passersby stopped and listened. Finally, he said, "You never asked if I were poor. You only assumed. Who was I to correct you?"

The neighbor shouted obscenities.

Later, Russ would send along some money to the man's family with a note: *From one poor soul to another.*

Because that was the way it was, Russ noted. He felt that way as a poor man and continued to feel that way when he became rich. There really wasn't anything separating a poor man and a rich one. Nothing meaningful anyway.

A lot of people acted as though amassing wealth were a great moral accomplishment, but it never felt that way to him. And besides, a lot of people who worshipped the wealthy would have been amazed to hear the kind of trash that came out of their mouths when they thought they were surrounded by like-minded people.

People who were wealthy and always had been were by and large some of the most despicable people Russ had ever met – and these folks were also blissfully unaware of their own depravity.

Russ was new money of course – and as such, he was suspect. But they still managed to assume that he felt the same way as they did. That he viewed rich and poor people as being fundamentally different. That he thought as a rich person he was superior to those who stayed poor.

No, no, that wasn't it at all.

People were people, regardless of how much money they had.

But his new "friends" kept on assuming he felt like they did and unknowingly embarrassing themselves with all their arrogant, superficial grandstanding.

But they never asked how he felt. And who was he to correct them?

"My father made a bet one time with a man in town. That he could take any old person off the street and turn him into a politician. Just pick one, he said, anyone, and I'll turn him into a leader.

The man in town took his bet. Singled out a drunk. My dad paid for a haircut, bought the man a good suit, wrote his speeches.

Within the year, the drunk was a state senator.

Later the man he made the bet with said he'd wished he'd asked my father to transform him instead. My dad's project became a US Senator, and the man who'd bet against them both lost everything he had in a house fire.

I learned a lot from watching that as a kid. The first lesson was that your luck was better if you could identify the real opportunity in any given situation. I also learned that you shouldn't waste your resources betting against other people when you could put those same chips down on yourself."

-*Campaign Speech, Russ Minot*

"Russ Minot is on," Chad said, pointing at the TV, which had been left running in the background while Minerva's boyfriends made dinner. "I love him."

Chad walked from the kitchen and settled in the living room, plopping down on the couch. Not that it made much of a difference, Minerva thought, since when it came to dinner Chad didn't do much hands-on work. He fancied himself a kitchen supervisor and preferred to stand around and tell her other boyfriends what was "wrong" with their technique.

Of course there was nothing wrong, but Chad felt compelled for some reason to correct other people when they weren't wrong. If anything, meal prep might go more smoothly with Chad otherwise occupied.

"Really?" Minerva said. "Russ Minot? I thought you'd go for someone who actually won elections."

Russ Minot had run for president of the United States twice, once in 1992 and again last year in 1996. Both times he was a third-party candidate, and while he managed to get more votes than any third-party candidate had before him, he'd come far short of what he needed to win.

Minerva scanned the chyrons that scrolled across the bottom of the screen. Minot was giving his opinion on the new presidential administration in an interview, discussing how things would be different if only he were in charge.

Chad rolled his eyes at Minerva. "The only reason he doesn't win is that people are too stupid to know he's the best. I mean, listen to the guy. He makes more sense every time he opens his mouth than all the rest of the politicians do combined."

Minerva wasn't so sure of that. Minot was folksier in his language, sure, and had an accent to match, but the substance of what he said didn't really impress her. He made about as much sense as the rest of them, when you stripped away the atmospheric elements that announced, "I'm one of you." There wasn't much left to Russ Minot when you took away what appealed to gut level populism.

Trouble was, Minerva noted, most people wouldn't bother to do that. They would be taken in, as Chad was.

"I don't think we've seen the last of him," Chad said. "There are big things in store for Russ Minot."

"Like what? Minerva asked.

"I dunno," Chad said. "We're a big state, with lots of resources. We could probably fend on our own. The federal government is useless."

"Secession?" Minerva asked. "You're saying we're going to secede from the union? And then what?"

"Well, we'd do our own thing. And Russ Minot gets to be our president, like he should be," Chad said.

"Oh sure," Minerva said, "That's really gonna happen. We'll secede from the union, become our own country. And then Russ Minot can be our first president."

She had meant it as sarcasm, but as she said it, the first two fingers on her right hand violently spasmed and crossed. The pain was intense. Her vision filled with stars. She suddenly felt nauseated and vertiginous. The world spun. Her legs felt weak.

She crashed next to Chad on the couch. He pulled her close to him and wrapped his arms around her protectively. She leaned against his shoulder, snuggling into him as she regained her strength.

She kept her eyes squeezed tightly shut all the while, part of her dreading what would be there when she opened them. If she kept them closed, nothing bad could happen.

It was an immature viewpoint, and she knew that, a lot like how children assume that so long as they can't see us, we can't see them.

But like a lot of irrational views, it provided comfort. In that comfort, Minerva screwed up her courage, steeling herself for what would be there when she opened her eyes.

A Career-Making Exclusive

When Minerva opened her eyes, she noted with great alarm that although Russ Minot was still there on television that the set behind him had changed – and even more shockingly, a different interviewer sat in front of him.

Quite a familiar one.

It appeared to be Regina Withers but heavily made over. The limp brown hair was now styled with tremendous body. Expertly applied makeup gave her a luminous glow.

Her clothes looked tailored and expensive.

Perhaps most notably, Withers seemed quite poised. Like a lot of interviewers, she didn't quite smile in the conventional sense but instead exuded the steady composure of a seasoned professional.

If Regina were nervous, it was buried deep below, where no one could see it.

"Thank you for taking time out of your schedule to come here," Withers said to Minot.

"Thank you for having me," Minot replied. "It's a pleasure to be here." He broke the fourth wall and craned his head amateurishly toward the studio camera.

It was a curious thing to watch, Minerva thought, a seasoned politician was acting green, and the young upstart reporter had all the poise and polish. The world *had* gone mad.

"President Minot," Withers began, "Could you tell us about some of your initiatives?"

Minot opened his mouth to speak. Out tumbled a slew of campaign jargon. At this point, English was almost his second language and this his mother tongue, the overwrought noncommittal rhetoric of politics that sounds like it answers questions but really doesn't, peppered with words that seem like they're promising something in theory but fall apart when you go to apply them to anything.

It was slippery speech, the kind that winds between true and false, belonging to neither and both all at once.

In general, Minerva found herself tuning out political talk, but even if she had wanted to pay attention to what Minot was saying at this moment, she wouldn't have been able to.

She was completely distracted by what Withers had said.

President Minot? When did that happen?

"...and the intuitive problem of course. That's a definite priority for my administration," Minot said firmly.

"The intuitive problem?" Withers asked.

"Well, everyone knows about the incidents. While I'm thankful to our psychic brothers and sisters for their aid in the War of Independence, that doesn't erase the fact that they pose a grave risk to public safety," Minot said.

"How so?"

"We're a young state of course, which complicates things. The police have a hard enough time keeping order without having to contend with extrasensory powers," Minot said.

"But so far, there's been no evidence that intuitives pose any risk to public safety or that they will," Withers pressed. "Why would you prioritize passing legislation that protects against problems that we don't have?"

"Would you rather I wait until we have those problems? Would you rather I let the psychics run free and burn our country to the ground?" Minot countered.

Withers paused, considered this, before trying another tack. "There are some who would say that it's noble to try to prevent issues before they occur. However, your critics would argue that there are plenty of other problems that are already here that need addressing first. What would you say to that?"

"I would say," Minot said, "that it's quite easy to criticize and much harder to lead."

"Which is why people look for a special person to lead," Withers said. "Tell us, President Minot, why you are that man."

Minot smiled. This was a question he wanted to answer. He did so at great length, singing his own praises.

After the interview segment was over, Minerva became acutely aware that her right index and middle fingers were throbbing and hot like they always were when she told a lie, except she noted with great alarm that this time the warmth didn't fade over seconds and minutes. Instead, the offending digits showed no sign of cooling down anytime soon.

The remaining two fingers and thumb on her right hand were fine. However, the index and middle finger no longer really looked like fingers but more resembled boiled sausages threatening to burst from their casings.

Within an hour, she also had a fever and found she had to lie down. At first the temperature was slight. The thermometer read 100 degrees Fahrenheit.

While a lot of the other families Minerva visited growing up were quite a bit more spleeny, her own parents had been largely unconcerned when it came to health matters. A large bottle of orange ibuprofen tablets sat in their kitchen cabinet. The bottle had been opened but was nearly full. Minerva wasn't sure who had taken the few missing pills and when. It was evident that the expiration date had been printed on the plastic long ago in black letters even though enough of the lettering had worn off that there was no indication whether the pills within were expired or not.

Not that it really mattered. The bottle was there just in case. Pain wasn't something to make a big fuss about. Pain was mostly a mental battle, Minerva's mother had impressed upon her when she was very young. It was a mental battle that tried to fool you into thinking there was something physical that needed attending to.

Yes, something physical had already happened, but in most instances, by the time you felt the pain, the actual threat was gone. The damage had already been done, and your job at that point was primarily to heal.

Sometimes there was no real threat at all – as seemed to be the case with most headaches.

Fever, too, Minerva's mother said, could be quite uncomfortable, but many times a fever could be helpful, provided it didn't get too high. Below 102 Fahrenheit, her mother had told her, and it was a therapeutic fever, there to burn out an invading pathogen.

The best thing for certain infections, her mother had taught her, was to let the fever burn. True, if a fever got too hot, it could pose a risk to her – because she was a living thing in danger of getting overheated.

But below 102? Bring it on.

When she saw a 100 reading on the thermometer, Minerva climbed into bed to rest and let her body burn its way into health.

She fell into strange dreams. There was no coherent storyline and certainly no place for her to lucidly explore the dreamscape. Instead, there was a mess of lights and sounds. Half-coherent recycled bits of the past few weeks.

She saw the faces of each of her lovers standing over her. As she lay there in a pool of her own sweat, she watched with bewilderment as their faces leapt from one body to another. They began to speak to her in a confusing battery. A familiar voice came from the wrong face. Sometimes as she watched there were multiples of one lover's face with other lovers conspicuously absent.

She tried to scream, but no sound came out.

She kept on trying to scream as their faces shuffled, and they all spoke grumbled nonsense at her with the wrong voices, wrong faces.

And when she broke through the dreaming world into the real one, it was the sound of her own screaming that she heard, continuous, uninterrupted, screaming that passed seamlessly from her dream self to her real self.

Minerva woke to unfamiliar surroundings. Before Minerva stood a woman who wore a skintight head-to-toe shiny black catsuit and clunky black leather boots with tall heels. She had to be over six feet tall, even without the getup, which made her seem considerably taller.

Her hair was so blond that it was almost white. It was also perfectly straight and fell to her waist. Across her forehead was an equally straight white-blond fringe bang.

"Minerva Cantor," this imposing figure said. "Welcome to the Coterie. I am Rire."

The Coterie? Minerva thought.

"I will tell you all about the Coterie," Rire said. "It is a large part of my job."

"Your job?" Minerva asked.

Rire nodded. "I am your orientation guide."

Minerva looked down at her hands and noted her fingers had gone back to normal, reverted to their normal size. Her fever had broken. She no longer felt ill.

The only thing amiss was that she was no longer in her room and the bed she was lying in wasn't her bed. She was someplace she'd never been before.

The Macomber Coterie

Any sufficiently advanced technology is indistinguishable
from magic.

-Arthur C. Clarke

"You'll find we're kind to visitors here in the Macomber Coterie,"
Rire said to Minerva as they strolled through a vastly open
outdoor square. The first thing she noted was how perfectly clean
everything in the plaza seemed to be. Although countless people
bustled back and forth, moving quickly and with great purpose,
the streets were immaculate.

Yet, as Minerva scanned the landscape, she saw no janitorial staff.
No indication that anyone ever cleaned up after what would be
an inevitable mess.

Curious.

Furthermore, Minerva had never seen so many people wearing
gloves. And every person she passed in the street was a woman.

Where were the men? Minerva wondered. She couldn't
remember when she'd spent this much time surrounded by
women. Usually there was a man or two kicking about if you got
enough people together.

"There are men here," Rire answered. "They're just not staff.
Think of them more as entertainment. We have our specific uses
for them, but we keep them tucked away where they can't mar the
scenery."

Minerva flinched. She wasn't used to having her thoughts
responded to.

"You will get used to having others hear your thoughts," Rire
replied. "It doesn't take long. Most of us can do it in the Coterie.
A lot of us are telepaths. Some of us are only that, some of us are

more. And some of us are other things. But we're all gifted in some way or another, in ways that people think are impossible where you're from."

Minerva didn't say anything aloud, but she didn't have to.

"Yes," Rire said, again responding to her unspoken thoughts. "I've done this many times. Guarded many prisoners. It's not the most pleasant job in the world, but someone has to keep order, don't they?"

"I'm a prisoner?" Minerva asked.

"In more ways than one," Rire replied.

"What's that supposed to mean?" Minerva asked.

"Well, quite literally, you're being held here. If you decided to make a break for it, it'd be my job to haul you back in. But in other senses, you're a different kind of prisoner. Of your own weaknesses, your own failings, your lack of will, your fear. Most of us are."

"How long has this place existed?" Minerva asked.

"Centuries," Rire replied. "And we've done a good job staying hidden... well, mostly."

"Mostly?"

"There have been incidents, times when we've been detected by the larger world, and it caused quite a stir."

"Like?"

"I'm sure you've heard of us before, although your understanding of what we are and what actually happened are likely inaccurate. That's on purpose. That's part of how we handled the incident and protected the Coterie."

Minerva shook her head. "I've never heard of anything like you."

"Sure you have," her orientation guide told her. "They called us witches back then, back when the trouble started."

"And they burned you at the stake?" Minerva asked, half-joking.

"Some of us," her guide responded earnestly. "It all depended on your station in life. How much money your family had. The poorest girls, yes, they burned. But the richer ones... well, they were our descendants. We Macombers come from good breeding."

"How did you escape?"

"The mobs in those executions were all paid actors. The blazes weren't real. And once the supposed inferno consumed the witch, we came in and brought her here."

Secret Societies

The prevailing theory about the origins of the Psychic Phenomenon traces its emergence to the late 1990s, at which time psychological research incidentally revealed the first evidence of precognition in a college-aged population.

However, while this is the most popular explanation, both in scientific circles and among the lay population, there are many other competing theories that dispute the idea that psychic powers spontaneously manifested in the population at the end of the millennium.

Instead, these theorists argue, intuitives have been with society for hundreds, if not thousands, of years, secreted away in collectives.

These claims are supported by numerous apocryphal reports of unusual abilities throughout human history. Some historians argue that magic is simply an alternate explanation for psychic ability as witnessed by non-psychic individuals prior to the development of the intuitive sciences.

Some theorists go even further, asserting that many of humanity's earlier scientific breakthroughs were secretly made possible via intuitive capabilities, or by non-intuitives who had at least fleeting contact with intuitive collectives.

Certain historians point towards the modern Four Families – the Skinners, Watsons, Ecks, and Macombers –suggesting that any of them, either singularly or as a combination, could be a potential outgrowth of early intuitive collectives.

Neither this volume nor its author takes a definitive stance on which origin story is the correct version. As far as mainstream intuitive taxonomy is concerned, it remains an open question.

from Insecta Psychica: Towards an Intuitive Taxonomy by Cloche Macomber

Minerva had never been much of a performer. Some children seem to have performing in their blood. They practically spring from the womb belting out power ballads or winding their way through intricate dance numbers, leaving their parents proud but mystified, wondering where their child picked it up.

Minerva was a different case when she was a little girl. She'd preferred to play quietly, making up melodramas in her head that involved her toys, but not announcing them to anyone in particular – and certainly never acting them out as herself.

She'd never once had that compulsion that plagues so many other children: Attention thirst. Look-at-Me-itis.

As an adult, she had been similar, content to write commercials at her former workplace, provide the lines for actors to speak on screen. She'd never once saw the ads being recorded and thought, *You know, I'd like to do that myself.*

Behind the scenes was where she was most comfortable. It suited her perfectly. It was where she wanted to be.

So, as she was trussed up in outlandish gear and had her face savagely attacked by a flurry of makeup artists, she didn't feel the excitement that a natural performer might, if put in her position. Instead, her stomach sank down into her tremendously tall lace-up leather boots, and despite her best efforts to breathe deeply and think of something else –anything else—her stomach stubbornly clung to her toe box.

Well, she thought, *I guess if I can't hide, then part of me ought to.*

She was hoisted up onto a parade float. It was decorated with a mess of red and yellow tulips. At first she thought they must be artificial. They looked too perfect, in full bloom and without a hint of insect damage. But as Minerva touched them with her hands, she noted that they didn't feel like polyester, foam, or cloth. They felt like actual flowers, oleaginous to the touch and even fragrant as she bent to smell one. Everything about them struck her as real, right down to the film of oil that clung to her hands afterwards, making her feel as though she'd washed her hands with soap and not rinsed them enough.

There were no mirrors available, but she looked down at the costume she'd been hastily wrapped in and noted blue, green, and purple in her skirt.

Against the flowers I'll look like a rainbow, she noted. She wasn't sure if this was a good or a bad thing. But it didn't seem as though she had much choice. Her orientation guide Rire climbed onto the float next to her.

"Oh, there you are," Minerva said, glad to see a familiar face, even if it was the face of her captor.

Rire nodded grimly. Something was off, Minerva noted.

As if to confirm this, Rire produced shackles, a design with four cuffs secured by several lengths of heavy chain. Expertly Rire secured the cuffs around Minerva's wrists and then her ankles. The bottom shackles took a little fiddling, as those needed to fit snugly over the comically tall boots Minerva had been made to wear.

"Is this necessary?" Minerva asked, feeling the metal chafe against her wrists. "I haven't made any effort to run. You can read my thoughts. You know I have no intention of escaping."

"These aren't to keep you from running," Rire replied.

"Well, what are they for then?" Minerva said.

"For show," Rire said. "They're part of your costume."

"They're pretty darn heavy for a costume," Minerva complained.

"Look," Rire said, taking Minerva's chin in her hand and staring into her eyes, "I know you're not running away. But *they* don't know that." She gestured around at the crowd that was already starting to gather for the parade. "And it's not like these people can enjoy the parade if they're worried about a criminal escaping and doing who knows what."

Minerva sighed. "I'm a criminal?" she asked.

"Of course you are," Rire replied. "We don't just imprison people for the fun of it."

"What's my crime then?" Minerva asked.

"That'll be explained later," Rire replied. "But first the parade."

Minerva sighed. "I'd really rather not do this."

"It'll be over before you know it," Rire told her. "And I'll be here the entire time."

"Is that supposed to be reassuring?" Minerva challenged her.

"It's the best I have," Rire said.

While up until this point Rire seemed so utterly unflappable and unmoved that it made Minerva wonder if the guide were in fact human, in that moment there was something so defeated and exhausted in her tone that Minerva felt a pang of guilt. It was awful to be a prisoner of course, deprived of her freedom, but was it ever pleasant for the guard she wondered? Arguably, a pure sadist could take pleasure in depriving another of their liberty, but for most people, being a guard would be quite painful. Perhaps there was something oppressive about being involved in such a dynamic, regardless of which side a person found themselves. Maybe the chain bound in both directions.

However, Minerva thought miserably, *only one of us has to bear the physical weight of it.* And that weight made a world of difference.

Thankfully, it was not too long before their float lurched to life and began the trip down the parade route. The crowds were thin at first, closest to their point of departure, but as they proceeded down the route, the groups got larger and larger. Minerva could hear the crowd's cheers as they greeted the float in front of hers, but as she pulled up, those cheers quickly turned to boos. All the while, Rire stood even taller than normal, holding up a length of chain proudly as though Minerva were a trophy she'd captured. Whenever Rire mimed strength, flexing a biceps or thrusting a fist into the air, the crowd would break from boos and begin to cheer.

Well, Minerva thought miserably, as children stuck their tongues out at her, *it's clear which of us they're booing.*

Their float was the third one in the procession, so by the time they reached the end of the route, there was still plenty of parade left to go.

Rire unlocked her shackles. Minerva rubbed the chafed bits of skin protectively. A team of attendants flooded in and quickly removed the parade costume, leaving her normal clothes that she'd been wearing underneath. Minerva was glad when her regular shoes were brought to her. It was good to be out of those ridiculous boots.

"Come," Rire said.

"What now?" Minerva asked.

"Watch the rest of the parade with me," Rire said.

It was phrased like a command, but there was a pleading tone in Rire's voice that Minerva couldn't help being moved by. While she probably could have made it a little harder on her guard, Minerva found herself complying without difficulty.

As Minerva watched the floats move by, she felt a little lost. She could tell from the crowd's reactions that the people who rode them were culturally important within the Coterie somehow, but their precise positions were lost on her, a newcomer.

Each float was appointed quite similarly to hers, covered with red and yellow flowers, with the riders in colorful outfits. A series of rainbows drifted past.

Rire stared at the parade, rapt.

Minerva thought idly of how easy escape would be at a moment like this, with Rire so fascinated by the parade and with the crowds on every side of them so ready and able to swallow an escapee running full tilt into them.

At this thought, Rire turned to her and gave her a grave look. "Please stop that," Rire said. "Enjoy the parade."

And she swiveled back to the procession.

Perhaps I could get into the crowd, but then what? I don't even know where I am. I don't know the edge of this territory. And I'd be wanted. People would be looking for me. Minerva sighed at the thought. *Besides, everywhere I went, Rire would have access to what I'm thinking. In a way she'll see what I see. It'd only be a matter of time before she found me.*

"Minerva," Rire warned again. "Stop thinking about escape."

Unless there's a range on telepathy, Minerva thought. *If I could just get out of range.*

"Do you want me to put the shackles back on?" Rire said.

Minerva frowned, rubbing her chafed wrists. "No," she said.

It was hopeless, she decided. Impossible to get the jump on a telepath. No sense thinking about it.

And when she gave up on her escape plan, Minerva noted that the corners of Rire's mouth turned up into a genuine smile.

At that moment, a dramatic fanfare began to play. It reminded Minerva of the trumpeting that introduced kings of old in movies set in medieval times.

The float that pulled up next was strikingly different than the others. There were no flowers on this float, which was stark, black, and mineral. Large black crystals jutted from every surface and formed not only the back of the float but a throne upon which a woman sat.

The woman on the throne was massive. Her hair was jet black but snarled into a chaotic shape that reminded Minerva of a claw. Her basic complexion was nearly white, but profuse red acne marked her face, rendering her complexion more polka dot than pale. Her features were all wrong for her face with eyes that were small, dark, and beady. Her nose was large and beaklike. She had a mouth that was wide but with thin lips that were pressed in a straight line.

She regarded the audience with thinly veiled contempt. It was clear that she felt that everyone was beneath her.

As she approached, the crowd fell to their knees. Rire dutifully kneeled and bowed her head. Some spectators genuflected even further, sprawling out on the ground, getting as low as they possibly could without sinking into the ground like spilled water flowing into cracks in the earth.

Minerva continued to stand, not out of defiance but because she momentarily forgot where she was and that she was even there. The whole thing felt like a strange dream.

"You!" an unpleasant voice cried.

Minerva realized the voice was talking to her. And that the voice belonged to one of this massive woman's attendants, attendants she hadn't even noticed, so transfixed she'd become by the woman sitting on the throne.

"Yes?" Minerva said.

"Kneel before the venerable Moche," the attendant commanded.

"Oh," Minerva said. "Of, of course." She kneeled and bowed her head.

"Bring her to me," another voice said. This voice was deep and dark, sonorous.

"Yes, your greatness," the attendant said.

Minerva found herself hoisted up by her armpits and lifted onto the float, which was now stopped in the middle of the road.

Rire did nothing as they took Minerva from her side. She didn't even lift her head. Her guard duties had clearly been overruled by the whims of a superior entity.

It was in that moment standing before Moche's immense presence that Minerva knew for sure she was having an audience not with a typical person in an elevated position but with absolute power itself, a force that was not to be questioned or crossed. When you were around such a person, Minerva thought, their will was akin to mind control.

Although, she thought idly, *in the Coterie it's possible that it's not akin to mind control. Here it could be actual mind control.*

"Look at me," the venerable Moche said.

Tentatively, Minerva inclined her head. Moche's face was even more pockmarked and scarred up close and her body more immense. *She could weigh half a ton.*

It was a rude thought – and one she regretted immediately – not only because it was unkind but also because she suspected she was surrounded by dozens, if not hundreds, of telepaths.

Under these circumstances, it was as though she'd screamed something similar in a crowded room.

She desperately tried to think of anything else, but her mind rebelled against her. The mind doesn't deal well with negatives, after all. While they can make a huge difference in everyday communication, the words themselves are small, easily missed.

Words like "not" don't have huge cognitive heft. Instead, more descriptive, evocative words are much more likely to make an impression, to shine through.

As Minerva tried to negate what she was thinking, she only strengthened the images she was fighting.

It was very much like how the adage, "Don't think of an elephant" easily conjures an elephant, despite the thinker's effort. The mind doesn't easily visualize negatives; instead, the mind introduces the object to be negated and *then* tries to destroy it or resolutely cross it out.

Unfortunately, even *this* doesn't always work. Just like a pencil eraser will leave behind pink smudges of rubber or vestiges of the original image, so too will bits of the not-elephant persist.

It is only an experienced telepath who can thought block effectively.

There was simply no hope for a non-telepath like Minerva. As she stood before Moche, the leader regarded her coolly watching a frenzy of images flicker through Minerva's mind.

The struggle taught her much. It was very much like watching someone feebly attempt to quickly clean up when you'd arrived at their filthy home for a surprise visit. Moche caught telling glimpses of what was shoved quickly under the psychological bed or in a mental closet. It was particularly easy because Minerva's hiding places kept rejecting the information, as though her mental closet had a broken door latch and flapped open, spilling contents into the main room.

Moche found herself smiling at one thought that kept bursting out repeatedly: Minerva was surprised that such a powerful Coterie leader wasn't conventionally attractive. It was the opposite of how things typically went in Minerva's world, with the beautiful being awarded stations much above their abilities and those who weren't so pleasing to look at having to work hard to overcome invisible penalties levied against them.

"You silly thing," Moche spoke aloud, "you may be one of us, but you don't know anything about women, do you?"

"What do you mean?" Minerva asked.

"There's only one reason a woman wants to be beautiful – and that's to use her beauty to control other people. If she can already control others, what need does she have to be beautiful? To a woman with other forms of power, beauty is just a liability."

Minerva felt ashamed. She didn't want to acknowledge the unacceptable thoughts she'd been having – let alone justify them.

"The trouble with you," Moche continued, "is that beauty is the only form of power you've consciously responded to."

"I'm not that shallow!" Minerva protested.

"Not that you know," Moche replied. "There are depths to you, contradictions that you will never see." She yawned. "I wonder what it's like to be so unobservant," she said. "To be so ignorant of your true self, to be so focused on only the parts of you that are easy to come forth and claim."

Minerva bowed her head.

"Get her away from me," Moche said.

Minerva felt herself lifted again by strong arms and placed next to Rire.

"Keep your head down," Rire said to Minerva, through gritted teeth.

Minerva did as she was told. For good measure, Minerva also closed her eyes. It seemed safer that way, more penitent. The fanfare blared again. The crowd cheered. Slowly, the music faded as the float traveled into the distance, far beyond the edge of the parade. They were taking the leader somewhere else of course. That was how it always went. Rulers traveled on parades that were longer and more prestigious – and whose endings were private.

Perhaps that's what true power was, Minerva thought. Being able to arrange the world so that no one ever saw you at a weak or unguarded moment.

She shook her still-bowed head violently as if to shake the thought out of it. No, she resolved. There was strength to vulnerability, to being able to show your weakness around others. It was just a different kind of power, a different form of strength.

Minerva wondered about Moche, what kind of power she had.

"It's not something we speak of," Rire said, answering the question she wasn't asking aloud. Another train of Minerva's thoughts hit her a moment later, and she responded to those as well. "There are some powers that aren't safe to speak of. If they're named, terrible things happen. The mayor is without peer, that's all you really need to know."

Minerva did her best to calm her thoughts, to level them off. There was no telling how many other telepaths surrounded her, after all. Rire was kind enough to let her know that she could be heard and to respond in a method that she could understand. She knew that would not always be the case, that there would be telepaths who would listen secretly and never let her know that they had heard.

Minerva slowed her breathing, tried to clear her mind. With her eyes squeezed shut, she let the seconds and minutes drift away from her, thinking as little as possible, just like a child who thinks if they can't see you, you can't see them. She was doing it again, and she knew it was silly, but she didn't know how to deal with what was happening to her any other way.

"It's safe now," Rire said.

Minerva inclined her head and opened her eyes. Night had fallen. Minerva looked up to the sky and noted that the constellations were completely different than when she'd last been at her home in Skinner. The Coterie was somewhere in the Southern Hemisphere, she reasoned. She silently cursed the fact that until now she hadn't traveled internationally at all and certainly not somewhere remote like Africa or Australia, anywhere that could give her clues as to where she was.

Well, that's if the distance involved was a matter of where and not *when*, she caught herself.

It was staggering how much she'd taken for granted, how much knowledge from her life before just wasn't going to help her here. As much as her teachers had impressed upon her that she'd need to learn certain subjects to cope with the real world, nothing she'd learned in school prepared her for where she'd suddenly found herself.

Perhaps there's no preparing for life, Minerva thought, staring up at the stars. *Perhaps there's only bracing for it and then reacting as well as you can when life inevitably hits you.*

"Where? When? What does it matter?" Rire asked her, answering the questions she wasn't voicing aloud. "You're in the Coterie now. That's all you need to know."

Terms of Imprisonment

Returning to the detention center with Rire as her guard, the reality of Minerva's situation began to set in.

On the trip out, there had been simply too much to take in at once and too much to wonder about. The questions would not stop coming. Who was Rire? What went on inside her head? Why was she here? Where was here anyway?

Minerva had barely had a moment to commit to wondering about the detention center itself. As she'd been led outside and towards the parade route, she had taken the structure as a given and had followed Rire without observing or questioning.

Now that she was beginning to acclimate to her predicament, she was noticing the detention center for the first time. It was a rather imposing structure. The base levels were encased in white concrete that reminded Minerva of a basement, except instead of being buried beneath the ground, they were superterranean.

"We have a basement as well," Rire told her, reading her thoughts. "That's where we keep those who need the most monitoring."

Minerva said nothing, but Rire nodded. "I will show you."

Atop this concrete base, a glass monolith loomed. Minerva wasn't sure how many stories high it was, but at a glance, it rivaled any skyscraper she had seen in downtown Skinner. The shape of the two structures together reminded Minerva of a tube of lipstick.

"The upper portion of the building is for administrative use," Rire said. "Very important matters are settled up there."

As they entered the building, Minerva was struck by how empty it was, how blindingly white the internal concrete walls were, and again how there seemed to be only women within. Women prisoners and women guards. Not a man anywhere.

"The men are kept below ground," Rire explained.

"This place is really lovely," Minerva said.

"Nicer than your detention centers?" Rire asked.

Minerva nodded. "Much."

"Well," Rire said, "here we don't try to make a profit from imprisoning people. It's not like where you're from with companies making money off captive customers. It's not difficult to hold people in nicer places if there's not a third party involved trying to skim money off the top. We actually use the resources we have on the people we're housing instead of diverting them to make other people rich."

As they moved through corridors leading to her cell, Minerva felt a profound heaviness enter her chest. She felt exhausted.

"Those are the demotivators," Rire explained.

"Demotivators?"

Demotivators

Demotivators are a very specialized type of intuitive. Essentially, their main power is the ability to make everyone around them extremely lazy.

As a power, demotivation can be quite subtle, and many demotivators are not fully cognizant of their power until well into young adulthood, when the tendencies are detected by a routine precollege intuitive aptitude battery.

Part of this delay in detection might be because demotivators are found primarily in underachieving families who live in underperforming school districts. While they don't possess any special scholastic abilities themselves and are quite average performers, as children they will excel at virtually every task relative to everyone who surrounds them, who simply will not try or apply themselves.

In adulthood, many demotivators find work as guards in prisons or mental institutions, anywhere that their powers of pacification will be advantageous in preventing riots or escape attempts. But their abilities aren't simply useful in this one particular context.

Perhaps the most famous demotivator of all is the world renown mononymous demotivational speaker Mallow, author of *Why Worry?*, and many high-end spas and resorts will employ at least one demotivator to help their clients to relax and more quickly go on "island time."

from Insecta Psychica: Towards an Intuitive Taxonomy by Cloche Macomber

Espoir Explains the Charges

When Minerva finally made it to her cell, she sank onto her bed. The last few corridors had been a real slog. There had been moments when she toyed with simply sitting down in the hallway and staying there, but Rire had given her such a sharp look that she hadn't dared.

"You'll get used to the demotivators eventually," Rire had said. "Well, a little. You can build up a slight tolerance over time, but you never really get completely used to them. I suppose that's the whole point."

It could be worse, Minerva thought. The heaviness had one practical benefit. It meant that she could get some sleep.

She had thought hypothetically before about being in jail, particularly often for someone who had never had a meaningful brush with the law. It had always been a thought experiment, not a fun one exactly, but one that her mind became fixated on after watching one too many movies set in prison.

In theory, she'd decided, there would be a few major problems with being in jail, other than the obvious loss of liberty that came with being confined. They were mundane problems that didn't get the same kind of focus and attention when Hollywood looked at them, but she knew they would irk her terribly.

One of these was having to be trapped in close quarters with others. Depending on the exact terms of confinement, the cellmate relationship could be particularly fraught. Minerva could think of few predicaments more unnerving than being assigned a roommate who was a much more hardened criminal than she was and from whom she couldn't meaningfully escape, impose distance, or enforce any sort of personal boundaries.

Minerva noted with great relief that she had a cell to herself. Not only that, but it was rather spacious and clean. There was even a bathroom stall with a door.

The other chief concern she'd had when theorizing about being in jail had been thinking about trying to sleep there. She'd imagined the stress would be incredible. The beds would be uncomfortable. The strange noises and unfamiliar surroundings would make it impossible to relax, let alone manage the precarious feat of falling asleep.

Sleep had always been rather mysterious to Minerva. She knew it was vital and that she couldn't function without it, but she never quite felt in control of how it happened or why. It didn't take much to throw her off her routine and make sleep elusive.

Thankfully, however, she noted that this wasn't going to be an issue. The demotivating atmosphere not only made it difficult to do things, it also seemed to relax her, acting like an anxiolytic.

She found herself struggling to keep her eyes open.

As she sank into her surprisingly comfortable bed, however, she heard Rire clear her throat. "It's not time to sleep," the guard said. "Later."

Minerva sat upright on the bed. "But I'm so exhausted."

Rire nodded. "I'll see what I can do." She left the cell.

Minerva glanced at the open door. It would be easy to escape in normal circumstances, but from her vantage point, it seemed like walking 500 miles with no shoes. She just couldn't summon the energy or concern required to escape.

In a few moments, Rire returned, accompanied by another rather imposingly tall woman dressed in the same shiny oil-slick black catsuit. "The demotivator should be moving farther away from us in a second," Rire told Minerva. "That should help take the edge off your lethargy."

"This is my colleague, Espoir," Rire said, introducing the woman next to her.

Espoir nodded politely. "Thank you, Rire," she said. "I am here to explain the charges against you."

"Are you my lawyer?" Minerva asked.

Espoir shook her head. "No, you will be meeting with your lawyer tomorrow morning. I am here for the Coterie's sake. I am more of a... counselor."

"Are you sure I shouldn't have my lawyer present?" Minerva asked.

Espoir raised an eyebrow and shot a quick glance at Rire. Rire smirked and shrugged. "This isn't part of your official proceedings," Espoir said. "So I'm not sure why that's a relevant concern."

"But you're not working for me, are you? You're working for the side that will try me," Minerva said. "How do I know you're not an interrogator?"

"Well, I'm not," Espoir said. "I told you. I'm a counselor. I am here for your benefit, even if I'm not going to be working in the court as your advocate."

Minerva chewed on her lip, thinking about this.

"It must be a cruel place where you're from," Espoir said.

"Why do you say that?"

"Everyone I meet who comes from your world, from your legal system, they're always asking for their lawyer, as though that's the only person that can help them. We don't think of things that way here. It is not so clear cut. Not so us and them. We are less committed to vigorous loyalties, the accused and the accuser. We aren't slaves to bias," Espoir said.

"Slaves to bias?"

Espoir nodded. "Where you come from, a lawyer will say practically anything to get his client off, regardless of its relationship to the truth. Here, we simply do not do that."

"So much for a vigorous defense," Minerva grumbled bleakly.

"Well, it works the other way, too," Espoir said. "Your legal system is supposed to be fair. Your prosecutors are *supposed* to adhere to fairness and rules of evidence. They're supposed to reveal everything that they find – and especially if it points towards the innocence of the accused." Espoir said. "But we know that people don't always do what they're supposed to do. I'm sure I don't have to remind you of the many scandals involving fabricated lab results and hidden exculpatory evidence."

Espoir shook her head. "It's not justice, what happens where you come from. You don't set two biased parties to war against one another and call that justice."

Minerva frowned. "Then why provide me a lawyer at all? Why hold a trial? Why go through any of it?"

"Because it's important to challenge one's assumptions," Espoir said. "Even if they are the assumptions of such an important and generally infallible body as the Coterie." She smiled.

"Anyway," Espoir continued, "that's not my role. I am simply here to explain to you why you're here and to facilitate your stay here as best as I can."

Minerva nodded. "Why am I here?"

"You really don't know?" Espoir said.

Minerva shook her head.

"You're in here because you've bent the truth, Minerva," Espoir said.

Minerva laughed.

"What?" Espoir said. "I don't see how that's funny."

"I'm sorry," Minerva said, as she calmed down her laughter. "But where I come from, that isn't a crime."

"Well," Espoir said. "Where you come from, people can't generally bend the truth the way that you do." She looked into Minerva's eyes in a way that felt profoundly invasive. "I'm not talking about normal fibs. Little white lies."

Espoir held up her own right hand with the index and middle finger crossed. "I'm talking about this."

Minerva looked away.

"You *do* know what I'm talking about," Espoir said.

"Yes," Minerva said. "But I didn't know at first. It just... started happening after my accident. I'd go to lie, and I'd be so much more convincing... so convincing that I not only got people to believe me, but I could actually change what the truth *was*."

Espoir nodded.

"But I didn't know what was happening when it started. I definitely didn't know what was going on. I just woke up that way. My body started doing it before I was even aware of exactly what it was. It took me a while to even catch on," Minerva said.

"But once you did, you didn't exactly stop, did you?" Espoir asked.

"No," Minerva admitted. "But by that time, it was hard to stop. It was like... I was addicted. The lies just kept feeding on themselves. The urge to do it kept growing." She shook her head. "By the time I realized what I was doing, I couldn't stop."

"Of course you could," Espoir said. "You always could."

Minerva shook her head. "No."

"You haven't done it once since you've arrived here," Espoir said.

"I haven't been here that long. And it's not like I haven't wanted to. I haven't been *able* to," Minerva confessed. "I've thought about it, but for some reason the urge is gone. I'm not sure why. I feel like it won't work here, so why even try?"

"She has thought about it," Rire corroborated. "Many times."

"Well, you're correct," Espoir said. "It won't work here. We've set the Coterie up that way."

"What way?" Minerva asked.

"The truth can't be reshaped that violently here," Espoir said.

"You can't lie here?" Minerva said.

"Oh, we can lie. Just not the kind of lie that you've been telling. We can lie with words, but we can't get the truth to conform to what we say," Espoir said. "There are a number of wards in place here in the Coterie, protections that prevent us from becoming like the outside world. It's safe here."

"So I'm being charged with bending the truth," Minerva said.

"Well, not exactly," Espoir said.

Minerva looked at her expectantly.

"You're going on trial for *breaking* the truth," Espoir said.

"Breaking the truth?"

Espoir nodded. "The truth and reality are actually fairly elastic. Most of the time, small alterations to their fabric won't affect the overall whole all that much. But enough lies – and big ones – well… here we are."

"So I broke the truth?" Minerva said.

Espoir nodded. "You gravely injured reality, actually, but yes, that's essentially right. You broke the truth. We didn't have a choice but to arrest you and stop you. We had to take you in."

"Because my crime was too great?" Minerva said.

"Well, yes," Espoir said. "That. And also because you were too much of a danger to society, to existence as we know it."

"Me?" Minerva said. "A danger to existence? Really?"

Espoir nodded. "You came really close to doing irrevocable damage, to bringing us to a point of no return." She cast her eyes down. "It's possible that some of the injuries you caused won't heal as it is. We couldn't exactly let you continue to wreak havoc on reality and make things even worse."

"How can one person do that?" Minerva asked.

Espoir and Rire both laughed.

"What?" Minerva said.

"I'm sorry," Espoir said. "I'm just not used to such naivete."

"It is rather precious," Rire agreed.

Minerva folded her arms. "Okay," she said. "So let's say that everything you say is true—"

"It is," Espoir interrupted.

Minerva glared at her. "Let's say," she began again and waited. Neither Rire nor Espoir interjected. "How can I possibly be held accountable for crimes I didn't know I was committing?"

"Well," Espoir said, "I do believe *that* is a matter that should be discussed with your lawyer."

"I thought you were above us versus them," Minerva challenged.

Espoir scowled. "I'm not a lawyer, but from what I understand of the legal system, you can break laws that you don't know exist. It happens all the time. Part of the social contract involves becoming aware of what the laws are and abiding by them. It is not the state's responsibility to educate you on them. When it comes to criminal activity, impact seems key. The matter of your intent seems to be more important in sentencing." She sighed. "But I'm not a lawyer of course and certainly not *your* lawyer."

"But I never signed a social contract with the Coterie," Minerva argued.

"Are you so sure about that?" Espoir asked.

Minerva wasn't sure what to say to that. She was becoming progressively less sure of many things she'd taken for granted only the day before.

"Anyway," Espoir said, "that's why you're here. You bent reality until it nearly broke. In particular, you circumvented the will of others, invaded dreams, meddled in life and death matters, and altered the course of history. You will be tried for these crimes."

The demotivator must be moving back in range, Minerva thought, as a wave of torpor hit her, forcing her to lie down on her bed.

Sneaky way of getting in the last word was her final thought as her eyes closed, and the room swam away from her.

Paper Guards a Rock Prisoner

It seemed as though only seconds had passed between the moment Minerva had closed her eyes and when she opened them again.

But it was certainly morning, easily discerned by both the quantity and quality of light that poured in through her cell window, which was small and high on the wall but did provide much-appreciated sunlight.

Rire was standing right next to her bed. Minerva wondered how long she had been there and if she had been staring at her while she slept. It was an unnerving thought.

The corners of Rire's eyes crinkled up as though she wanted to smile, while her lips persisted stoically in a straight line. This was not an easy combination, Minerva thought, having tried a similar maneuver herself in her former professional life when she worked at the marketing firm.

It was after a lecture by a consumer psychologist, who had informed them all of the difference between a genuine smile and a forced one. In both forced and genuine smiles, the zygomatic muscles would flex, raising the corners of the mouth. However, it was only in the Duchenne smile, which was genuine, that the *orbicularis oculi* muscle would also come into play, causing wrinkles to form at the corners of the eyes.

Most people could fake the upturned mouth, but smiling in your eyes was hard to do voluntarily. In a series of informal experiments in front of her bathroom mirror, Minerva had also found it difficult to suppress the upturned mouth when she was genuinely smiling.

And yet here Rire was, somehow accomplishing it.

She was disciplined, Minerva had to give her that.

"Good morning," Rire said. "Today you are going to meet with your lawyer for the first time, but before you do that, I must keep the promise I made to you."

"Promise?" Minerva said.

Rire nodded. "To show you the subterranean levels of this building."

"Do I have a choice?" Minerva asked.

Rire shook her head.

Minerva frowned. "Well, is there at least some way I could wash up first? And maybe change my clothes while I'm at it." She gestured to her outfit. "I've been wearing this for too long. I even slept in it."

"Of course," Rire said. "We have a facility that you can use, and I will make sure you have clean clothes for the day." She walked toward the door, gesturing vaguely. "Come."

Minerva followed her out of the cell and down a corridor she hadn't yet walked through. It seemed to lead deeper into the facility, although if pressed she couldn't be sure. The layout was quite labyrinthine, and while the walls and floors were marked with a system of strange symbols, it wasn't anything she recognized.

"If you stay with us long enough, we will make sure you are properly taught how to read runes. We value literacy," Rire explained in response to Minerva's thoughts.

At the end of their short walk was a large room with an array of sealed stalls. On each door, there was a control panel with a variety of buttons and a large light-up display. Rire led Minerva to a stall in the center of the bank and navigated a complex series of prompts, entering a 12-digit number when prompted that Minerva supposed was either Rire's ID number or some kind of authorization code. Whatever the case, Minerva only caught the first three numbers in the series, and even then, she wasn't 100 percent sure that she had those digits correct.

"You don't," Rire said.

"I'm surprised you rely on passwords for security," Minerva said.

"Why's that?"

"Wouldn't telepaths simply be able to pluck the correct input from your mind? I had a hard time figuring it out of course, but that's because I had to watch you visually. It seems like it'd be fairly easy to retrieve someone's password from their mind as they were entering it."

"It is," Rire said.

"Then why use them?" Minerva asked.

"They're only one part of our security," Rire said.

"What else do you use?"

"If I told outsiders," Rire said, "that would make it significantly less secure, wouldn't it?"

Minerva shrugged. "I suppose."

"Let's just say," Rire said, "that there are multiple ways that our machines are set up to recognize me. The password is more there to ensure that I approve of the transaction, not that I'm the one using the machine."

"That makes sense, I guess."

"Plus," Rire admitted, "we put a lot of thought into which guards oversee which prisoners. I wouldn't be assigned to guard another telepath. It just wouldn't be considered a suitable pairing."

"It's a bit like rock, paper, scissors then?" Minerva asked.

"What?" Rire said.

"You haven't heard of rock, paper, scissors before?"

Rire shook her head.

"It's a game people play, usually to break stalemates. Each player selects one of three choices: Rock, paper, or scissors. These elements all have relationships with one another, strengths and weaknesses. They're all about equally strong because of this. What wins the day depends on context. Paper covers rock. Scissors cut paper. Rock breaks scissors," Minerva explained.

Rire nodded slowly. "I think I see what you mean. Yes, it's like that. I guess you could say I'm a paper guard and you're a rock prisoner and that there's no way they'd have paper guarding paper."

"Or paper guarding scissors," Minerva offered.

"Sure," Rire said. "Whatever you say." She opened the door to the stall.

Minerva peered in and saw a shower setup that led deeper in than she would have guessed looking at the stall bank. Behind the door were two small but complete rooms. In the closest room was a small bench and what looked like a trash can. There was also a fresh towel hanging on a hook on the wall, as well as a small cubby. Minerva peered into the cubby and saw that it was at the end of what seemed to be a long chute. She couldn't see too far into it, however, since it curved up at an angle.

Rire gestured toward the trash can-like structure. "That's where you put your clothes."

"Do I just drop them in?"

Rire nodded. "Yes."

In the adjoining room were a shower and various toiletries. There was also a control panel on the wall that looked very similar to the one Rire had used to open the stall. "I hope you don't mind, but I took the liberty of specifying soap, shampoo, and conditioner for you based on your hair type and skin oil profile."

"I don't mind," Minerva said. "That was very thoughtful of you."

"Well, you could potentially use that panel on the wall to select it yourself, but since you're not exactly literate enough to use it, I thought it was best to make some selections for you," Rire explained. "Don't touch the panel by the way."

"Afraid I'll escape?" Minerva asked.

Rire shook her head. "No. I've programmed in a soothing temperature for you and an adequate water flow length. If you change the settings, you might scald yourself or end up with a cold shower. Or, worse, run out of water altogether fairly quickly. Really, you'd only be hurting yourself if you messed around with the console, so please don't do it."

"Okay," Minerva said.

"When you're ready for the water to start, just press the green button on the lower right," Rire said.

"And when I want the water to stop?" Minerva asked.

"Don't worry about that," Rire said. "The water will stop on its own." She stepped away from the stall. "Have a nice shower," she said, before closing the stall door.

Minerva waited a few seconds and tugged on the internal handle of the stall. It didn't budge. *Of course*, she thought. Well, it had been worth trying.

She stripped down quickly, throwing her clothes into the bin, which made a slightly disconcerting sucking noise, as though there was vacuum pressure involved.

She slunk into the shower area, noting that the floor tiles felt good on her feet, and pressed the green button.

The water came on and hit her back. She cringed away from it instinctively, having been conditioned by years of showers in which the water took a minute or two to warm up, and the first water out of the tap was always bracingly cold.

There was no need in this case. The water was the perfect temperature. This, too, was unusual as Minerva typically found that in her home shower it took experimentation turning the hot and cold dials to find the right mix via trial and error. Even when she managed to achieve it, she found that often her skin would acclimate to it, and she'd have to futz with the mixture again.

Not so in this case.

She noted with great surprise that the water seemed to be self-modulating through a programmed range of temperatures that effectively made it so that her skin's temperature receptors never got used to it and habituated. Therefore to her it always felt to be the same temperature, the perfect temperature.

I could get used to this, she thought as she sighed happily before she reminded herself that she was in jail and that she was effectively locked in this shower room with an imposing telepathic leather-garbed guard posted right outside.

The perfect shower made it easy to forget many things, she mused.

She turned her attention to the wall, which held a series of three tubes partially filled with colorful substances. The tubes were labeled with runes, but that was of no help to her. The rightmost tube was filled with a violet-colored concoction. Minerva dispensed this using an installed button. With the gel in her palm, the shower smelled strongly of lilacs. She rubbed the purple substance between her hands under the water and noted it lathered quite profusely.

Soap. She was almost certain of it. She put it all over her body, lathering it up even more, before rinsing herself clean.

The middle tube was full of something that was royal blue. Dispensing it, she noted that it smelled clean but not in a way that hinted at anything in particular. Clean linen? The ocean?

It smelled clean and blue. Testing it in the water, she guessed it was shampoo and washed her hair with it.

The final tube held yellow material. It was significantly less transparent than the first two. When dispensed, the substance was very thick.

It reminded Minerva of vanilla pudding. It didn't smell of vanilla *per se*, although the odor was pleasant and a touch sweet.

Probably conditioner, she concluded, working it through the tangles in her hair.

It always astounded her how snarly her hair could get in a single day, without constant brushing. She wondered if she would be brought a brush if she asked, if that were permitted.

Up until this point, it hadn't even occurred to her to ask. There had been much more distracting things to contend with.

Just as she was satisfied that she was clean and all the products had been washed off her body or out of her hair, the water stopped.

Rire had delivered. The shower was the perfect length.

The Subterranean Level

As Minerva emerged from the shower room into the adjoining dressing area, she spotted a fresh set of clothes in the cubby set into the wall. They were not the clothes she had arrived wearing, nor the clothes she had worn in the parade. She noted with amusement that they were all black, even her undergarments.

"I guess that's the team color," she muttered aloud, laughing, before feeling doubly silly for not only talking to herself but laughing at her own joke.

However, as she did, it occurred to her that the line between thoughts and spoken words had been obscured by the presence of telepaths. Given this, she wondered, was intentionally voicing her thoughts aloud all that different from thinking them?

Perhaps this was another clear upside of psychic society, she mused. Not only had they perfected the shower, but here it could be argued that it was perfectly acceptable to talk to yourself, that we were all set up to do it anyway with the automaticity of thought.

"Now you're getting ahead of yourself," she said, as she slipped into the fresh set of clothes. She noted that they fit perfectly. Strangely, the outfit managed to both be completely form-fitting and comfortable all at once.

You had to hand it to psychic engineering, she thought. While the rest of the industrial world frittered away its energy on trivialities like inventing more flavors of potato chips, they've been over here – wherever *here* happened to be – perfecting what really matters in life: Showers and comfy clothes that still looked sexy.

Well, she imagined she looked sexy. She wasn't quite sure.

As Minerva thought this, a mirror folded out from a compartment in the wall, one that had been so skillfully incorporated into the design of the tile that she hadn't noticed it before.

She studied her reflection. The wet hair looked a little sloppy, but yes, the rest of it was rather chic.

She looked like one of them now. She looked like she belonged in the Coterie. Well, other than the wet hair.

Still, the effect was quite striking.

With that, she heard a hiss as the pressure locking the door to the outside released. She stepped out.

Rire was standing there outside her stall, with her arms crossed. She nodded her approval. "You look good, Minerva."

"Like one of you," Minerva said.

"I wouldn't go that far," Rire said. "But this is a definite improvement."

Minerva smirked as Rire led her to a far corner of the building, where they reached another dead end. There was a large locked door with a series of runes on it.

I need to get someone to get me a basic reading primer or something, Minerva said. It was funny how much you took being able to read for granted. She was sure she'd experienced similar frustration once upon a time when she was a little girl, but that time existed in a fuzzy part of her memories.

Whenever she'd recall those years, she never quite knew if she was accessing a memory of something that actually happened or something made up wholesale, either guided by what she'd been told by relatives about when she was a little girl or by creating stories from photographs she'd been shown later. Some of it could even be dreams. It was hard to tell.

"They're expecting us," Rire told her, as they waited together in front of the door.

A few moments later, the door swung open, revealing a staircase. "You need to be careful down here," Rire said. "If you get your heart set on doing something stupid, I can't protect you down here the same way I can other places. Stay with me up on the platforms, and you should be fine."

Minerva nodded, not quite knowing what she was getting herself into.

"I mean it," Rire said. "If you're going to make an escape attempt, this is absolutely the worst place for you to do it. Not for me but for you. It's harder to escape from here, and you're a thousand times more likely to get hurt."

"I understand," Minerva said.

Rire studied Minerva's thoughts for a moment. Confident that she was telling the truth, she led her charge down the long stairwell.

Minerva noted as they descended the stairs that the walls got rougher and rougher in quality. The air changed as well. It was dustier, less pleasant to breathe.

And as they reached the final few flights, Minerva began to smell sweat and unwashed bodies.

Finally, the stairwell opened out into a wider viewing area. Underneath their feet was a black wire meshwork, a platform that looked down on what appeared to be a quarry. Opalescent rock jutted out from the sides of a pit, rock that changed color depending on the angle that the lanterns hanging throughout the area hit it.

In the pit were dozens of near-naked men. They were wearing only the briefest slip of cloth between their legs. The back portion of this outfit was a thong, and so their buttocks were mostly exposed.

They struggled with heavy mining picks, chipping away at the rock face and lifting the fragments into wheeled buckets.

It seemed as though these men hadn't seen the world outside in quite a long time, as many of them were disconcertingly pale, so pale that their bare bottoms caused a glare when caught in lantern light.

Their heads had been shaved bare, another source of glare as the light glinted off their bald heads.

"To prevent lice," Rire explained, again answering the question Minerva hadn't voiced aloud. "They do it themselves. It's part of their training."

"Training?" Minerva asked.

Rire nodded. "In the Coterie, everyone is put to good use. Most of the men who end up here don't possess the extrasensory powers that our society requires. It's self-serving bias, you see. The men who come here are rife with it. There's something about the other world, the world you come from, that puffs them up, gives them the worst egos. That overconfidence interferes with any natural psychic ability that they might have. The purpose of this area is to break them of that. To wear down those biases, their attitudes, so that they can actually access their true potential."

"So all of these men have psychic powers that they suppress because they can't get past their own egos?" Minerva asked.

Rire shook her head. "Not all of them," she said. "But some of them."

"Why are the other ones down here then?" Minerva said.

"Because we have other uses for them," Rire explained. "We've found that with the proper training, men become good servants."

"Servants?"

Rire nodded. "Some aid in domestic tasks. Others serve at the pleasure of leadership."

"What does that involve?"

"Anything leadership wants," Rire said. "I'd rather not go into it. Some of it is rather unsavory."

Minerva's stomach turned. This didn't seem ethical at all, but clearly Rire seemed to have no problem with it. Neither did any of the guards stationed down here, come to think of it. Minerva watched them on duty. They wore the same basic uniform as Rire but also carried long whips in their hands. For the most part, they looked happy and relaxed, however, chatting to one another as they presided over their charges.

"Why did you warn me? They don't look dangerous," Minerva said.

"It's been a while since there's been any sort of uprising," Rire explained. "But one never knows. For the most part, this batch is a bunch of old-timers. We haven't had any fresh recruits for a while, and new prisoners do tend to be more defiant. Feistier. But there have been incidents in the past. A hostage situation or two. You never know what a desperate man is capable of. Any of those recruits could take one look at you and decide you're their ticket out of here."

They look completely beaten down and defeated, Minerva thought.

"Some of them are only acting," Rire said.

"Why would they do that?"

"To get the jump on their guards," Rire said. "Pretend you've given up, and they'll let their guard down, and then that's your chance." She lowered her voice. "Too bad for them that there are always telepaths around. And demotivators if they get far enough."

"What are they mining?" Minerva asked.

"Does it matter?" Rire asked.

Minerva frowned.

"It's about the work, first and foremost," Rire said. "They're the real products of the work, not the ore."

Minerva felt sick again. She'd had about enough of this. "When can I meet with my lawyer?" she asked Rire.

"Now, if you'd like," Rire said. She stared at Minerva for a moment, listening to her thoughts. "You can judge us if you like, how we do things. You can think you're better than us, but it doesn't make you right. There's plenty in your world that is wrong that you turn a blind eye to. At least we're honest about it down here. We're not always pretending that things are equal or are about to be. We're not constantly patting ourselves on the back for all the steps we've made forward. I know it looks crazy to outsiders who are not used to our ways – or even *evil* as you keep thinking, but you'll get used to it. You'll see that we're bringing out the best in people, no matter what it takes. And when you do, you'll understand."

"I'd like to see my lawyer," Minerva said.

"Certainly," Rire responded, leading her back up the stairs. They walked a long way in silence, up the many flights of stairs to the ground level, through the winding hallways to the building's exit and out into the streets surrounding the jail.

As they did, it occurred to Minerva that it was awfully difficult to give a telepath the silent treatment. Rire smirked at this thought but said nothing in response.

The Unvarnished Truth

"I'm here to see Gentille," Minerva said to the woman sitting behind the desk.

Well, Minerva said it to the woman's hair anyway, which was swept up on her head, pulled into the same severe bun Minerva had seen on many people she'd encountered since being pulled into the Coterie. As Minerva arrived at the desk, this receptionist was bent over dramatically. The fingers of her left hand were splayed out with cotton balls between each digit. In her right, this woman held a bottle of nail lacquer. To Minerva, it appeared to be colorless, very much like a topcoat intended to protect nails and not to change their fundamental color.

What the polish lacked in color, however, it made up for in smell. The fumes were incredible. Minerva immediately felt dizzy.

Perhaps that's why she's hunched over like that, Minerva mused. *Maybe the fumes got to her.*

"Oh good, you've arrived," the woman beneath the hair and behind the fumes said in an oddly expressionless voice. To Minerva, it sounded like she was concentrating on her nails, and the words she spoke next confirmed that suspicion.

"The important thing is to keep the layers thin and let them completely dry in between coats," the woman said.

Minerva waited, not knowing what to say.

"If you don't, you risk ending up with stucco nails, and no one wants that," she continued.

"No, I suppose you don't," Minerva replied, more to be polite than anything else.

She watched as the woman put the finishing touches on her pinkie. She set the bottle down and blew on her fingernails.

Satisfied by the job she had done, she looked up and met Minerva's gaze.

"Ms. Cantor," the woman said. "I am Gentille. It is nice to meet you. I'd shake your hand, but..."

Minerva blushed. "You just painted your nails," Minerva finished.

"I'm not the receptionist by the way," Gentille said.

"Of course, you're not... I..." Minerva started. She sighed. "How did you know?" she asked.

Gentille smiled. "I hear in a different way than you're used to is all."

"You're a telepath, too?" Minerva asked.

"Too? You've met more of us then. I guess it's only inevitable. Telepathy is the most common psychic ability in the Coterie. Although I never think of it as telepathy myself," Gentille said. "I prefer to think of it as having really good hearing. Hearing beyond the range that many others can, being able to pick up frequencies that people don't always realize they are broadcasting on. You are fascinating by the way." She extracted the bits of cotton from between her fingers and wiggled her nails, admiring them in the natural light from the office window.

"Fascinating?"

"The things you think. Your assumptions. I haven't been outside the Coterie in ages. A person forgets how it is out there. It's like another planet, really," Gentille said.

"So, you're saying my thoughts strike you as alien?" Minerva said.

Gentille laughed. "Yes, something like that. Alien." She smiled.

If you can read my thoughts, do I even need to talk to you at all? Minerva thought, very intently and purposefully.

"Well, no," Gentille answered. "But I've never gotten the hang of thought implantation. Or, one could say, my telepathic speech is limited relative to my hearing abilities. So, I have to speak in the traditional way of course, by making sound. Otherwise, you'd have no clue what I'm thinking in response, which would be a good way to annoy you but not to communicate. And while telepathy is quite common in the Coterie, it's far from universal. It's important to keep those skills sharp, to make sure I can work in both methods, even if I'd rather listen to thoughts most days than to sounds."

"Talking is different than thinking," Minerva said.

"Yes," Gentille replied. "Thinking is better. It's more honest." She slapped herself on the forehead. "But what am I saying? Honesty isn't exactly your thing, is it?"

Minerva frowned, hurt but not exactly sure what to say.

"Oh dear, I didn't mean any offense."

Minerva said nothing but instead stewed silently.

"Honestly, I didn't." Gentille stopped. "Again with the H word. I'm incorrigible."

"You're something," Minerva muttered.

Gentille frowned. "Perhaps I'm not what you would have chosen for a lawyer, but frankly I don't know that I would have chosen you as a client. In any event, Ms. Cantor you're what I have. I'm what the Coterie has appointed for your defense, and so we must work together, one way or another. There's no replacement process for either of us, I'm afraid. I don't make the rules. We must find a way to get through this case even if we'd rather be doing so with other people."

Minerva stared out the window, lost in thought.

Gentille concentrated and surfed these thoughts with her. Neither spoke for a few minutes. Finally, Gentille said, "I'm not exactly sure what *Law & Order* is, but it looks fascinating."

"That wasn't an actual episode," Minerva said.

"Episode?" Gentille asked.

"It's a TV show."

"So, you're an actress," Gentille said.

"No," Minerva said, shaking her head. "Not an actress, more of a dreamer. I was just imagining how my situation would play out if I were on *Law & Order* instead of stuck in this miserable place."

She could see it unfold vividly before her. The emblematic theme song would play with its forceful percussive hits, funky keyboard riff, the Guitar of Madness, and what she'd come to think of as the Clarinet of Reason. After the opening theme and a spectacularly smooth fade, the first half of the show would center around law enforcement, who would uncover some unfortunate crime and attempt to piece together facts to build a case. But her mind didn't dwell on that. Instead, it jumped briskly to the second half of the show, when the trial would start.

And there she would be sitting at the defendant's table with a team of counsel. The judge would sit there before them, perhaps a bit wry and salty but witty and fair-handed. He would admonish both sides in turn.

Minerva would sit in a lilac pantsuit as her competent lawyers eviscerated the thin case built against her. Eventually, it would be her turn to take the defense stand, and she would do so looking radiant and emotionally devastated.

"Objection, your honor, badgering the witness," her defense attorney would cry as the prosecution laid into her unfairly.

"Sustained," the judge would say. "Knock it off."

She would be found not guilty and the true culprit would be apprehended in another episode, a to-be-continued multiparter.

Yes, that's what this was. This was a to-be-continued multiparter.

Gentille began to sing the theme music. This snapped her out of her thoughts.

"You were doing it again," Gentille said.

"Well," Minerva said, becoming increasingly annoyed. "Perhaps that's just something I do then. Maybe it's something that's not worth commenting on." She glared pointedly at Gentille.

Gentille smiled. "I knew there was a spine buried somewhere under all of that."

Minerva's lips snaked into a frown. She refused to dignify such condescension with a response.

Gentille, however, didn't care. "Okay, so I've had a chance to review your case," she segued, unfazed.

"And?" Minerva prompted.

"Looking over the nature of your crimes, your personal situation, and the fact that this is your first offense, I believe the best approach is to plead guilty," Gentille said.

"Plead guilty?" Minerva said. "But I'm innocent."

"Hardly," Gentille said. "You are guilty. Guilty as sin. You did everything you've been accused of… and probably more that we missed."

"How can I be guilty if I don't know which laws I've broken? How can I be guilty if I've done something and didn't know it was wrong?"

Gentille raised an eyebrow. "Surely, you've heard the saying 'ignorance of the law is no defense.'"

"Of course," Minerva said. "But—"

"You're special? This is a special case?" Gentille interrupted.

Minerva nodded.

"I don't think the Special Snowflake Defense is going to cut it, Ms. Cantor. Especially not with Judge Cloche," Gentille said.

"Judge Cloche?" Minerva said.

Gentille nodded. "The head magistrate. She oversees most of the cases here in the Coterie since we generally don't deal with enough crime to occupy more than one judge. She was elected to the post last year. A real nail biter of an election actually. She was a controversial pick to say the least."

"Why's that?" Minerva asked.

"Are you sure you want to use your allotted legal advisory time talking about our politics?" Gentille said.

"Well, you were content to use that time to finish your manicure," Minerva shot back.

Gentille winced. "Touché."

"And besides," Minerva continued, "I'm a newcomer here. I don't know what I don't know. It can't hurt to know more about the political climate – and particularly the judge trying my case."

"Sensible," Gentille said, nodding. "Cloche Macomber is a strange one. She's not like any magistrates that preceded her. She's very self-contained… she does her own thing. Very analytical, very categorical, academic." Gentille paused to gather just the right words. "Cloche is a nerd."

"Aren't most judges?" Minerva asked.

"Maybe where you're from," Gentille said, "but in the Coterie, it's a little different. We tend to look for a different kind of mental acuity. Psychic prowess, if you will."

"And Cloche doesn't have psychic powers?" Minerva said.

"Well, I wouldn't say that," Gentille said. Minerva could swear she heard harried backpedaling in progress. "She's... technically psychic."

"But not very?" Minerva prompted.

Gentille nodded. "There are degrees to psychic power. Just like some of you have keen vision and others not so much. Or like how some people in your world can hear quite acutely and others hear very little and might wear a device to amplify the sound." She chose her words very delicately. "Cloche's perceptive powers are very faint."

Minerva thought about that for a second. "That has to be very challenging, living in a psychic culture and yet having limited perceptive powers."

"Perhaps," Gentille said. "On the other hand, what Cloche lacks in depth, she makes up for in breadth."

"Meaning?"

"Judge Cloche is a psychic generalist, the rarest form of intuitive of them all. She has just about every manner of insight you can imagine – precognition, telepathy, eideticism, what have you. She can even truthshape, believe it or not. But her power only ever comes in short flashes, and it's not under her conscious control," Gentille explained.

"Is it considered a good thing or a bad thing to be a generalist?" Minerva asked.

"Yes," Gentille answered, her face and tone serious. "Good, bad, it all depends."

"Maybe it will work in my favor," Minerva said.

"How do you figure?" Gentille pressed.

"Who better to understand me than someone who has experienced it all? Who better to judge me than someone who's been both powerful and powerless? I can't think of a luckier break," Minerva said.

"You don't need luck," Gentille said. "You need to plead guilty. If you plead guilty, we can work out a deal. That is your best chance for having some say in your fate. I know the court will be lenient on you if you admit what you've done. All you have to do is take some accountability. These TV shows you watch have clouded your judgment. They've prepared you for a world that doesn't exist – not in your own society and certainly not here, in the Coterie. They've set you up to believe that it's best to fight the charges before you as hard as you can, to not give an inch. In the real world, plea deals are nearly always the best way to go. A plea deal is in your best interest here."

Minerva scowled. So much for the dream of a defense lawyer who would be a vigorous advocate. She found herself missing Darren. At the time he'd represented her in her personal injury case against the trucking company, she hadn't appreciated him properly, she realized. Something within her had relegated him to the role of good-looking ambulance chaser and had rounded down his litigation strengths to undetectable levels. She hadn't realized how lucky she was to have him in her corner after the accident. At the time she'd had no idea how shoddy legal representation could be, how indifferent, how ill-fitting.

"I'm not convinced Darren would know how to navigate our legal system," Gentille said, working from her unspoken thoughts.

It would take some time among the telepaths, Minerva reflected, before she got used to that. Every time it happened, she second-guessed herself, wondering if she had spoken her thoughts aloud without realizing it. The lack of mental privacy was hard to get used to. She made a mental note to never take it for granted ever again.

"Okay, against my better judgment, I have to ask. What realistically would I be looking at if I did plead guilty?" Minerva said.

"Well," Gentille said, "it all depends on the prosecution and how flexible they are, but going by past cases, you probably would be confined for a bit in our prison system so your attitude could be adjusted and you could be monitored. I'd imagine that would be for about a year, perhaps two or three if you took a while to adapt. After that time, the court would find you suitable transitional housing while you were tested for vocational aptitude and we placed you in some job training, so you could become a productive member of our society. Once you got a full-time job and stable long-term independent housing, you'd be able to stay in the Coterie with minimal restrictions. There would be mandatory visits from your parole officer of course but nothing too troublesome. Check-in interviews mostly, just to make sure you were sticking to any court guidelines and appropriately contributing your talents to the Coterie."

Minerva nodded in understanding. "And when would I be able to leave the Coterie? When could I return to Skinner?" she asked.

"Return to Skinner?" Gentille said.

Minerva nodded.

"Never. They'd never allow that."

"What?"

"You're here. You know we exist. Every day you know more about our inner workings, our strengths, our weaknesses. It's too dangerous. Too great of a security risk. You can't go back. Not as a reformed criminal. No, they'd never trust you to do that," Gentille said. Her tone was flat as though she were speaking something obvious and not giving Minerva the worst news she had ever gotten.

Minerva felt all the blood drain from her face. Her stomach lurched as though she were falling from a great height. "But what if I get acquitted?"

Gentille thought about this. "If you get acquitted?" she repeated. "I honestly don't know."

"I thought you were a lawyer," Minerva said.

"I am," Gentille said. "It's just never happened before – not with such serious crimes. My role in these cases is typically to facilitate the plea deal." She frowned. "Acquittal would be unprecedented."

"So my fate post acquittal would be up to Judge Cloche's discretion?" Minerva said.

"I suppose so. She'd get to set the precedent," Gentille said, nodding.

"Then I'm going to take my chances," Minerva said. "No plea deal. No guilty plea. We'll see what the judge does once all of the facts are before her."

"You're going to gamble your entire life on this?" Gentille asked.

"If I plead guilty, life as I know it is over anyway," Minerva said.

"But for all you know, the new life you *could* have would be much better," Gentille said. "In fact, given what I know about your world and its barbarity, its misogyny... I can almost guarantee a new life here would suit you."

"Well, it doesn't matter what you think, does it?" Minerva snapped. "You're working for me. You're my defense, aren't you?"

Gentille nodded. As she did, she felt a deep sadness descend upon her. It was incomprehensible, that Minerva would fight starting over in the Coterie, unencumbered, surrounded by people who were more like her, finally being able to receive proper training and education for her obvious gifts.

"Minerva, we are your people," Gentille ventured. "This is your new home."

"Not guilty," Minerva said again. "End of discussion."

It's legal suicide, Gentille thought sadly. Aloud she said, "Understood. I'll file the appropriate motion."

Under the Cloche

The Honorable Judge Cloche Macomber glided through her Coterie-provided efficiency in bare feet.

Her dwelling was the only place she would ever be seen without her shoes. Her shoes were her armor. She didn't speak of it frequently, but she liked having an extra two or three inches of height. It made her feel more powerful.

Judge Macomber shied away from thinner heels, preferring nondescript black boots with hidden platforms, or perhaps a chunky thick-heeled Mary Jane. It was a little incongruous on a magistrate, more like what a prison guard would wear. But it was what she liked.

Not that it mattered too much what they looked like, obscured under her floor length black robe.

Still, she liked to feel prim and steady. In control. Level.

She'd take any advantage she could get, given the circumstances. It was a large burden acting as head magistrate and not what she'd trained for.

She was and always would be a taxonomer at heart. Sorting things into categories had always soothed her. Cleaning up messy realities and gingerly directing them into much neater, discrete divisions. Never mind that sometimes you had to force something into a place where it didn't quite fit. Never mind that there were times when elements of an idea, person, or incident would strain under this force, wriggling like a trapped insect's back legs when the car window goes up.

Taxonomy was satisfying. It grounded her. It was her first love.

But being a judge wasn't too different than being a taxonomer. It involved sorting things into the appropriate categories. In the law that could sometimes be difficult. Boundaries were blurry. And bias was an ever-present threat.

Every head magistrate before her had also had psychic powers. But Cloche was different, and this difference pained her. It made her doubt herself. Her predecessors had all been specialists, and Cloche was a staunch generalist.

She could do a little bit of everything. But not much more.

Still – and most importantly – she was accustomed to doing as much as she could with what she had.

Resourceful. That was what they had called her in her earlier years, when she was a mere student. Resourceful.

Perhaps that was what they should call her now, Cloche mused. The Resourceful Judge Cloche Macomber. Because to her, the "Honorable" moniker often seemed a stretch. This was likely because she was privy to her own thoughts. She knew the failings and frailty that lurked within her.

If others saw it, well, she'd be unmasked in a second, Cloche thought. The key to her success had been learning to hide it. Learning to fence it in. To give her wickedness places to play that would remain private. Pose no consequence to her social life.

This could be quite a feat regardless of who you were, but for the elite in a secret psychic society... well...

She had been forced to become resourceful, if only to have a modicum of privacy and to retain a sliver of her humanity. She had to be resourceful in order to never pay the price for her imperfections.

Part of this was ensuring that no one ever had a reason to look underneath her surface. No reason to think there could be anything untoward lurking beneath her smooth, flawless façade.

It was a wonder she ever got anything else done. Fitting in was such a difficult job sometimes.

But she made it work.

Because she was, after all, resourceful.

"How'd it go?" Rire asked Minerva after she exited Gentille's office.

Minerva shook her head slowly, not sure where to begin recounting the encounter. Thankfully, Rire was adept at rifling through the jumble of her thoughts and methodically reordering them. Reading people's thoughts could be difficult, she reflected as she did this, but only if you didn't learn to calm your own thoughts and emotions and keep them in check. Otherwise, you ran the risk of mixing up what you were feeling and thinking with what was going on inside of the mind of your subject.

Rire steadied herself with a few deep breaths and moved Minerva's thought fragments into a logical sequence. At once, she saw it, how the meeting had gone – more or less, fed through the filter of Minerva's consciousness. The revelation was as satisfying as working out the solution to a daily jumble in the newspaper.

"Gentille is a character," Rire commiserated.

"That's one way of putting it."

"She isn't a bad lawyer," Rire said. "Just one who is used to doing things a very specific way. She's not to blame though."

"No?"

Rire shook her head. "A lot of people are used to doing things a very specific way. We're particularly prone to it here in the Coterie."

"Why do you think that is?"

"We have utopia. Why mess with it?" Rire said.

"Utopia's a matter of opinion," Minerva muttered.

"It's not your utopia," Rire said. "Of course it's not."

"Because I'm from out there?" Minerva said, gesturing vaguely
off into the distance. As she did, she thought how strange it was
to not even know if she were pointing in the right direction, to
not know how she even got here, let alone where *here* actually
was.

Rire shook her head. "No, because you're not a person who gets
used to doing things a specific way."

"What do you mean by that?"

"For most people, the world as it is suits them just fine. The world
– this little world, the outside world, probably even other worlds
we don't know about – is built so that it works for most people.
That's how things are set up, how all the decisions to build a
civilization are guided. The trouble is that people are simply too
different from one another for one size to ever fit all. There's no
world that works for everyone. There will always be people who
don't really fit in the spaces that are supposed to fit everyone.
People who have to constantly change something in order to
make it work, whether that's changing themselves, somehow
changing the world, or changing their expectations. You're one
of those people who don't fit, Minerva. I'm sure you've known
it your entire life, sensed that the world is a poor fit for you, and
that the world that you belong in doesn't really exist. What makes
you different from most people in your position is that you went
to greater lengths to change the world than most."

"None of that makes me sound like a criminal," Minerva said.

"Well, you wouldn't be," Rire continued, "except when you
reshaped the world to fit you, you broke it for an awful lot of
other people. And yes, I know you didn't realize what you were
doing at the time, but you can do a lot of harm without realizing
it."

Minerva didn't know what to say to this. She let her thoughts
wander. As she did, it occurred to her that she was growing
strangely comfortable with Rire. *Perhaps this is how Stockholm*

Syndrome sets in, she thought. But she let that thought drift away and flew onto others. And as she did, she didn't care that Rire could see it all. Let her look. Let her hear. What did it matter?

"I know what might help," Rire said.

"What's that?"

"There is someone you should meet," Rire said.

Perhaps the plush purple carpeting in the anteroom should have been her first hint that she was off to see someone important. The well-built mahogany furniture. Expensive paintings hung on walls made of smoothly polished black stone, walls that appeared oddly contiguous without visible joints or seams. Such tricks of the eye often cost a fortune.

But Minerva was still surprised when Rire walked her into the judge's chambers, of all places.

"Minerva Cantor," Judge Cloche acknowledged her. "Do sit down."

And so, Minerva did. There was a tenor in Cloche's voice that firmly emphasized that the guidance she gave was not up for question. Something finite and hard to place. But certainly there. And Minerva certainly heard it.

She'd heard it before, she realized. Cloche spoke with the same heft that Moche did. Perhaps it was fitting that their names rhymed, Minerva mused, as their energies rhymed as well. Their voices were almost like echoes of one another, although Cloche's was in a higher register.

"I would say it is good to meet you, but I'm afraid I can't," Cloche said. "Because it's not good to meet you. I wish you had never come to the Coterie. I wish we never would have had to bring you here. That we could have left you out in the wider world to live a normal existence. One that would have harmed nearly no one and no one meaningfully. But that is not the case."

Minerva dropped her eyes to her lap.

"I wouldn't want to meet my gaze either, were our positions reversed," Cloche observed.

Minerva said nothing.

"I'm disappointed in you of course," Cloche said. "I had hoped for better. From you. From the world. From..." She paused. "From the nature of things."

Minerva still said nothing.

"In hindsight, I suppose it's foolish to demand anything of existence, as though it could be socially pressured to comply." Cloche screwed up her face in disgust. "Still, you do form expectations of reality, don't you?"

Minerva nodded weakly. "I had, yes."

"And then you began to subvert them," Cloche said.

And though it wasn't a question, Minerva found herself nodding at that, too.

"It's funny how that works," Cloche said. "You don't know what you believe until it's challenged, do you?

Minerva thought about that.

"No need to answer, Ms. Cantor," the judge said.

"Where's Gentille?" Minerva asked suddenly. "Will she be joining us?"

Cloche stiffened up, sat ramrod straight in her chair. "Are you formally requesting that your counsel be present?'

"No," Minerva said. "I just... I don't understand why I'm meeting with the judge without my attorney."

"I can have her summoned if you like," Cloche offered.

Minerva scratched her head. "I'm not sure what I want. I just..." She stopped to think of how to phrase it. "I don't know if it's... proper to talk to the judge without an attorney?"

"Proper's a funny thing," Cloche said. "It's all contextual. Depends on where you are, who you're dealing with."

"Well, here," Minerva said. "Here in the Coterie, is it proper for the accused to speak to the judge without an attorney?"

"Here in the Coterie, it doesn't much matter," Cloche said. "I know it's quite different in the legal system you're used to though, so I understand your confusion. And we're more than willing to accommodate you, act closer to what you're used to in your culture."

Minerva realized uncomfortably that she didn't really have much experience with the legal system in her everyday life, not even in her "culture." In this case, her sole cultural experiences were episodes of *Law & Order.*

"Anyway, we're here to discuss something straightforward today. We could do it in open court if you prefer, but now that you're here, perhaps we could get the matter out of the way as quickly as possible," Cloche said. "And truthfully, I thought you might like a chance to spend some time out of your quarters a bit."

Minerva smiled. "Thank you. That was quite kind of you."

"Well, I know that the place we keep prisoners is a bit spartan. Nothing cruel of course. You have all the amenities. But yes. Quite spartan. I thought you could use a bit of fresh air," Cloche said.

"I do appreciate it," Minerva said.

"You're very welcome," Cloche said. "There are some among us who think it's important for criminals to suffer as much as possible, that it will lower the rate of recidivism, lead to fewer repeat offenses, but I'm not one of those. It flies in the face of all the science on the matter. Harsher punishments do little to deter crime, and a bit of kindness and humanity at the right time can help someone go straight, as it were. We want it to be tidier than that. We want to think that fear of awful punishment will prevent crimes, but unfortunately the mind doesn't really work that way. There has to be some kind of consequence for harmful actions of course. There must be justice. But justice doesn't have to be extreme or cruel to be effective. And it's up to society to provide a path back. Whether that's a society like yours – or the Coterie's."

Minerva felt very encouraged. The judge held a similar viewpoint to hers regarding reform, which was always a good feeling, being in the company of someone who had a similar value system to your own. It had a way of making you feel just a little bit less alone, something she desperately needed. Not only that, but it boded well for her case.

This was a person who was not only capable of showing mercy but preferred to. Judge Cloche was clearly someone who wasn't motivated to punish but to reform.

I couldn't have gotten a better judge, Minerva thought.

"Anyway, that's not why we're here, to hear my thoughts on the state of our prisons or how I'd prefer them to be. We're here today because I wanted to consult with you on an important matter," Cloche said.

Minerva nodded.

"Would you like me to summon Gentille before I go any further?" Cloche asked.

Minerva shook her head. She'd been unimpressed with her useless lawyer at their initial meeting, and even though it flew in the face of everything she'd been told about talking to authorities, this was the Coterie, after all. Things seemed to work quite a bit differently here. Besides, she suspected having Gentille here would only complicate the discussion with Cloche.

"What matter did you want to discuss?" Minerva asked.

"You have an important choice to make: Whether you want a bench trial or a jury trial. I'm sure you're familiar with jury trials. I've been informed about your penchant for fictional legal dramas," Cloche said.

Minerva blushed.

"Don't be embarrassed. I reviewed a few episodes myself so I could better understand your point of view and make sure we accommodate you. I noted that jury trials were much more common. Bench trials, in which a judge hears the evidence and renders the verdict, were quite rare. So I suspect that you will probably want to go with a jury trial."

"I'm not sure," Minerva said.

"Oh?"

"Well, typically, a jury trial is when you're tried by your peers, and I don't know... given the circumstances... if that would be possible. I don't know if I have any peers here."

Cloche furrowed her brow. "But you're surrounded by your peers here. There are plenty of people like you."

"People who grew up in the outside world and were forcibly brought here after being arrested for crimes they didn't know existed?" Minerva challenged.

"I suppose you have a point," Cloche said. She did her best not to chuckle, although she wanted to. Minerva had quite a colorful way of putting things into perspective. It was a little disarming – and unexpectedly amusing.

"Right now, especially after our meeting today, I'm leaning towards the bench trial," Minerva admitted.

"Oh?"

Minerva nodded. "It might sound kind of hokey, but I've got a good feeling about you. I feel like you will be reasonable. That you'll be fair."

"That's high praise," Cloche said.

"It's how I see it," Minerva said. "Do I have to decide right now?"

Cloche shook her head. "Not at all. You have a few days. I believe Gentille will be heading to the detention center tomorrow morning, and you can always discuss it with her then." She smiled broadly. "But it was a good excuse to get you out of your cell for a bit, wasn't it?'

Minerva returned the broad smile. "That it was."

"Duty calls," Cloche said, gesturing to the towering mountain of paperwork perched on the corner of her desk and then waving at the door behind Minerva. "Until we meet again."

Minerva nodded, as she rose and left the judge's chambers. Rire stood there, quite alert, with her eyes trained on the door.

Minerva knew the way back to the detention center, but Rire walked closely next to her, ostensibly so she could grab Minerva or call for help should she make a break for it.

Or even think of making a break for it, Minerva realized. That was probably why they hadn't cuffed her since the strange parade that had heralded her arrival. For that matter, they didn't use similar physical safeguards that were standard at prisons outside of the Coterie. A telepathic prison guard served as an early alert system for escape attempts. In a lot of ways, they were superior to physical restraints.

Minerva supposed it didn't hurt that she simply didn't feel like doing much of *anything* when she was locked up because her cell block was guarded by a psychic demotivator.

Walking back to the prison, Minerva and Rire passed a newsstand. Minerva thought at first it was a line of mirrors because her own face reflected back at her in the newsprint.

Minerva the Liar! One headline read. *The Trial of the Century!*

"Looks like you're famous," Rire said.

"I never thought that magical beings would dig trash so much," Minerva remarked. "I can't believe you even have tabloids."

"Are you kidding? We're insatiable for it. Like all people of substance, we crave trash," Rire said.

Passersby cringed away from Minerva with a newfound intensity. *That's her*, their body language said. *That's the criminal.*

For the first time since she'd entered the Coterie, Minerva felt like a *persona non grata*. Being paraded around, held in a cell, brought up on charges, assigned a lawyer, and meeting with the judge – none of that had made the reality of her situation sink in.

But being shunned in the public square... that was what really brought it home.

That certainly said something about crime and punishment, Minerva mused as Rire shot warning glances all around them at folks who dug out cameras and looked as though they might want to take a picture of the fallen woman being escorted back to prison.

Rire had an uncanny knack of identifying them even before the cameras were drawn, Minerva noted. Ah yes, telepathy worked just as well to stave off photography attempts as it did escape attempts.

Still, Minerva had a feeling that this wouldn't be the last time she felt like something on display. The parade wasn't over now, was it? It would go on for quite a while yet. Something deep within her suspected that the media circus was only just beginning.

How was it possible, she wondered, that some people went all of their lives lusting after fame and doing everything they could to obtain it and still languished in obscurity, while some who never wanted fame found it descend upon them without their consent?

And how could we continue to worship fame as though it meant something when its whims were so arbitrary?

"No pictures," Rire growled over and over again at each potential photographic offender as they approached the detention center.

Minerva breathed a sigh of relief as she was walked back to her cell, and she felt the will to do anything – let alone escape – leave her.

It was good to not be seen.

She clung to that memory, that feeling of invisibility, at the arraignment hearing that followed. Much to her lawyer's chagrin and despite much last minute cajoling from counsel, Minerva pled not guilty, and bail was denied.

All the while, a large crowd gathered in the courtroom gaped at her as though she were an exotic animal in captivity. Perhaps she was, Minerva thought, as she was brought back to her cell. And perhaps they all were captive animals, the crowd, the lawyers, the judge. Perhaps they just didn't realize that they were stuck in enclosures, too. Maybe they were all prisoners, too, whether they recognized their respective prisons.

Minerva knew it was a stretch, but the thought gave her hope. In a certain sense, she was just as free – or not – as anyone else.

The Role of Bias

The emergence of the Psychic Phenomenon played out quite differently than anticipated by centuries of storytellers.

Fictional depictions of psychic powers demonstrated such abilities as infallible and their wielders omnipotent.

It was quite a shock for the public to realize that not only did psychic powers exist – and were more widespread among the population than they would have guessed – but that psychic powers were less straightforward than originally conceptualized. The activation of powers themselves could be quite idiosyncratic, differing from individual to individual. Some practitioners merely needed to mentally concentrate and could effortlessly manifest their abilities. Others needed a more tangible focusing agent, typically some sort of talisman that aided the discharge of psychic energies. Still others were somewhere in between. They could perform without the aid of additional props but might need to assume a certain physical stance or position.

These variations exist regardless of the type of psychic power in question.

Furthermore, fictional accounts of extrasensory perception and intuitive feats failed to take account of what would become a major mechanism in the activation of psychic power: Bias.

Bias, or the inclination for or prejudice against something, often in a way that is unfair and not in line with reality, posed the greatest threat to accurate use of intuitive powers and indeed to psychic vitality itself.

Some psychic practitioners have been known to go to great lengths to mitigate the effects of bias. As of the time of this edition's writing, it is currently quite popular for psychic intuitives interested in reducing the impact of bias upon their powers to seek out methods of increasing their levels of self-awareness. For many individuals, this means pursuing talk therapy. Others participate in ordeals designed to foster epiphany and personal growth. An entire ordeal industry has sprung up to satisfy the increased demand.

Regardless of the popularity of these interventions, however, there is little evidence at the current time that they are helpful.

Bias has been observed to interfere with the activation of practically every psychic power, although it has been noted that the magnitude of its effects is larger with certain power sets than with others.

Notably, precognitionists, intuitives with the ability to see potential future outcomes, are profoundly affected by bias. As a result, a precognitionist can never accurately predict a situation of which they are an integral part. They can *try* to predict the future, but if it's a future that directly affects them, their predictions are much more like guesses than actual second sight.

For a precognitionist or the related class of clairvoyant to be as accurate as possible in their readings, they must be separate from the future they're studying.

This means that precogs either do best if they stick to readings of specific matters that do not involve them, or if they must work globally, they should ideally be as isolated from the rest of society as possible.

Only then will their readings have a chance of being accurate.

from Insecta Psychica: Towards an Intuitive Taxonomy
by Cloche Macomber

Minerva's next visitor didn't walk into her cell but was instead hauled there like a piece of heavy equipment. He was a miniature man, about the size of an old radio, the sturdy kind you never saw anymore. This kind of radios inevitably fill the garages of very old and very young men. The old men are surly and devastated that time has moved forward and despise that much has changed. The young men typically celebrate how much technology has moved on since then but want to stay connected to the recent past, feeling they owe a lot to their still-living ancestors and that they also have a lot they can learn from the modest niches those ancestors carved out.

He was about as heavy as an old radio, too, this tiny man, Rire reflected as she carried him into the cell. Squat, with clumsy proportions. If he had been pixelated, it would have been easy for Minerva to mistake him for video game sprite art. He seemed to be a person forced into his particular blocky form rather than one who had spontaneously grown this way.

Viewing him, she wasn't sure if he had been carried into her cell because he came to see her reluctantly or because he was physically unable to walk. His legs seemed inadequate length to propel his body forward, suggesting immobility, but then again, he also scowled in such a dour way that Minerva got the impression that he would rather be doing anything else.

"Same shit, different day," he said in a surprisingly deep voice given his small stature. To his bearers, he said, "Can we get this over with? I'm not your toy, you know."

"Sure, Bad Touch," Espoir said to the tiny man. "Just do your thing and we'll have you back to..."

"Whatever it is that you do," Rire finished.

Bad Touch's scowl deepened. Minerva wondered idly how many layers of irritation this small man could manage to wear at one time. He was quite good at being annoyed.

"Thank you for stopping by," Minerva said to Bad Touch in as warm of a tone as she could muster.

"I'm not your friend, lady, so I'd cut it out with the charming crap," Bad Touch replied.

"Look," Minerva said, "it's clear you don't want to be here. I don't want to be here either. Maybe we're not friends, but we have that at least in common. Neither of us wants to be here. But here we are."

Bad Touch paused, considered this.

"Anyway, I've never met a... uh... whatever it is that you are... before." Minerva suddenly felt foolish. Clumsy.

"Of course you haven't," Bad Touch said proudly. "There's only one of me, after all."

"And that is...?" Minerva said.

"I'm a homunculus," Bad Touch replied.

"A homunculus?" Minerva asked, with an unintended tone of amusement in her voice.

She hadn't meant any disrespect, but Bad Touch scowled anyway.

"Uh, yeah," he said. "Is she slow or something?" he asked Espoir and Rire.

"No, she's not slow," Espoir replied. "That's the trouble, really. She's a little too talented for her own good."

"Could have fooled me," Bad Touch replied.

"That's not terribly hard," Rire jabbed.

"Go ahead, insult the help," Bad Touch snapped at her. "And they wonder why I hate my job," he said to Minerva.

"For what it's worth, I don't wonder at all," Minerva replied. "I'd hate your job, too."

"The Coterie created him long ago," Espoir explained. "He's the result of cross-species fertilization. We gestated him for 200 years. Well, I'm not sure that gestated is the right word, even. We did use a womb though... to prepare him."

"The womb of a horse," Rire interjected.

Espoir nodded. "Right."

"You didn't have to tell her that," Bad Touch said, frowning. He looked embarrassed. "She didn't have to know that."

"Gestation isn't quite the right word, no. I would say that fermentation would be a better way to put it. Bad Touch was biological material composted in the womb of a horse for 200 years, just rotting and rotting, and then one day he clawed his way out, and here he is," Espoir finished. "In all his... glory." She smirked.

"It wasn't quite that easy of course," Rire continued. "He wasn't quite done when he freed himself. His skin was transparent, more like a sac, and he had no self-awareness. The Coterie nursed him with a steady supply of blood and bile, and then he developed into the charming character that he is today."

"You seem proud of him," Minerva said.

"We are," Rire said. "He's our pride and joy."

"Bad Touch is our child... in a way. All of us," Espoir said.

"At the very least, he is our collective creation," said Rire. "The product of many generations of Coterie members. We passed him from one assembly to the next, never quite sure if he'd eventually come to life. It was all a leap of faith. And something we had to hide from the outside because they would have thought we were crazy, brewing up a child from spare parts. But here he is. And we're ever so proud now."

"Even if, like an unruly child, he doesn't always act in a way that pleases us," Espoir added, shooting him a sharp look.

"Although I suppose it's quite a different relationship if you look at it from another angle. In another way, he's our father," Rire said.

Minerva frowned. "How is that even possible?"

"We weren't psychics back then, back when we... created him? Seeded him?" Espoir said.

"Planted him," Rire offered.

"We were enthusiasts of the refining arts. Scientists who were working without a map but filled in our lack of plan with passion," Espoir said.

"I believe the word you would use for what we were is 'alchemists,'" Rire explained.

"We were eager to change the world, even if we didn't know where our changes would lead. Bad Touch was simply one project of thousands. But many of those other experiments fell by the wayside. They didn't ultimately go anywhere. Bad Touch is different. He's one of the few that actually was successful," Espoir explained.

"Glad to hear *you* think I'm successful," Bad Touch moaned.

"You see," Espoir said, "Bad Touch has psychic powers. We believe he is the first being who ever did. Others soon followed him of course. Psychic contagion. That's what we call it. The spread that happened. To this point, we've managed to keep it a secret. But people like you threaten that. Psychics who are running around changing enough that people might start asking questions."

"Enough that people might find us and make our lives miserable," Rire said.

"Oh, boo hoo," Bad Touch mocked.

"Know your place," Espoir scolded him.

"Oh I do," Bad Touch said. "It doesn't mean I have to like my place."

"Anyway, Bad Touch is here as a consultant, of sorts," Rire said.

"Of sorts," Bad Touch said, grimacing.

"He's reality's witness, you see," Espoir clarified.

"Reality's witness?" Minerva asked.

Espoir nodded. "He can detect rips in the fabric of reality. He's a bit like…"

"A cadaver dog," Rire offered.

Bad Touch winced at this comparison. Minerva didn't blame him. It was literally dehumanizing.

"Exactly," Espoir said, clasping her hands together, seemingly oblivious to Bad Touch's chagrin. "Just as a cadaver dog would sniff out a hidden body, our friend Bad Touch here, he will point the way towards the damage you've done to reality."

"Why do they call you Bad Touch?" Minerva asked the tiny man directly.

He met her eyes.

"You don't have to answer that," Rire said.

Bad Touch ignored her. Of course he didn't have to answer Minerva. They treated him like a child. No, worse than a child. They treated him like an animal. Not a pet either, but like a workhorse. Like the kind of animal you kept and fed for years and didn't name because they were intended to one day be consumed.

No, it was worse than that. They'd given him a ridiculous name instead of not naming him at all.

"It's a joke," Bad Touch said.

"Your name is a joke?" Minerva asked.

He nodded gravely. "A bad one, too."

"I told you," Rire said. "You don't have to explain it."

"Has it ever occurred to you that I might *want* to?" Bad Touch asked her, his voice growing louder.

Rire's eyes widened.

"No, of course not. Because no one ever thinks about what I want," Bad Touch said.

"What was the joke?" Minerva pressed.

"It was my first time acting as reality's witness. Long before either of these clowns were even born," Bad Touch said.

Espoir audibly scoffed at this, but Bad Touch ignored her.

"I was brought in, and the first thing the former prosecutor said was 'show me on the homunculus where that mean lady touched you.'"

Rire and Espoir laughed.

"See what I mean? They act like it's a funny joke. But it's not. It's lazy, disrespectful. Pointlessly offensive. I'm not a doll. I'm a living person. And molestation is nothing to laugh at," Bad Touch said.

Minerva nodded. "I do know what you mean."

"Anyway, they all started calling me Bad Touch. Everyone in that first trial, the prosecution, the defense, the judge, even the accused. And the name stuck," he said.

"Why don't you change it?" Minerva asked.

"Change it?"

"Yes. If you hate it so much, why don't you change it?" Minerva said.

Bad Touch considered this for a moment. "I suppose that could be a possibility." He thought for another moment. "It's hard to start over again though, once you've made a certain name for yourself. Even if it's one that you wouldn't have chosen in the first place."

"Well, I don't know about that," Minerva said.

Bad Touch smiled.

"I think you're selling yourself short." As soon as the final word –*short*—had left her mouth, she regretted it.

Bad Touch's lips curled into a sneer. "That is *NOT* funny!" he said.

"Good one," Rire said.

"No, that's not what I meant at all," Minerva said. "I just meant that you should give yourself more credit. I think you're more than capable of starting over."

Bad Touch's expression softened. "It's a thought. Now the session begins."

He grabbed one of her hands with his two tiny ones and closed his eyes. He looked straight into her past, present, and future and dutifully noted everything he saw there. Painstakingly, he moved reality a centimeter to the left and performed the same function, thin slicing the most adjacent alternate universe. When this was finished, he moved another centimeter to the left.

He imaged each reality, noting the dimensions of each as well as the reality of each dimension, marking down the stream of numbers in neat columns that he held inside his mind, just beneath his tiny forehead.

The procedure took no more than three minutes. When it was over, he let go of Minerva's hand and nodded at her.

"It's been a pleasure to meet you, Minerva Cantor," he said.

He nodded at Espoir and Rire. "My work here is done. I'll have the report prepared shortly."

Rire lifted him and took him from the room.

"I wonder what he saw," Minerva said to Espoir.

"Everything," Espoir replied. "He saw everything." She paused. "That's what he does."

The Difference Between Clairvoyance and Precognition

Although often confused by the layperson, there's a world of difference between precognitionists and clairvoyants.

As discussed elsewhere in this volume, precognitionists are psychic practitioners skilled with discerning the future, and most precisely, possible futures. They are particularly adept at foreseeing events that do not involve them directly.

Clairvoyants, conversely, do not predict *per se*. Instead, they simply see and see quite clearly, regardless of the matter in question. Their function is implied by their etymology, *clair* being French for "clear" and *voyant* French for "seeing."

Clairvoyants are less bound by temporal causality than precogs and see past, present, and future about equally well. Indeed, many clairvoyants struggle with meaningfully differentiating between the three states and may instead find themselves interacting inappropriately in a temporal sense. For example, a powerful clairvoyant might find themselves easily emotionally "stuck" in a past predicament and never able to move beyond it meaningfully since time doesn't have the same mitigating effect in their emotional inner lives.

While precognitionists are among the most common psychic practitioners observed, clairvoyant powers are exceedingly rare.

The most powerful clairvoyants possess a pseudo-secondary precognition for what's come to be known as Reality Momentum. Such a clairvoyant can not only see past, present, and future clearly, they can also see all possible futures clearly and account for the differences between them, generating strikingly accurate actuarial tables.

These gifted few are the closest real life has to the fictional accounts of all-powerful intuitives.

Only a handful are believed to exist, and all are kept in near-total isolation, employed in the service of the State and affiliated organizations.

from Insecta Psychica: Towards an Intuitive Taxonomy by Cloche Macomber

The War of Independence

"Simpler beings dream of power, never realizing the pursuit of power is more thrilling than the possession of it."

The voice was familiar but at the same time impossible to place. The problem was that it didn't sound like it belonged to any one person. Instead, Minerva noted, it sounded like a whole chorus of voices harmonizing tunelessly, performing a melody not meant to be sung.

It was a different form of hearing than she was used to, she also realized. It wasn't sound exactly.

Then what was it?

Of course, Minerva realized. She was telepathic. This was what being telepathic was like. She now understood why Gentille compared it to having acute hearing.

She swiveled to see the person speaking to her and was instead met with a vaguely human-shaped hazy blob. If she squinted, she could make out more details, but a pervasive glare made it difficult to focus. She kept having to look away from the form, and every time she looked back, the details she caught seemed to have changed.

"You asked me who I am," the form said. "It's simple, really."

Minerva waited.

"I'm the deepest darkest pit of despair," the blob said.

And in that moment, the shape snapped into focus. Standing before her was Espoir. She wasn't wearing her normal black leather Coterie uniform. Instead, she stood in a long white flowing robe. The sleeves hung beyond her hands. The waist was belted. It was difficult to know for sure, but judging by the bare legs and feet that could be seen where the bottom of the robe gaped open, it appeared to Minerva that Espoir wasn't wearing much, if anything, underneath.

"You don't look dark to me," Minerva said. "Not right now."

"That's how I get you." There was a sadness to her face, as though it hurt her to say it.

"Can we talk about the dreams?" Minerva asked. Even as the words left her mouth, she wasn't quite sure what she meant by it. Whether she was referring to her crimes, Espoir's dreams, or some other dream.

As the words left her mouth, they, too, sounded like chords, harmonies. She meant every possible meaning of every possible word. All at once. And yet none of them.

Espoir nodded as if she understood this. But then she said, "Why would you want to do that?"

Espoir snapped her fingers, and the whole world went white. Light flooded Minerva's eyes in a millisecond, and she reflexively squeezed them shut, stumbling backwards.

When Minerva opened her eyes, Espoir was gone. Rire stood in her place. She licked her lips. "Come," she said, beckoning Minerva to follow with an outstretched finger.

Rire popped her hips as she walked, reminding Minerva of a salsa dancer. It was curious, really, Minerva thought, as she followed Rire. Their surroundings were moving, but it didn't seem like they were going anywhere.

Instead, it was like walking in place on a treadmill while the setting swept past them, like the world was rolling along a reel. Perhaps it was.

The scenery graduated from light to dark as they walked. They started out in an open green meadow bathed in sunlight. Stepwise the sky darkened nearly imperceptibly and the sun set, until they found themselves in a dark forest grove. The sun had gone down. Ordinarily, Minerva would expect it to be very difficult to see Rire under these conditions. However, Rire glowed softly as though she were lit from within.

They weren't alone in the grove, however. Minerva was taken aback by the sea of naked bodies. They'd happened upon an orgy, she realized.

She averted her eyes quickly, feeling as though she had stumbled upon something not meant for her.

"No," Rire said. "Look."

Her body obeyed Rire's command. It wasn't up to question. Minerva found herself moving before she even realized she was doing so.

As she looked closer at the bacchanalia laid out before her, she realized there was some kind of ritual in progress. It lacked the chaos of a spontaneous affair. There were six women, all seated upon identical chairs, lined in a row, holding leashes. At the end of those leashes were six men wearing collars. Each man knelt before the feet of a different woman.

Minerva wasn't sure if she recognized any of the orgiasts. The women's faces were twisted into such strange shapes that their features transformed. The men's faces weren't visible at all, buried into laps, hard at work.

Each participant glowed as Rire did, as though they were illuminated from within.

Rire smiled at Minerva as she locked eyes with her. Even as the women in the grove moaned and even screamed, Minerva found she couldn't look away from Rire's face. She felt as though she were about to tumble into Rire. Into her mind.

Minerva's body began to respond. An ache rose within her. It tormented her. Rire subtly contracted the upper corners of her eyes, and Minerva started to feel a delightful friction, as though she were being stroked. The ache grew. It yawned.

Rire pursed her lips.

Stars clouded Minerva's vision. She fell to the ground. The ache bloomed into a full body spasm that seemed to last forever.

Minerva lie there stunned for a while with her eyes closed, catching her breath, feeling completely sated, satisfied.

It took her a few moments to realize that the grove had gone silent around her.

She opened her eyes to find that she wasn't in the grove anymore. There were no trees. No ground.

She found herself lying in a black void. Or perhaps "levitating" was a better word for it since there didn't seem to be any ground below or any sky above.

She was floating. And there was absolutely nothing around her. Rire was gone.

"Good morning." It sounded like a chorus again, like a tight braid of voices rather than any voice in particular.

"Good morning," the chorus of the void said again.

"Good morning," Minerva called back, confused.

"Good morning," the chorus said. This time the sound was sustained, held like a musical sostenuto. One by one, each choir voice dropped away until a single voice remained.

It was Cloche, Minerva realized. The moment she knew this, Minerva found herself in the judge's chambers.

"Yes, it's appropriate to meet without your lawyer," the judge said.

"I never asked for any of this, you know," Minerva responded.

"Of course you didn't," Cloche said. She smiled, her shoulders quaking a little as though Minerva had said something funny.

Minerva shook her head, confused.

"You would think that having psychic powers would be a boon, wouldn't you?" Cloche asked. "In some ways it is." She smiled, but it was a smile that was sad at the corners. One that sagged. "But you adapt so quickly, you hardly get to enjoy it. It becomes your new normal. You don't notice it anymore. And you're stuck with all the problems of a normal life and the burden of power on top of that." Cloche shook her head. "No, you don't get to enjoy it. You really don't."

"I'm sure I could find a way," Minerva said. She startled from how curt it sounded as it escaped her lips.

"Children never understand." Cloche was no longer looking at her.

What is she looking at? Minerva wondered.

"I'm looking into myself," Cloche replied.

Of course you can understand, Minerva thought.

"That's the trouble with children," Cloche continued. "They have to experience it for themselves." She sighed. "So be it."

And before Minerva had a chance to react, Cloche reached out and placed her hand on her forehead.

Minerva fell into darkness.

Before her was a blank expanse, not a void because it possessed sky and ground, but quite empty nonetheless. What was laid before her was otherworldly in its blandness. Lacking even the casual touches of a desert. The stray cactus. An anxious lizard.

Instead, this was like an ink outline of a desert. What a child might draw.

The beginnings of a new world. Outlined quickly, dreamt up, but abandoned before it could be fully realized.

Minerva stood on the apex of a hill, looking out upon it all. As she did, she felt sadder than she could ever remember being.

"A landscape without pain is little different than one without pleasure," the choir of voices said. "Monotony is monotony. It might come in different flavors, but it's ultimately the same basic formulation. You can never expect it to sustain you for very long."

Minerva blinked and found herself back in Cloche's office, seated before the judge.

"That is the true essence of the Psychic State. That is what you've done, the result of your crimes."

"The Psychic State?" Minerva asked.

"Oh dear," Cloche said. "You really don't understand, do you?"

Minerva nodded. It occurred to her that she wasn't sure exactly how long she'd been held, first for questioning and then waiting for her trial.

"You lied the Psychic State into existence, Ms. Cantor. You set off this chain of events when you lied to Chad Anderson about secession. The United States now has 49 states. The Psychic State is a separate country, and Russ Minot is its first president. Thousands of people died in the War of Independence, all because of you."

Minerva jolted awake in her cell. She was drenched in sweat.

Oh, she thought, *that was just a dream.*

She looked up to find Rire and Espoir standing over her. Rire shook her head slowly.

"Not just," Rire said. "Not just a dream."

Minerva shivered.

"It was a dream, yes. But not just."

Espoir laughed. "I was tasked with explaining the charges to you, wasn't I?"

"Do you think you're the only one who can invade people's dreams?" Rire asked her.

"So the Psychic State..." Minerva couldn't bring herself to finish the question. But she didn't have to. She knew the answer.

The Trial Begins

The courtroom was absolutely packed the morning of the trial. Instead of limiting attendance, however, Judge Cloche seemed to welcome a larger audience. She ordered the bailiffs to prop open the doors to the courtroom, and a mass of people spilled into the hallways outside.

"Don't make me close those doors," the judge admonished, a smirk creeping onto her face. "I will if it gets loud enough."

Minerva wanted to sink down in her chair and disappear. Gentille gave her a disapproving glance and shook her head, motioning for her client to sit up.

Minerva did, feeling like a naughty child. Really, this whole experience made her feel like a naughty child – except now there were adult stakes to contend with.

Minerva hoped that the crowd would be too loud and that the doors would have to be closed for the proceedings, but there was no such luck.

As soon as the trial was called to order, the ambient murmurings ceased. The audience even managed to breathe quietly.

Minerva silently cursed her own luck.

The prosecutor rose to deliver her opening argument. "What would you do if you could get away with anything?" Punit began.

Minerva studied the prosecutor carefully as she paused dramatically, letting the silence blossom into theatrical perfection. Punit's face was generally impossible to read. Minerva had gathered as much during the preliminary hearings leading up to this point.

Well, that wasn't exactly right now, was it? You could read Punit's face, Minerva mentally corrected herself, but never anything that she didn't intend you to read on it. Punit didn't seem to do involuntary facial expressions or give herself, or her true intentions, away.

No, there was something utterly disciplined about the way she carried herself, which spoke of a highly ordered emotional inner life.

This was a sharp contrast to her own lawyer, Minerva noted. Gentille was polished and professional when it came to dress and demeanor, but her face often betrayed her true thoughts. For a lawyer she wasn't a very convincing liar.

I might be the one on trial here, Minerva thought, *but I think Punit could give me a run for my money. She'd be an excellent liar.*

Not that she had to lie. Minerva noted with great alarm as Punit gave her opening arguments that when it came to the basic facts of the case that Minerva didn't disagree exactly. It was only when it came to personal culpability and what should be done about the situation did she really disagree with the prosecutor, who seemed quite intent that Minerva be nailed to the wall.

Well, not literally, she corrected herself. *Hopefully not anyway*, noting that she was still an outsider here. For all she knew, there was another place like the subterranean work camp that Rire had shown her, a place where people were tortured or even crucified. She shuddered at this idea, causing Gentille to turn towards her and stare her down sternly.

Right. It wasn't exactly professional or courteous to do anything but sit quietly while the trial went on. It looked bad to the judge. She'd have to work on that.

She nodded quickly at Gentille, hoping to communicate this. Gentille broke eye contact and returned to jotting down notes. Minerva wasn't sure if her lawyer understood. She stole a quick glance at the legal pad to see what it was that Gentille was writing. However, it was all in the runic language.

As Punit continued to lay out the Coterie's case against her, Minerva struggled for a point of contention, something they could easily dispute, but she kept coming up empty handed. However, Gentille continued to scribble furiously, which gave her some hope. Her attorney would surely launch a brilliant legal argument, one that would completely disrupt the prosecution's case.

Punit didn't speak for all that long, perhaps 15 or 20 minutes at the most. She was thorough but made good use of the time, moving from point to point in an organized fashion.

"Once you have heard what the prosecution's witnesses have had to say, your honor, we are confident that you will find the defendant guilty of all charges. Thank you," Punit concluded, before sitting back down.

"Thank you, prosecutor," Cloche replied. "Defense?"

Gentille smiled and rose. "Thank you, your honor."

Minerva took a deep breath, steeling herself for their opening argument.

"The defense is confident that by the end of this trial we will have created reasonable doubt to the prosecution's claims," Gentille said.

Gentille didn't sound nearly as confident, or as practiced as the prosecutor. Well, Minerva thought, that's fine. She probably didn't prepare as much, knowing that she would have to respond to the prosecution's argument as it unfolded at trial. While a lot of that information would have been made available to Gentille during discovery, a pretrial process where the defense would receive evidence and information related to the prosecution's case, it was understandable that Gentille might want to leave the exact language of her arguments flexible until she knew exactly how the prosecution would word things.

Minerva waited for Gentille to say something else. The defense attorney riffled through the papers on her desk, hesitating a few moments.

Minerva's heart began to beat loudly in her ears. With each subsequent pulse, her anxiety grew.

Finally, Gentille spoke again, "Thank you, your honor," she concluded, before sitting back down.

Minerva fumed. Her face reddened. Two sentences. Two sentences? And both of them generic and canned?

"Very well," the judge replied, before acknowledging the prosecution.

"The prosecution would like to call its first witness." Punit said.

"Ms. Drake," the judge said. "Would you please come to the stand?"

Minerva turned around and felt her stomach lurch as Rosie Drake walked up to the front of the courtroom and was sworn in.

Rosie Takes the Stand

"Witness, would you please state your name for the record?" Punit had a way of making the most mundane statements seem profound, Minerva noted. The prosecutor had all the marks of a great orator.

It would be something to have a lawyer like that, Minerva thought. You would be reassured every time they talked, no matter what they said.

"My name is Rosalyn Aurora Drake," the witness said. "But my friends call me Rosie."

"And would you consider Minerva Cantor such a friend?" Punit said.

Rosie nodded. "I would."

"How did you and the defendant meet?"

"I am a ceramics instructor at a place called Skinner Makes. Minerva took classes from me," Rosie said.

"Do you make it a habit of befriending every one of your students?"

Rosie shook her head. "Not typically."

"What was it about Minerva that made you want to befriend her?"

"I didn't at first," Rosie said. "I suppose you'd say Minerva grew on me over time."

"Grew on you?"

Another nod. "Yes," Rosie said. "I find it usually happens that way. You meet someone, and you don't exactly say to yourself 'there, that person is a friend,' but they show up, and the interaction goes fine, and then later you both end up in the same place again, and that goes fine. After a while of being in the same place, maybe you find that you actually enjoy their company. Over time, you become friends, whether that's something you saw happening at first or not. This is especially the case when your social circles overlap, when you start having people in common."

Minerva glanced at Gentille. Why was she not objecting to this line of questioning? It hardly seemed relevant. Any *Law & Order* defense attorney worth their salt would have leapt to their feet and interrupted this meandering testimony. However, Gentille sat demurely with her hands folded in her lap, acting as though nothing at all were amiss.

Once again, Minerva found herself questioning if her lawyer were a dud or if this were just another difference between the legal system that she had come from and the one she was currently navigating.

"Is that what happened with you and Ms. Cantor? Did your social circles overlap?"

"Yes," Rosie said. "Skinner Makes is an environment conducive to that. There are a number of different clubs there, but membership isn't firm. Anyone can take a class in any department. One class or twelve. They come and go. Even though I teach in ceramics, I take classes in other areas."

"And you're not the only person in your household who has been a member of Skinner Makes, are you?"

Rosie shook her head. "No, my girlfriend Regina is also a member." She paused, correcting herself. "Well, my ex-girlfriend, I mean. We broke up since then. But we were all members at the same time, Minerva, Regina, and me."

"That would be Regina Withers, correct?"

"Yes."

"Did Ms. Withers take any classes with Ms. Cantor?"

"Yes. There was an acting class they took together. It was called Beautiful Liars."

"Who taught this class?"

"Darren Delvecchio."

"And to your knowledge was there any connection between Ms. Cantor and Mr. Delvecchio?"

"They were lovers," Rosie said.

Minerva glanced again at Gentille. What did any of this have to do with the actual case?

"Was Mr. Delvecchio Ms. Cantor's only lover?"

Rosie shook her head. "No, absolutely not."

A soft murmuring swept through the crowd assembled behind them in the court room, a gathering who up until this point had been perfectly silent.

Really? Minerva thought pointedly. An assembly of psychic dominatrices who formally oversaw a labor camp of scantily clad men were clutching their pearls at the mere mention of non-monogamy.

It seemed strangely prudish and small minded for a group whose collective powers seemed beyond her comprehension.

"How many lovers did Ms. Cantor have?"

"I'm sorry," Rosie said, turning to the judge. "I'm going to need some clarification on that issue."

"Ask whatever you need to know," Cloche instructed her.

"Well, when?" Rosie asked Punit.

The prosecutor cocked her head. "When?"

"Yes," Rosie said. "The number varied over the time that I knew Minerva... err... Ms. Cantor."

"Were there a lot of breakups?"

"No, not at all," Rosie said. "Additions mostly."

"How about a minimum and a maximum then? What was the range?"

"Well, when I met her, she wasn't seeing too many people. Chad, Max, and Darren. So that would be three. But by the time she was arrested, oh geez...." Rosie's voice trailed off. She appeared to be counting on her fingers. "Twenty-two," she said finally. "I think. There may have been others I didn't know about. Those are just the men I know."

"Were her lovers all men?"

"Yes, although it was clear – crystal clear – that if she could have had it a different way, then she would have. She would have taken some women as lovers."

Why wasn't her lawyer objecting? Minerva looked over again at her attorney, who appeared to be lost in thought. Gentille was looking at her right hand. The fingers were splayed out widely, as though she were admiring her manicure.

Thankfully, the judge was on the ball. "Ms. Drake," Cloche said, "please try to stick to the matter at hand."

"Sorry, your honor," Rosie said.

"Your honor, if I may," Punit said, "I think this is related to the matter at hand. If you'd just allow me to explore this topic, I'm sure it will pay off."

"Fine," Cloche said. "But I'm warning you, prosecutor, if this goes nowhere, it will hurt your case."

Minerva sat up straighter. Did she detect a hint of annoyance in Cloche's voice? It was subtle, but it sparked a tiny hope within her.

"Of course," Punit said. "Ms. Drake," she continued, "what makes you say that Ms. Cantor would have taken women as lovers as well?"

"It's simple," Rosie said. "I was one of those women. She tried awfully hard to seduce me and my former girlfriend."

Another audible gasp swept through the room. Really, Minerva thought bitterly, these people needed to get out more. Perhaps this was the effect of being stuck in the Coterie, isolated from the outside world. Utopia re-sensitized you to scandal. It made you think so many relatively tame things were beyond the pale when most folks outside of the Coterie were inundated every day with far worse via the tabloids and the Movie of the Week.

"Seduce you?" Punit asked. "How?"

Rustling swept through the room again, as the listeners prepared themselves for tales of debauchery.

"One night all three of us went out as friends and got drunk at a bar. When we got back to my place, she attempted to join my partner and me in bed," Rosie said.

"Not to sleep, I take it," Punit said.

"No," Rosie said. "She came in and stared at us."

"Did she ask to join you?"

Rosie shook her head. "No, she didn't. She said, 'I'm part of this' in this cold, dead voice and crossed her fingers."

"What happened then?"

"I felt reality starting to give a little, like she was bending it, rearranging the night so that she would be in the bed with us, so that all three of us would be lovers."

"How did you know that this was happening?"

"Because I'm a truthshaper, too," Rosie admitted. "Not as powerful as her, but I have the ability. I know what it feels like, even if I haven't done it myself for many, many years."

"And when you sensed reality starting to warp, what did you do?"

"I pushed back," Rosie said. "I braced against the force. I bent the truth back at her. She didn't have my consent. I wasn't about to let her lie her way into my bed."

"And you were successful?"

Rosie nodded. "Yes."

"Even though you aren't as powerful as her, you managed to fend her off?"

"Yes, I did."

"How?"

"I'm sorry."

"How did you do it?"

Rosie thought about it for a second. "I'm not sure exactly, but I suppose it helped that she was so drunk." She fidgeted as she pondered it some more. "Plus, I had the element of surprise."

"Surprise?"

Rosie nodded. "I could be wrong about this, but I got the distinct impression that no one had ever fought back against her before. She wasn't prepared at all for the possibility."

"I see," Punit said.

Minerva's head swam. It sounded so damning coming out of Rosie's mouth. It was true, but she didn't want it to be true. She had never seen herself or her actions that way before. She wondered if she would ever unsee it.

"Did it end there?" Punit continued.

"Did what end there?" Rosie asked.

"The attempts to seduce you."

"No," Rosie said. "That was the worst part, really."

"What was the worst part?" Punit pressed.

Rosie hung her head. "The dreams," she said.

"Can you tell us about these dreams?" Punit asked.

"They were all very sexual in nature," Rosie said. "Both Regina and I kept having them. Minerva was in every one. They were... very graphic."

"So you started dreaming about Minerva?" Punit said.

Rosie shook her head. "No, I didn't start dreaming about her."

"But you just said—" Punit began, frustrated.

Rosie waved her hand. "With all due respect, counselor, I know what I said."

The courtroom murmured excitedly at this pushback.

Punit stood stunned. She hadn't expected this witness to behave in such a fashion and wasn't sure what her next move should be.

Cloche stifled a laugh, as it wasn't befitting a judge, but she felt amused nonetheless.

Maybe Rosie can help me after all, Minerva thought.

"What I said," Rosie continued, "was that Minerva was in our dreams. But that's not because I was dreaming about her. Instead, she came into our dreams. She invaded them. And while she was there, she had her way with us sexually."

"Had her way with you?"

Rosie nodded.

"In what way?"

A synchronized creaking could be heard as most of the audience leaned forward in their chairs, anticipating lascivious details.

"Every way you can possibly imagine," Rosie said, "and perhaps a few more."

"I don't know, Ms. Drake," Punit quipped, "I'm rather imaginative."

"I thought I was too before the dream invasions," Rosie said. "Minerva's depravity shocked me."

And me, too, Minerva thought sadly. She was suddenly aware that the assembled crowd was eyeing her suspiciously, and could she blame them? In their eyes, she was a likely sex offender.

Minerva repeated that to herself mentally, trying to come to terms with it. *I'm a sex offender. I'm on trial for it, on my way for being convicted.* It was something she thought she'd never be saying to herself.

She scowled at the thought. If only she hadn't had such a worthless lawyer. No, she corrected herself. If only she hadn't done it in the first place, any of it. If only she'd known what was going on and could have made informed, responsible decisions. They had all seemed like easy throwaway acts at the time. She'd had no idea what the consequences of such small actions would be.

But as she thought this, she stopped herself again. If she had understood her powers and what was going on, would that have prevented her from abusing them? Or would she have simply abused them more cleverly, found ways of skirting around the rules?

Would she have been able to resist temptation? Sometimes, she reflected sadly, there were situations in which more knowledge didn't help you because the issue wasn't what you did or didn't know but more elusive qualities like willpower and self-control.

Question by question, Punit drew the sex dreams out of Rosie, who appeared mortified, re-traumatized by the ordeal.

Minerva lost track of the words of the testimony, lost in her own thoughts. She suddenly understood why her lawyer had urged her to plead guilty.

This is all my fault.

As soon as the thought hit her head, Minerva regretted it immediately. She could feel several heads turn her way in unison and countless sets of eyes boring into her.

It was dangerous to have self-doubts around telepaths, she decided.

Change's Testimony

After a short recess and a quick lunch that looked like a work of abstract art but contained no individual food elements that Minerva could recognize either by sight or by taste, the trial reconvened for the afternoon.

The man who sat on the witness stand looked almost completely unfamiliar to Minerva... except... well, it was hard to pinpoint what she recognized. Perhaps there was a little something around the eyes.

Yes, they reminded her very much of the strange man who had been painting by numbers in her living room. And also of the long-tailed grackle that had spied on her the night her father, or something that looked like her father, had visited her.

But other than the eyes, he looked completely different. He sported a different hairstyle and cut. She could have sworn the last time she had seen him that he'd been taller.

And the nose was all wrong.

But as he spoke while being sworn in, Minerva was sure of it. It was the same voice, the same man.

"Witness, would you please state your full name for the record?" Punit asked.

"Change Patterson," the man said. He sounded a bit bored, as though he didn't want to be there.

"No middle name?" Punit said.

Change shook his head. "It's a bit over the top even having a surname, to tell you the truth, but I found it made life a lot easier since so many people expect you to have one."

"Why not Macomber then? You've worked for the Macomber Coterie for...?" Punit let the statement trail off to the point where it became a question.

"Longer than you've been alive, prosecutor," Change said, answering and non-answering the question at the same time. "My employment for the Macomber Family is precisely why I don't want to take their last name. I wanted a certain degree of distance from them. It's important to have work-life balance."

Even without the benefit of telepathy, Minerva could tell he was holding something back with his explanation.

"Have you met the defendant before?" Punit asked.

Change nodded. "Yes. Quite a few times." He learned forward and smirked. "Although I'm not sure if she'd recognize me."

"Why wouldn't she recognize you?"

"Well, I look different sometimes," Change said playfully.

"And by this, you mean you wear disguises?" Punit asked. Her tone indicated she was frustrated with him. Watching them, Minerva got the distinct impression that this wasn't their first time working together. There was something about the way they spoke to one another that hinted at a long-standing back history between the two of them.

She felt as though they had done this exact same dance before, perhaps in an earlier trial, with another defendant.

Change shook his head. "No," he said. "I have the ability to drastically alter my appearance at will."

"What would a layperson call someone with this ability?" Punit pressed.

"Any number of things," Change said. "Sometimes I am referred to as a changeling, but I prefer the term shapeshifter if I'm being honest." He considered stopping his statement there, but something compelled him to continue. To Minerva, it seemed as though he were used to being asked certain questions after he said certain things, and because of this, he had become so well trained that he now answered the phantom questions even when they weren't asked.

"Changeling is so infantilizing," he clarified. "Shapeshifter is a great deal more dignified and respectful."

"So you visited the defendant in a professional capacity?" Punit said, visibly annoyed. Minerva imagined that if the prosecutor had one of those oversized vaudeville canes, she would have deployed it on the witness without hesitation, yanking him off the stand with a quickness.

"Yes," Change said. "I was told to check on her after the dream invasion incident."

"Who asked you to do that?" Punit said.

"My superiors in the Coterie," Change said. "My boss. And I was told, not asked. It's a very important distinction."

"By dream invasion incident, you're talking about Minerva's attacks on Ms. Drake and Ms. Withers?"

Change nodded. "Yes."

"And when you found Ms. Cantor, what did you do?"

"I watched her for a few weeks," Change said.

"Watched her?"

He nodded. "I kept my distance. Blended in. It was easy to escape detection, particularly at Skinner Makes, where she spent a lot of her time. While she has a lot of friends at the organization, it's difficult to impossible to know everyone there, particularly because there are new members all the time. I posed as a new member and observed her."

"Is that all?" Punit asked.

"No," Change said. "I also paid her a few visits."

"Was that in your orders?" Punit asked.

Change shook his head. "No, my orders were to watch her from a distance, gather information, and bring it back to the Coterie."

"Why didn't you follow your orders?"

"Sometimes in my line of work, you'll see things that mean you have to intervene. It's not pretty when it happens. Not something I look forward to either. It means a helluva lot more work for me whenever it happens."

"And this was one of those times?"

Change nodded.

"What did you see?" Punit asked. "What happened?"

"She messed with life and death," Change said.

"By she, you mean Ms. Cantor?"

Change nodded. "You're never supposed to do that. That isn't just a truthshaper thing. It's not just a psychic thing. It's a rule for everybody. You don't mess with life and death."

"What exactly do you mean when you say she messed with life and death?"

"Her father died unexpectedly. She got the call, and instead of actually dealing with it and grieving like a normal person, she lied to others and herself about it. For most people, this wouldn't be a big deal, but Ms. Cantor is a truthshaper. Her denial just doesn't stay within her, like it does for most people. Her denial isn't harmless. Instead, her denial spreads out and overtakes other people's consciousness, and given enough aptitude, that denial can actually infect reality and change things that shouldn't be changed."

"What were the consequences of Ms. Cantor's denial about her father's death?"

"Her father un-died."

"When you say her father un-died, you mean that he came back to life?"

Change shook his head. "Not quite. It was more unpleasant than that. He was still a corpse. He just didn't know he was dead, and he was moving around acting like he wasn't. It was like he got stuck between life and death, confused. Nasty business, if you ask me."

Minerva swallowed hard, remembering the strange being that had come to her when she was in the basement apartment. It had seemed rather confused, certain about the wrong things. It looked a bit like her father but not quite. It didn't speak like him, and it had smelled awful.

With Punit's urging, Change recounted the next big lie, when Minerva had somehow undone the zombification of her father, when she'd managed to lie him back to inertness.

"In all fairness," Change said, "I do believe that second lie was well meaning. I imagine she panicked, that she knew what she had done was wrong, and she wanted to undo what she'd done."

Minerva looked at Gentille. No hearsay objection. Of course not. That would be too helpful, Minerva seethed. She knew this was probably bad form, to think such negative thoughts with so many telepaths present, especially since she suspected that the judge was at least somewhat telepathic herself, but she couldn't help it. It was all too unfair.

"The trouble," Change continued, "is that it doesn't work that way. Bending something one way and then bending it back the other isn't the same as undoing it at all, is it? You change the nature of the object as you bend it. Perhaps this strengthens the object. Perhaps it weakens it. It's possible that this last bend is too far, and it breaks. In any case, you alter whatever you're bending again. You don't set anything back to the way it was. At best, you are just establishing a different new normal that resembles the old normal as closely as you can muster. But it is not the same. It will never be what it was. So whatever her intentions were, she altered life and death twice. I saw the whole thing."

As Punit wrapped up Change's questioning, Minerva felt a sense of profound violation set in. She had wanted no one to see that interaction with her father's remnants... ever. It had been a low point, something she had been loath to admit even to herself had happened. It shook her to her core to know for sure that this virtual stranger had seen the whole thing, and now he'd recounted the ordeal to an audience that largely considered her a tabloid figure, an object of entertainment and ridicule.

Minerva wondered if Change had also seen her talk with her mother after she'd dismissed her father's remains. That had been a private moment as well.

It did not come up in his testimony, so she had no way of knowing.

That was always the hardest part, when you suspected something but couldn't be sure. It had a way of looping your brain in circles.

Sometimes it hurt to know a difficult truth, but once you knew, then you could start to get over it. Your body and mind could begin the process of forgetting, however long it took. The brain had a way of fixating on issues that were open and tucking away ones that were finished.

This is why it was emotionally difficult to not know something for sure. The ambiguity made it stick in your brain for much longer, wasting space and slowly driving you mad.

As the judge adjourned proceedings for the day, Minerva expected it would be a long night.

The judge rose and exited towards her chambers. The prosecutor quickly followed suit, as did the crowd who had been watching the trial. As the room emptied out, Minerva and Gentille sat, lingering behind. Gentille made no move to pack up her things or to leave. She was staring straight ahead motionless with a blank look on her face.

Rire stood poised at the back of the room watching them, ostensibly ready to act as escort when it was time for her to head back to her cell.

"How do you think that went?" Minerva asked her lawyer.

"As best as could be expected," Gentille replied.

"Is that good or bad?" Minerva said.

"You really didn't leave me with many options," Gentille said.

"Well, you could try defending me for a start. Just saying," Minerva said.

"There isn't a defense for what you did," Gentille replied.

"You know," Minerva said, "you are probably the worst lawyer ever."

"And you're not much of a client," Gentille replied.

Minerva laughed. "You're a defense attorney. I thought you'd be used to clients who aren't perfect."

"It's not what you've done, Minerva," Gentille said. "It's how you refuse to take accountability. Or to listen to my advice."

"I get a choice. I get to decide. That's how it goes. It's my neck on the line, not yours."

Gentille sighed. "It was a bad day for us, yes. Pretty damning." She began to pack up her things. "But tomorrow will be even worse."

"Worse?" Minerva said.

"Yes," Gentille confirmed. "They're bringing in an expert witness. He'll offer indisputable evidence."

"Indisputable? Like a security camera recording of the crime? A videotaped confession?"

"Worse than that," Gentille said. "You're up against the reality auditor. Bad Touch."

"The little person who came to my cell?"

Gentille nodded. "Get some sleep," she said, as she rose and left. "You'll need it."

"Yes," Rire said to Minerva as she escorted her back to her cell, responding to her thoughts. "You're right to be worried."

Nothing But Guards This Entire Time

Minerva came to suddenly, crashing awake. She knew at once she wasn't alone, that someone was standing over her. A quick glance up told her at once that it was Rire.

This wasn't that unusual all by itself. Rire's face was typically the first one Minerva saw when she rose in the mornings. She'd grown accustomed to the sight of the towering guard holding a breakfast tray that looked tiny in her hands on account of Rire's relative size. The food, too, underwent the same sort of optical illusion while the tray was held by Rire, although ultimately transformed when Minerva held the tray herself. Not a moment before, however. Until the tray was actually in her hands and Minerva had a chance to tuck in, her meals reminded her for all the world of the tiny plastic fake food that she'd seen in children's play sets.

Minerva noted that this time Rire had nothing in her hands at all. As sleep began to lift and her consciousness caught up with the fact that she was indeed awake, Minerva realized that it wasn't morning either. What time was it? She wondered.

"It's 3 a.m.," Rire told her, snatching the question from her mind.

"What are you doing here?" Minerva asked.

"You have a visitor," Rire said.

"At three in the morning?"

Rire nodded.

"Who visits a jail at three in the morning?" Minerva asked.

"Rosie Drake," Rire said.

"Rosie?" Minerva asked.

Rire nodded again.

"What is she doing coming to see me at three in the morning?" Minerva said.

"Should I send her away?"

Minerva shook her head. "I'll see her."

Rire left the room. She was only gone for a few minutes, but the seconds dragged. Minerva looked out her tiny cell window, noting that there was a new moon this night. Her cell wasn't dark exactly, but the lighting that Rire had activated was soft, set to about 10% of full power. She looked down at her hands and noted they seemed to glow in this light.

When Rire reappeared, Rosie was following close behind. Rosie had dressed like a person who was striving to be incognito, but she had overdone it to the point where it came off as cartoonish and more conspicuous than if she hadn't bothered trying to camouflage herself at all. Even though it was the middle of a warm night, she was wearing large dark sunglasses that obscured her eyes and a scarf that covered her hair. The rest of her body was hidden under a giant trench coat that was clearly too large for her and also too long, as it dragged on the floor in a way that guaranteed it would eventually fray. Because of this, it was impossible to see her shoes or even if she had feet underneath.

For all an observer knew, Rosie was gliding around like a ghost.

No, Minerva thought suddenly. Gliding into rooms was Regina's forte now, wasn't it? Not Rosie's.

This stray thought punched her in the gut. It was another reminder of a life that seemed further and further away with each passing day that she spent here, surrounded by dominatrices, alchemists, and what she would have until very recently called wizards.

She had taken her old life for granted, Minerva thought, as Rosie carefully disrobed and handed her unwanted outerwear to Rire.

Rosie didn't take her sunglasses off right away, however. It was unnerving to not be able to see Rosie's eyes. It certainly set her at a disadvantage, but after all this time conversing with telepaths, it didn't seem all that bad.

"You're probably wondering why I'm here," Rosie began.

"I am," Minerva said.

"I couldn't go back without talking to you first," Rosie said.

Minerva said nothing.

"There's so much I need to say to you and even more that I'd *like* to say to you," Rosie said. "I'm not even sure where to start."

"Well, you could start by explaining what you're doing here at this hour," Minerva said.

Rosie sighed. "I didn't want to attract a bunch of attention."

"Waltzing in here in that getup you had on? Really? You thought that was discreet?"

Rosie cast her eyes down to the cell floor. "Maybe it was a little over the top."

"A little?"

Rosie smirked. "You have no idea what I'm going through right now."

"Enlighten me."

"I know you don't have a lot of respect for the Coterie, that you view us as outsiders, as the other…" Her voice trailed off.

"Us?" Minerva asked.

Rosie nodded.

"You're in the Coterie?"

"Yes."

"But your last name isn't Macomber," Minerva said. "And you don't live here."

"Not in the outside world, no. There I go by my married last name. Drake. I kept it in the divorce because it makes it a bit easier to blend in. That's my whole purpose, really. To blend in. Not everyone who is in the Coterie actually lives here. There are some of us who do what I do."

"And that is?"

Rosie considered the question. "I don't know if there's a word for it outside of our runic language. Probably the closest would be…" She thought about it for a moment. "Agent," she finally decided.

"So you're a spy?"

"Well, that's a nasty way of putting it."

Minerva shrugged. "It's a nasty thing to do."

"What is?"

"Spying on people," Minerva said.

"I don't *spy*," Rosie insisted. "I just keep tabs on important matters. I monitor the outside world. My job is to make sure there aren't any imminent threats, anything that would put the Coterie at risk."

"That sounds very much like a spy."

"Or a security system," Rosie replied.

Security. The word flashed into Minerva's mind. When you really got down to it, the past few months had just been a long line of guards. First there had been Security escorting her out of her old job when she was fired. Then there had been Chad and his demands. Followed by Rosie, who was keeping tabs on her. Then Change, sent to warn her and yes, spy, on her. And finally came

Rire and the entire infrastructure of the detention center where she now sat, waiting for her fate to be decided.

She'd been a prisoner this entire time, but she hadn't known it. She'd had the illusion of freedom before, but that's all it had been. An illusion. The epiphany struck Minerva hard.

"Are you even listening to me?" Rosie snapped, making Minerva realize she had gotten lost in her own head.

"Sorry," Minerva said.

"Anyway, you'd understand completely if you were one of us. Well, you are one of us. That's the sad thing, really. You just don't want to accept it. You keep fighting it. If you just had an open mind and let yourself accept that you belong here, you'd realize why I do what I do. Why there's a need for people like me," Rosie said.

"Try me," Minerva said.

"I'd probably be wasting my breath," Rosie said.

"Awfully open-minded of you," Minerva jabbed at her.

This got a surprised laugh out of Rosie. "We're very powerful, Minerva," she explained. "But we're not invincible. There's a delicate balance to the entire system. We're not the only faction out there either. There are other Families like this one who are just as powerful. We have to be careful and make sure we're prepared. We're a lot more vulnerable than we seem. And it's not just the Families that are a threat… there are so many other dangers, systems that could enslave us, bring us to harm, scatter us to the winds, destroying hundreds of years of hard work. We have to watch out for governments and large corporations. Even smaller organizations could cause problems."

"Smaller organizations? Like Skinner Makes?"

Rosie nodded. "Sure. Pretty much any community group." She thought for a moment. "And cults. Cults are a big focus now in my work."

"So you watch? Is that it?"

Rosie forced a smile. "I can't really get into the details of what I do."

"I get that. But generally speaking, I mean. No details. No names. Just... do you just watch?"

Rosie shook her head. "No, I don't just watch." She thought about it for a moment, and Minerva swore she could actually see the deliberation playing out on Rosie's face, as she considered how much she could safely reveal about what she did and what the best way would be to say it.

For a moment, Minerva thought she understood what it must be like to be a telepath. This struck her as the free trial version.

"I don't just watch," Rosie repeated, before adding, "I also set things right."

"That doesn't reveal all that much," Minerva said.

"Good," Rosie replied. "Because I shouldn't be telling you all that much."

Minerva laughed.

"Anyway, none of this has been easy. I didn't want to testify against you. I didn't want to press charges," Rosie said.

"Then why did you?"

"You kept doing it," Rosie said. "If it had just been once, the one time you tried to force your way into bed with us, I could have forgotten. I could have forgiven you. We were all drunk. You misread the signs. It happens. Was it wrong to try to use psychic leverage to force your way into our bed? Yes. Absolutely. Without a doubt. But until I pushed back on you, I didn't know that *you* knew it was wrong. Once that happened, I couldn't give you the benefit of the doubt anymore. Even if you had just invaded one dream, maybe I could have looked past it. But Minerva..." Rosie looked out the window at the moonless sky.

Minerva waited for her to finish.

"You didn't stop. You did it over and over again."

"And that's why they sent in Change?"

Rosie nodded. "I wanted to have you brought in then, but I was told it wasn't enough."

"It wasn't enough...?"

Rosie shook her head. "Yeah. Pretty insulting actually. You violated me. Violated Regina. Over and over again. And the Coterie said it wasn't enough to bring you in. They said you'd need to do more than that, as though what you did to me, and to Regina, meant nothing. They only started to really care about it when they realized I could be a vital building block in a bigger case. Then that got their attention."

"How's she doing by the way?" Minerva asked.

"Regina?"

"Yeah."

Rosie shrugged. "I don't know. I haven't talked to her."

"What?"

"When you bent the truth, you pulled her away from me. I've seen it coming for a long time. I've known. But it still doesn't make it feel any better." Rosie removed her sunglasses and rubbed her forehead with her hand.

"I'm sorry," Minerva said.

"Are you?" Rosie asked.

Minerva didn't answer the question. She had a hunch that no matter what she said, she'd only end up offending Rosie more.

"The only way I'm making it through this is by remembering that Regina's happy. If there's one thing she wanted more than love, it was this. To make it big. To become famous. And she's going to be huge. There's no doubt about that."

Rire entered the cell.

"Is my time up?" Rosie asked.

"If you want to leave without anyone else seeing you, yes," Rire said.

Rosie smiled. "You always seem to know just what's on my mind, Rire," she said. "It's simply uncanny."

"Ms. Drake, that joke hasn't been funny any time you've ever told it," Rire said as she smiled.

"I'm hoping one of these days it'll just get so unfunny that it wraps back around and is funny again," Rosie replied.

"You'd have to live an awfully long time," Rire said.

"Now, that," Rosie said, "is a funny joke."

Bad Touch's Lament

Bad Touch was frankly sick of being the butt of every joke.

"The butt, the abdomen, the head, shoulders, knees, and toes of every joke," he found himself saying quite forlornly... but only when he could be reasonably sure no one was listening to him.

Resentment without power often manifests this way, in quiet complaints that echo in solitude but never reach a source that can either meaningfully accept or reject them.

It was true that the very existence of the homunculus was an oddity and therefore a reliable source of discomfort to many a new acquaintance, but he was a living being worthy of respect, and somewhere along the way, his guardians had forgotten that.

Somewhere along the way, they had grown addicted to delivering the witty punchline and had turned their backs on substance.

What a perfectly infuriating thing it was for the law to be without scruples, Bad Touch reflected. Law had always struck Bad Touch as a sanctimonious profession, the very act of forming and delivering edicts put a judicial body into the role of unsolicited advice-giver.

Everyone hated someone who was giving advice without say-so beforehand.

Except somehow judges were forgiven. Somehow magistrates were exalted and considered superhuman, beyond reproach.

Perhaps this was the greatest injustice of all.

Sometimes Bad Touch found himself ruminating on what the world would be like if social gravity were to suddenly reverse. What would it be like if smaller creatures such as himself were put in charge?

And of course in this scenario untouchables like Coterie magistrates would be forced to be the butt of every joke.

"The butt, the abdomen, the head, shoulders, knees, and toes," he reminded himself, singing the last bit, and imagining a clunky dance corresponding with the lyrics, with hands pointing to each bit of anatomy in turn.

He imagined a team of judges doing that dance. Synchronized. They would be perfectly synchronized. And wearing matching outfits of course.

And Bad Touch would look down on them as they did so. He would supervise them from on high, sitting atop a tiny throne – one boosted up much higher with the aid of a system of luxurious risers.

Yes. King Bad Touch.

He could see it all so clearly.

It wouldn't take much. Just a little adjustment to his math. A bit of fancying up of figures.

Presto-change-o on the old report.

He thought about it for hours. He thought about it for days.

They trusted him. It would be a simple matter to fudge the numbers.

They'd never know. He knew how to do it so that they'd never know.

Except…. He'd know. It had been a few hundred years since he'd last lied, but he could still remember it. He hadn't been caught. That, too, had been an easy matter. Changing a few minor details around. That time he had done it in vengeance. The accused had mocked him, treated him as though he were subhuman, sub animal.

A thing.

Nothing more than an instrument.

And though he was used to such treatment from the Coterie guards, lawyers, magistrates, and jurisprudents, it had been simply shocking to be treated that way by a common criminal.

Well, an alleged criminal anyway.

When Bad Touch had examined reality, used his Reality Momentum to calculate the effects of her actions, the number had been trace. Infinitesimal.

Within his margin of error. This meant that the accused's actions hadn't changed anything, really. Certainly nothing worthy of a sentence had transpired. The report could easily exonerate her.

But a curious whim had seized him, and when he made up his report, he exponentially raised that figure by making a few quick substitutions.

It wasn't difficult. *There*, he thought spitefully, as he submitted the doctored report, *something better than justice will be done here.*

And yet... when the verdict was handed down, Bad Touch had felt an unexpected pang of guilt. He realized then that he had let a momentary impulse cheapen his trade, cheapen his art. With a single act, he'd tainted his very purpose for existing.

Perhaps if he'd confessed then, the verdict would have been overturned and the convicted would have been afforded a new trial, this time with accurate information.

But Bad Touch couldn't bring himself to confess. His particular crime had never happened before. How would the Coterie's legal system try an arbiter of truth? The consequences of such an objective source proving fallible could be immense.

He anticipated that if he came forward that every case he'd weighed in on – and there were many of those now – could be subjected to scrutiny and the verdicts questioned, even though Bad Touch knew for certain this was the only instance he'd strayed from his duties. This was the only time he'd altered a report.

Double checking his otherwise flawless work would be an immense undertaking for the Coterie. A senseless one.

No, he couldn't confess. Instead, he let the convicted sit in jail, knowing all the while that it was only his own insecurities that had landed her there. True, she had been nasty to him – but rudeness wasn't a crime that merited life imprisonment.

It was a relief when her natural life finally ended, when Bad Touch no longer had to think of her sitting alone in her cell.

She never knew it was Bad Touch that had landed her there. She had no way of knowing that the report he'd written was inaccurate.

But he had certainly known. And it ate at him.

This time could be different, he thought. Perhaps if he made a guilty woman look innocent, it would be penance for putting an innocent woman away.

It was an attractive prospect, achieving closure this way, but he couldn't shake the reality of one of his least favorite sayings: *Two wrongs don't make a right.*

Nasty reality, that, Bad Touch frowned. If only we could repair what's wrong with another wrong – or even a flurry of wrongs. If only it were that easy. Because wrongs were plentiful and found everywhere.

He tried to convince himself for days that it might just be that easy. But he couldn't quite believe it.

After several days of deliberation, he came to a compromise. The report would be submitted unaltered, but he would argue on Minerva's behalf despite its damning findings.

Perhaps this bit of unprecedented kindness would make up for what he'd done in his past.

It would have to do because confessing his earlier deed was well out of the question.

Bad Touch Takes the Stand

Reality Injuries or Reality Offsets

It may be difficult for many readers to fully conceptualize Reality Injuries. In general, the lay population is conditioned to think of reality as monolithic, staid, and unchanging.

This is only natural. Beings who live linearly are accustomed to thinking of cause and effect as being singular and sequential.

However, reality theorists and certain kinds of intuitives are acquainted with a different model of reality, one that includes contingencies, twists and turns, and a multimodal system in which there is not simply one reality but scores of different realities, all hung upon one axis.

The multiplicity of reality is one of the many reasons that predicting the future is a great deal more complicated than many non-intuitives realize. It is also what allows certain intuitives such as truthshapers to change the present, past, or the future.

These changes, however, never come without a cost. Commonly, this cost is framed as Reality Injuries. When one version of reality is swapped for another with great force and without reason, the whole system bears the strain.

Truthshapers may have great power to shape reality, but they lack precision. The act of re-shaping reality in one area will frequently lead to rebounds in other areas, unintentional changes in past, present, or future. These rebounds are known as Reality Injuries.

There are some who say that after a certain amount of damage is sustained, the system finds it very difficult to repair itself.

However, this concept is quite controversial, and there are others who say that Reality Injuries are at best a political invention, meant to caution individuals against attempting to upset the *status quo*. They argue that the term is a misnomer and that a better name for the observed dynamics would be Reality Offsets, for this seems to better describe the phenomenon. Reality, they argue, is never truly injured but simply offset in another area.

Nevertheless, manipulating reality is universally considered quite dangerous and taboo territory, and those who would attempt to do it are subjected to harsh punishments.

from Insecta Psychica: Towards an Intuitive Taxonomy by Cloche Macomber

🤞

Gentille met Bad Touch's gaze as he was carried to the witness stand by Rire. She nodded politely at him, and he returned the gesture.

He was a fixture in the trial court, but Gentille had never quite gotten used to him, the novelty of his size and unusual proportions, or his unfailingly bad temper.

If he had been larger, such a scowl would have likely been intimidating, but on a being of his size, this expression had quite the opposite effect.

Bad Touch, frankly, looked adorable – especially today costumed in a miniature suit, short tie, and tiny loafers. Iridescent threads in his jacket caught the light whenever he shifted. Whoever had made his clothing had put a lot of thought into it, Cloche observed.

The bailiff adjusted Bad Touch's standard adaptive equipment, a lift that elevated him so he could comfortably testify on the witness stand and be seen and heard by everyone in the courtroom.

"Do you swear to tell the truth, the whole truth, and nothing but the truth, so help you God?"

"I *am* the truth," Bad Touch replied huffily.

"Do you?"

"I do," he snapped. "Of course I do."

Once he was sworn in, Punit rose to question him.

"Would you please state your qualifications for the court?" the prosecutor said.

"Certainly," Bad Touch replied. "Although I'm not sure it's the best use of the court's time."

"Not the best use of the court's time?" Punit said.

"My credentials are well known of course, and they're also recorded in many trial transcripts housed here."

"We thank you for your service," Punit said robotically.

"I am the Coterie's resident reality auditor. I was specifically created for this purpose, and I have been working in that capacity for many centuries." He smirked. "I suspect I will be doing it for centuries more."

"What is a reality auditor?" Punit asked.

"You don't know?" Bad Touch said.

"For the record, sir," Punit said tersely.

"As a reality auditor, I analyze the state and flow of current reality as well as all contingent and dependent realities. I compare this sample against a calculated theoretical normal."

"An average?" Punit said.

"Sort of," Bad Touch said. "More like an average of averages."

"And what does this comparison tell you?"

"It tells me whether reality has been left to flow naturally or if it has been disturbed," Bad Touch said. "Whether its momentum has been disrupted."

"Is this a common occurrence?"

"Is what a common occurrence?" Bad Touch asked.

"For the momentum of reality to be disrupted," Punit clarified.

"I don't know I'd say it's common," Bad Touch said. He smiled. "But it happens enough to justify my existence."

"And did you have occasion to review Ms. Cantor's case, the case in question?" Punit said.

"I did," Bad Touch replied.

"And?" Punit said.

"And what?" Bad Touch shot back.

Punit shook her head, caught off guard. She had worked with Bad Touch many times over the course of her career. He was an experienced expert witness, well acquainted not only with the customs of the court but with her as an attorney, and today he was acting like a rank amateur.

What had gotten into him? She had never seen him act this way on the stand, not in any of her cases and not in any she'd observed.

"What were your findings?" she said, annoyed but doing her best to keep her voice perfectly level. The homunculus clearly had a bug in his craw, but there was no sense in making it worse, irritating him further.

"I put my findings in my report," Bad Touch said. "It was submitted into evidence."

Punit sighed. He was going to play this game, was he? Well, fine. There were plenty of ways to deal with this. She politely asked for the report to be given to Bad Touch.

"Witness," she said, "would you please read your conclusion summary on page 92?"

Bad Touch rolled his eyes but flipped to the appropriate spot in the report. He read the summary aloud verbatim but in a dull monotone voice that made it harder than normal to follow, which was saying something as the report was very academic to begin with.

"In your expert opinion–" Punit began.

Bad Touch rolled his eyes again and slouched.

"Would you say that there were severe Reality Injuries sustained in this case?"

Bad Touch shrugged flippantly. "I guess it depends on what you mean by 'severe.'"

"Surely there must be some system of classification in your field," Punit pressed.

"Well, we have standards and means and things like that," Bad Touch conceded.

"How do the injuries in this case compare to the standards?"

Bad Touch hesitated. "They don't," he said.

"I'm sorry," Punit replied. "I don't quite understand what you mean by that. Perhaps you can explain it to me. Why don't the injuries compare to the standards?"

"They just don't." Bad Touch held firm.

He wasn't lying. Punit could tell as much. But how to get at the truth?

"Okay," she said. "Looking back on your illustrious career, do you by any chance know the average level of disruption in the cases you've handled?"

"Yes," Bad Touch said.

"Including this case or excluding?"

"I know both," Bad Touch said.

"How does the level of disruption that Ms. Cantor caused compare to the earlier average?"

Bad Touch hesitated. It was damning, but it was all there in the report. "It's about a thousand times greater," he admitted.

"Did I hear that right?" Punit said.

"Of course you did," Bad Touch said.

"One thousand times?"

"Yes," Bad Touch said.

"That's quite a bit more severe than any other case you've analyzed, isn't it?"

"You could say that," Bad Touch said.

"Would *you*?" Punit pressed.

"Prosecutor," the judge said, with a warning wrapped into her voice.

"Withdrawn," Punit said. "No further questions." She sat down.

It took Minerva a full minute to realize that Gentille was actually going to cross-examine the homunculus.

It was the first time, after all, that the defense lawyer had done so to a trial witness. Minerva had grown accustomed to seeing Gentille pop up from her station for just long enough to say "no questions" before sitting back down.

But there Gentille was on her feet in the midst of an argument, looking more lawyerly than she had all trial and speaking with a great deal more conviction.

It was as though she'd found an opening at last, Minerva noted, growing excited at the prospect.

"I sensed some reluctance just now, Mr. Touch, as you were testifying to my colleague," Gentille said. "But I am not an empath. Not by a long shot."

This got a rolling wave of laughter from the courtroom. Minerva felt as though she were missing out on some private joke, something important about Gentille's reputation in the community.

"Would you say that you feel torn about this trial?" Gentille asked Bad Touch once the courtroom had again quieted.

"I'd say that's fair," Bad Touch replied earnestly.

"Is this common for you, to experience ambivalence in your line of work?" Gentille asked.

Bad Touch shook his head. "Not at all."

"What is it about this case then that instills you with such mixed feelings?'

Bad Touch took a moment to consider the question. He turned to the judge and noted that she was gazing intently at him, hanging on his every word. This was the first time he could remember that she had regarded him with such respect. Cloche Macomber, the high and mighty magistrate, hanging on his every word!

It was a good feeling. Intoxicating. He suddenly felt much taller than his stature, and so the words came easily.

"Because to be honest, I am not so sure about my line of work anymore," Bad Touch said.

Gasps could be heard throughout the courtroom. Bad Touch frowned. Of course they would be surprised. They regarded him as little more than an automaton, a tool. To them, his experiencing uncertainty would be like a robot having a midlife crisis.

Gentille nodded at him. She considered asking another question but could see in his body language that the homunculus was just on the verge of saying more, so she waited for him to continue.

"I am happy to have employment. That's not it at all. But I have my doubts about Reality Injuries as a theory."

"Really?" Gentille prompted.

Bad Touch nodded. "It just doesn't make any sense. Reality always repairs itself. It always finds a way to offset what was done to it. Yes, you can end up on a different strain of reality than you were originally on. Yes, worlds and people can collide who were never meant to occupy the same space. That's all true. But the laws of the universe hold fast. There is no destroying them. There is no injuring them. I only measure movement – or displacement, if you will. I do not measure injury. And to call it injury all of these years has been a great disservice to science."

"So you're saying that my client didn't actually hurt anything when she moved reality? When she bent it?"

Bad Touch nodded. "No, she didn't injure anything. She simply moved a few things around."

Murmurs spread throughout the crowd. Cloche banged her gavel on her desk. "Quiet," she admonished, "or I'm not only closing the doors but kicking you all out."

That did the trick. The room hushed.

Minerva noted that the magistrate was quite pale. She'd been relatively unflappable for the entire proceedings. The judge had sat poised and unmoved and had also notably tolerated quite a bit of ambient noise during the trial from those who watched. But the words of the homunculus had clearly perturbed her deeply and tested her patience.

"Really?" Gentille asked. "And in your opinion, would it be possible to move it back?"

Bad Touch considered this. "I'm not sure," he admitted. "It's never been done."

"But we don't know for sure, do we?"

"I suppose not," he said.

"Thank you, Mr. Touch," Gentille concluded. "No further questions."

Minerva Takes the Stand

"The prosecution would like to call its final witness," Punit said.

"Proceed," the judge said.

"Ms. Cantor," Punit said.

As Minerva rose and walked to the witness stand, she felt more at ease than she had for several days. Bad Touch's testimony had been the first real coup they'd had in her defense.

Minerva had thought it peculiar when she'd first found out that the prosecution wanted to call her as *their* witness, but Gentille told her that it was a game that Punit often played with defendants, a tactic she used to psyche them out. "It's to make you feel that your case is so hopeless that your testimony will build theirs up. That sort of thing," she explained.

Normally, defendants declined. They either testified in the defense portion or not at all.

But Minerva had opted to accept Punit's invitation. "I want to let her know we're not afraid," she had said to Gentille.

"You know," her lawyer had said, "I think this is the first legal decision you've made that I've really respected."

"I'm not making a huge mistake, am I?" Minerva had asked.

"I think it's the one thing you're doing right," Gentille had said. She pointed out that they weren't calling any other witnesses for the defense, that Minerva would have been the only one to testify on her behalf as it was, so it was the same order of witnesses anyway.

"Just this is the power move version," Minerva had observed, and Gentille had agreed.

It was a great time for a power move. As Minerva was sworn in, she felt as though she were rallying off Bad Touch's strong testimony during Gentille's cross-examination.

"Please state your name for the record."

Minerva said her name. She'd heard it said that people universally love the sound of their own name more than just about anything else. You could see it on brain scans, research studies said. Parts of the brain would light up to demonstrate this.

If she thought really hard, she could just barely remember a time when that was true, when she loved the sound of her own name. It had to have been when she was a little girl. Somewhere along the way, however, it had stopped feeling good to hear her own name. Perhaps her name had been associated with too many stressful experiences. Too much shame, too much disappointment.

She'd had a friend who was fond of responding, "That's my name. Don't wear it out." It was a joke, but as Minerva sat there on the witness stand waiting for the questioning to begin, she wondered if there weren't some truth to it. Could other people wear out your name? Could they make hearing your own name an anxiety-provoking experience instead of an enjoyable one?

She certainly thought so. She noted as she said her name for the record that she had reached the point where it made her wince when even *she* said it.

She had expected a barrage of questions from Punit. An onslaught.

But the prosecutor was standing there studying her, not saying anything.

"Your question, prosecutor," Judge Cloche prompted.

Punit nodded slowly, as though Cloche had said something profound.

"Are you sorry?" Punit asked.

"Sorry?"

"Are you sorry for what you did?"

"I... I'm innocent," Minerva said. She shot a glance to Gentille hoping that she would object but noted the defense lawyer was filing her nails.

"Are you saying that the other witnesses are liars?"

Objection, badgering the witness, Minerva's brain screamed. *This would never happen on* Law & Order.

In the real courtroom before her, no one objected. Her defense attorney barely paid any attention to the proceedings. The judge was listening attentively, as she had been the entire trial, but no emotion showed on her face.

Minerva bit her lower lip. "I'm not saying they're liars. That's their truth."

"And your truth?"

"It's different," Minerva said.

"There's a special word for someone who insists on having their own truth, regardless of whether that lines up with other people's truth or with reality," Punit said. "You're a liar."

"Prosecutor, that's not a question," Minerva replied.

Yet the court was unmoved. No one was coming to her rescue. She found herself wishing she could reshape reality again. That she could just cross her fingers behind her back and make it so this entire ordeal had never happened.

She wouldn't have to be back in the big house with dozens of boyfriends. She would be happy with a smaller life, settling down with one or two of them. She was okay with reality picking companions for her, so long as it didn't pick Chad. The one thing she'd learned from the past few months was that life with Chad wasn't as good as she'd been trying to believe it was.

If only she could do it one more time, cross her fingers and bend the truth – undo this mess.

Minerva felt the crowd stir. Of course. The telepaths knew what she was thinking. Like always. They'd been listening to her private ruminations all trial, after all.

It was ironic, she thought, as she sat there feeling the intensity of so many eyes on her, watching her, listening to both her public testimony and what should be private thoughts. She was on trial for bending the truth, and now the truth was her only option.

There was nowhere to hide. To lie before such an assembly would be like trying to claim you were wearing a fur coat when those you stood before could clearly see you were naked. It had only worked for the emperor in the fairy tale because he'd had leverage. Power.

And even then, a small child had managed to break through those defenses and point out the obvious.

The power to lie was gone; all that was left to her was the truth.

She hoped it would be enough.

"I didn't know what I was doing," she said, and even as she heard herself speak the words aloud, she knew that a legal expert would scream at her to shut up, that she was incriminating herself, ruining her chances at any sort of reasonable defense, even on appeal.

"I didn't know I was a truthshaper," she continued. "I didn't know truthshapers existed, that someone could even do that."

"You never suspected something was off? How could you not notice the energy flowing through your body or the ways that things would just change?" Punit pressed her.

"I didn't at first," Minerva said. "At first, it was easy to dismiss. I thought I was imagining things. My memory has never been all that good. I just assumed I had gotten things wrong. That I was remembering things wrong."

"But surely it reached a point where you noticed," Punit said.

Minerva shrugged. "Well, sorta."

"Sorta?"

"I knew something weird was going on, but I didn't know exactly what. And I wasn't sure that it was coming from me," Minerva said, but she felt doubt as she said this.

The crowd's energy rippled as telepaths noted the stray doubt passing through.

Minerva sighed, knowing she'd have to address it. "Again," she said. "Not at first."

"But you *did* figure it out eventually?" Punit pressed.

Minerva nodded. "But I didn't want to admit it to myself."

"Why not?"

"Because then I'd have to do something about it. And I had no idea where to even start."

"Couldn't you have asked for help?" Punit asked.

"Who would I ask?"

Punit clicked her tongue on the roof of her mouth. "Very good, Ms. Cantor. The ignorance defense. You say you lacked resources and knowledge. That you had no awareness of your condition. You think that makes you innocent and that the court should take pity on you."

"That's pretty much it, yes."

"You're so close, Ms. Cantor. But 'so close' doesn't cut it in a court of law," Punit said.

"What are you talking about?"

"You were warned. Change Patterson came to see you specifically for that reason. And you ignored him. Rosie Drake, same story. She even told you what you were... and what did you do? You pursued her and her lover sexually, tried to subdue them against their will, by chasing them into dreams where their defenses were lower. And even that wasn't good enough. You had to go and change the course of history."

"I didn't know what I was doing," Minerva said.

"Why did you do it anyway?" Punit asked.

"Do what?"

"Why did you form the Psychic State?" Punit said.

"It was an accident. A complete accident. I made some throwaway comment about politics, and my fingers acted on their own."

Punit gave her an incredulous look. "Your fingers acted on their own?"

"I know it sounds crazy," Minerva said. "But it was starting to happen involuntarily. My body would lie before my brain even knew what was going on."

"So you're saying you lost control?" Punit said.

Minerva nodded. "I think my body became addicted to lying," she admitted. "It might sound weird, but I've almost been having... withdrawals." She bowed her head. "It's been strange being held here, not able to shape the truth anymore. It's like part of me was amputated."

"It's still there," Punit said. "Just deadened. Constrained. Dormant."

"Could have fooled me."

"So," Punit said, "your defense is that you didn't know what you were doing at first, and by the time you did, you had completely lost control?"

"Yes," Minerva said. "That's the truth."

"The truth about the lies?" Punit asked.

It was a cheap shot, intended to wound. *This would never happen on* Law & Order, Minerva thought again. But she didn't fight it. "Yes, the truth about the lies. I know it's not much of a defense, but the court should find me not guilty."

"But you say that you can't control yourself. You say that your body lies before your brain catches up. Given this, aren't you basically admitting to the court that given a chance, you're going to reoffend?"

Minerva froze. She didn't know what to say to that. "Surely there must be rehabilitation programs. Places where I could learn how to control this, where I could turn it into a strength rather than my weakness."

"Rather than a threat to society," Punit corrected her.

"Sure," Minerva said.

"Your honor," Gentille said, rising suddenly. "May I approach the bench?"

Cloche allowed this, and Minerva watched curiously as both lawyers clustered close to the judge.

"I'd like to request an audience in chambers," Gentille said.

"On what grounds?" Punit challenged her.

"So that the proper steps towards a plea deal can be reached."

A plea deal? The hair stood up on the back of Minerva's neck.

"No plea deal," she said to the attorneys and the judge, interrupting their impromptu benchside conference. "I'm innocent."

"But what you were describing... entering into a rehabilitation program, learning how to control your powers, integrating into our society... all of that could happen, and quite easily, if you would just enter into a plea agreement and throw yourself on the mercy of the court," Gentille said.

"But that would be lying," Minerva said.

Punit raised an eyebrow. Minerva didn't have to be a telepath to understand what was going on in the prosecutor's mind. The liar was suddenly concerned about lying. Well, let her gawk.

"I'm not going to plead guilty when I'm innocent," Minerva said.

Cloche sighed. "Counselor," she said to Gentille, "your request is denied. It appears that your client is not amenable to this course of action at this time."

Gentille's eyes narrowed, and her jaw tensed. "Yes, your honor," she said.

"No further questions," Punit said, smiling broadly.

The floor was yielded to Gentille. She sat in her chair at the defense table with her arms folded across her chest. She didn't even rise to speak.

"Your witness, Gentille," Judge Cloche prompted her.

Gentille shook her head. "I'm done with her," she pronounced.

Minerva's stomach fell. She felt abandoned by her lawyer once again. *Perhaps she's just confident in our case,* Minerva thought, trying to reassure herself, but she didn't believe it at all. The days when she could convince herself of something that untrue were over.

There was very little new in Punit's closing argument. It was shorter than Minerva expected it would be, perhaps 10 minutes. The prosecutor laid out the same series of events she'd detailed in the witness testimony, emphasizing the most damning facts: That Minerva had bent the truth repeatedly, in a multitude of ways, and continued to do so after being repeatedly warned.

"But I don't have to tell you this," she said, concluding the main narrative. "You've been here, you've listened. You know what she's done. Even Minerva admits it. But what you don't know, well, that's even worse."

The judge leaned forward with great interest at these words.

"Even as Minerva Cantor sat on the witness stand, telling you that she wanted to be rehabilitated, that she shouldn't be held accountable for what she'd done because she couldn't control herself, her inner thoughts told a different story."

Minerva felt a pang of confusion. She'd stuck to the truth. What on Earth was Punit talking about?

"As she sat on that witness stand, she kept thinking to herself that she wished she could lie this entire trial away. That she could just get rid of any accountability or responsibility for what she'd done. The only thing stopping her was the fact that her powers don't work here in the Coterie. If she could have bent the truth and freed herself, she would have done it several times."

Minerva lowered her head. It was true. And awfully damning when spoken aloud instead of thought silently. The difference between an urge that was given into and one that was resisted was *huge* normally, but telepathic scrutiny had a way of shrinking the size of such a distinction down to a rounding error.

It was much easier to claim pure intentions than to actually have them. You wouldn't know it listening to people defend themselves and their mistakes, but people rarely had purely good or purely bad intentions. Instead, most people had a mix of good and bad intentions in just about every situation.

Normally, if bad intentions made up a minority of the picture, they had a way of receding into the background and not mattering, unspoken, overshadowed by voiced good intentions and extenuating circumstances. But in a telepathic court, they stayed detectible, impossible to forget.

"The defense is asking the court to take a chance and have mercy on a defendant who won't even admit that what she did was wrong. She wants the court to invest the time and resources to rehabilitate her but won't admit to her guilt. Do you see a problem here? I do."

Punit shook her head. "Ms. Cantor can't have it both ways. If she can't admit her guilt, then the only sensible thing left for the court to do is to convict her and punish her appropriately. Not rehabilitate her but punish her. Ms. Cantor has demonstrated that rehabilitation would be wasted on her. Effective rehabilitation takes humility, a willingness to admit you're wrong. There is no rehabilitation without accountability. If Ms. Cantor can't take accountability now, in a situation that is this dire and this stark, what hope would she have in an informal rehabilitation setting?"

Punit smiled. "But I'm getting ahead of myself. That's a matter for sentencing, after all. Which is something that will be decided at Your Honor's discretion of course."

Cloche nodded.

"The verdict is the current matter at hand. It is obvious. By the actual legal definition of the term, Minerva Cantor is guilty. She performed all the elements of the statute, and she has presented no compelling defense other than to claim that the term guilty means something other than what it does. This is not a legal argument. It's pedantry. Ms. Cantor will not lie her way out of this, as much as she'd like to. She is guilty. Thank you."

It was Gentille's turn to speak. "I will keep this brief," she began.

Of course you will, Minerva thought. It wasn't as though her attorney had put up a vigorous defense.

"The Coterie's case is largely proven and true. We do not dispute the facts or the witnesses' statements. There are minor inaccuracies, sure, details that are remembered differently by my client, but nothing that's out of step with what you would expect due to the normal imperfection of memory."

"I am not going to stand up here and say that my client didn't bend the truth. She did. She freely admits to that fact and did so on the witness stand."

"The good thing is that we don't have to deny what happened. Opposing counsel says that these acts Minerva committed were crimes in that they violated our legal statutes and possess all elements of that crime. That's not exactly true. And that's where our case differs from the prosecution's."

"In order for a crime against reality to have been committed, great harm must have been perpetrated."

Gasps were heard through the room.

"Causing a civil war seems to meet that standard, doesn't it?" Gentille said. "Open and shut case, right? Slam dunk. Well, think again."

"If you'll recall Bad Touch's testimony, the fabric of reality wasn't damaged at all by Ms. Cantor's antics. Were things changed by what she did? Certainly. Everything she did had consequences."

"But as I stand here before you, I cannot see that reality has been permanently damaged whatsoever. Were individual lives lost? Yes. But reality is still quite intact. A single person cannot throw the universe completely off its rails. It doesn't work that way."

"So why is my client on trial then? A number of reasons. Prejudice is surely at play, since she comes from outside the Coterie. Oh, sure, some might point at the dubious ethics of psychosexual conquest or wishing people alive or dead. But that's sound and fury, signifying nothing. No, the real matter here is fear. Political fear."

Cloche sat up straighter in her seat.

"The creation of the Psychic State poses a great threat to those in power," Gentille said. "It poses a great threat to us, to the Coterie, and to the other Families who have been able to stay hidden until this time. Not only do we now have another powerful body to answer to, diluting our relative power, but our secret is no longer safe. Psychic power is no longer a legend, a conspiracy theory only espoused by lunatics. Psychic power is now a mundane, verifiable reality – in a world that doesn't know how to handle that information. And that scares the Coterie. That scares the court. Because it upsets the *status quo*."

"My client is not a criminal. She is a political force," Gentille said. "And any society that convicts her is indicting themselves in the process."

"I believe in the Coterie, in our pride and our power of course, but also in our bravery. We are not guilty of such small-mindedness. We do not act out of fear. We would not punish an innocent person simply for presenting us with a challenge, no matter how existential a threat that the challenge poses."

"I believe that when you think through the matters at hand, think beyond petty concerns, you'll see that no harm has been done. There are no victims here. And therefore my client cannot have committed any crime."

"As such, you must find her not guilty. Thank you."

Punit rose and gave her second and final closing argument. It was the prosecution's prerogative to go first and last so that they could make an impression and also leave one. She spoke for only a few minutes, this time moving down a series of bullet points rapidly, as though she were trying to leave them marked indelibly in the judge's brain.

The judge looked a little bored, which Minerva took as a good sign.

When Punit was done, Cloche nodded. "I'm ready to render a verdict," she said.

Surprised murmurs spread through the courtroom. It was so soon. No deliberation needed whatsoever. Not even a short recess.

The judge launched into a long legal spiel that sounded to Minerva like a magic spell. Perhaps it was, she thought idly. Or something just a few months ago she would have mistaken for magic anyway.

The judge spoke without inflection, reading the charges and introducing the verdict, quickly, automatically. It reminded Minerva of how people sounded when they prayed in large groups, mumbling with great speed, sounding brainwashed to outsiders who didn't grow up with those same prayers.

When the judge got to the important part, however, her voice slowed down, and she paused before speaking the verdict itself.

"Guilty," the judge said, making eye contact with Minerva. She continued to speed through more mumbled legalese, but Minerva couldn't hear it over the sound of her heart beating in her ears.

"Now that we have a guilty verdict on the table, it's time to start talking about sentencing," Gentille said.

"Do I have to?" Minerva asked.

Gentille frowned. "Look, I advised you that a plea bargain was your best bet. You didn't listen to me. And you see where you ended up."

Minerva shook her head slowly. "Fair."

"Will you listen to me?" Gentille said.

Minerva nodded again.

"Judge Macomber has a lot of freedom to impose pretty much any sentence she would like upon you. Anything from probation up to the death penalty."

"The death penalty?" Minerva said.

Gentille nodded.

"But all I did was tell a few lies," Minerva said.

Gentille sighed. "It's that sort of lack of remorse that'll get you in trouble, Miss Cantor," she said.

Minerva didn't say anything.

They talked over strategies. Seeing as everyone Minerva had ever known lived outside of the Coterie, bringing in witnesses was logistically untenable. Bringing in their testimony would be deemed time consuming and cost prohibitive by the judge.

"Especially for a convicted felon," Gentille said.

"A felon," Minerva said, hardly able to believe that the word now applied to her.

"Our best approach will be a written statement for the judge to review. A way for you to give your side of the story without all the theatrics of the courtroom."

"But I don't know what to say," Minerva protested.

"You don't need to," Gentille reassured her. "Leave it to me. I'll prepare the document."

"Will I get a chance to review it before it's submitted?" Minerva asked.

"Of course," Gentille replied. "You can look over it and approve it with your signature."

After Gentille left her cell, Minerva sank to the floor, weighed down by the heaviness of it all.

She couldn't believe the death penalty was on the table. These didn't seem like people who would execute others. And particularly not for something that wasn't a malicious crime spree but the acts of a person who didn't ask to be gifted with truthshaping powers and certainly wasn't aware of what they did.

Would she one day be making a request for her last meal? She'd read about that tradition. The funny thing about last meal requests was that prisoners often didn't get what they even asked for, she'd learned.

The death row last meal tradition wasn't really about doing something nice for the prisoner but was primarily instituted to assuage the guilt of the person executing them. Paying a small kindness to the condemned could help guards and the system distinguish themselves from the murderers they were putting down.

Both killed, but the murderer did so in cold blood. And the executioners? Well, they did it in a more orderly detached fashion – and served refreshments beforehand.

It was funny that they often didn't follow through on granting the last meal request, given this. Basically, the act of even offering a kindness to the condemned was enough to make executioners feel better about themselves. Following through on what they offered was strictly optional.

It's a lot like how when many people see another person suffering, they're quick to ask, "Is there anything I can do to help?" But they don't want the other person to actually name something they can do.

Offering to help makes them feel better. They don't actually want to help that person. What they actually want is to feel better about the reality that someone else is suffering.

The Long, Dark Night of Cloche's Soul

Knuckles rapped on the door gently, as though the person attached to them were asking a question by knocking and not making a statement.

Cloche lifted her head. "Come in," she said.

The servant entered pushing a meal cart in front of him. His head was bent meekly as he avoided eye contact. Cloche didn't recognize his face. A new server. No wonder he was so tentative. He hadn't yet had time to become accustomed to his position. He didn't yet know what kind of charge she would be, friend or foe, heaven or hell.

If he'd been telepathic or empathic, he certainly would have known that such caution was unnecessary. A full year into her appointment as magistrate, Cloche still found herself amazed that she was waited on. She didn't see herself as the type of person who would have servants – and yet here she was.

Cloche waited as he set the silver tray down on her desk, setting up silverware and a red wine glass. He poured pinot noir into it with mind-numbing slowness. Cloche also noticed that his hands were shaking. She wondered if he would spill wine on her desk.

But he didn't. And he even seemed to find his confidence at the end of this brief service.

With a triumphant flick of the wrist, he lifted the silver dome of the cloche to reveal her evening meal waiting underneath.

"Thank you," Cloche said.

"Do you require anything further?" he asked.

"That will be all," she replied.

He bowed and rolled the cart out of her office.

Cloche studied dinner. It looked appetizing. Someone in the kitchen had given a lot of thought to presentation. The food was arranged quite symmetrically on the plate, varied in color. A whorl of purple sauce filled the right upper quadrant.

It was a pity, she thought, for such effort to go to waste. But she wasn't hungry.

She pushed the plate to the corner of her desk and picked up the wine glass. She inhaled. The scent was fruity, a bit more tannic than what she had come to expect from Coterie pinots, but complex.

She swirled the wine in the glass and noted it had good legs as it dripped down the sides.

Closing her eyes, she sipped. Yes, it was good.

She drank half of this glass before she realized that the wine wasn't doing what she wanted it to. Her mind was still stuck on the case and running in circles about the sentence that she would announce at tomorrow's hearing.

She would need more than wine to distract her. Quite a serious situation indeed.

She pulled out her work in progress, what she hoped would be her magnum opus. After training for all those years as a taxonomer, it had been a strange turn of events to find herself as magistrate. Her sister Moche's lot in life, as mayor, seemed much more natural, more inevitable.

Moche was born to lead in precisely that way. There had been something mayoral about her even as a child, something imperious and executive.

And the unspeakable power she'd demonstrated... well, mayor had been an obvious appointment.

Cloche still had trouble understanding why the Coterie had insisted she take up as magistrate. She'd shown no desire to lead and certainly no desire to interpret the law and make rulings.

She had been a prim and officious young girl. Content to organize and take copious notes on the world around her. But not one necessarily to judge or to impose any judgments she made on others.

She liked to sort what she found, to make order out of chaos.

And she was a generalist. She had been back then, and she was still.

Taxonomy had been a natural fit. It was her true passion, not law.

But here she was.

Insecta Psychica, the cover of her work in progress read. She wondered at this title. Perhaps it was a bit too abstruse, bombastic. The idea was to create a taxonomy manual that could be used by as many people as possible. She envisioned something that would be of use to academics and experts in the field of intuitive taxonomy, but she also hoped it would have some practical application – and perhaps even popular appeal.

Such a title could be off-putting, she thought. It didn't *sound* like a beach read.

No matter, she told herself. It was a working title. Not set in stone. It could easily change in the future.

She looked over a chapter on Reality Momentum she'd been working on, fretting over the phrasing. Was the language too imprecise? If she went more technical with it, she could risk losing the lay person. But there was no utility in a book that was wholly inaccurate, was there?

She debated by herself in her empty office until an hour had been swallowed up. Sighing, she closed the draft.

She wondered idly if she'd ever finish the manuscript to her satisfaction. There were so many minor points of execution that presented conflicts. Even as she adopted her judge's brain and presided over them, she found that she didn't feel confident in the way that she resolved them. Instead, laying down judgment felt more like a game of eeny-meeny-miney-moe where she cycled through approaches and at some point arbitrarily settled on one. In the choosing game, it was always a matter of timing and place in sequence. In her own mind, she was surrendering to some emotional impulse, some feeling that what she had selected was "right."

Sometimes she convinced herself that her sense of what was "right" and what was "wrong" was a result of her intuitive powers, a whisper of Reality Momentum showing through. A generalist's gift.

But even as she did, she found herself questioning her own bias. Far more powerful intuitives than Cloche had experienced significant bias interference. If that was the case, what hope was there for a generalist with softer powers to resist?

"Eeny-meeny-miney-moe," she said, shaking her head.

Besides, she thought, would a perfectly executed manual of psychic taxonomy really change the world? Taxonomy was just the beginning. When it came to the impending intuitive uprising, there was so much more to contend with than taxonomy.

Everything was going to change. Minerva had changed a lot on her own, and it was only going to get worse. What the truthshaper had started was going to build on itself, send them all further astray.

In the face of all that impending chaos, Cloche wondered, what could one little book do?

The Minerva incident had made it impossible to keep the psychic and non-psychic worlds separate. They wouldn't be separate for very long at all. Certainly not forever.

The best a person could do was delay.

She smiled at this thought. That took the pressure off. She knew what she must do.

When the worlds merged, the first thing that would be needed would be proper classification. Not a scientific system but a practical one. Society would need designations for each psychic citizen and their individual freedoms or lack thereof.

A system that paid homage to psychic history would be best, a system that remembered its successes and failures as well as the public's quest to unearth psychic powers, efforts that had only recently begun to bear fruit.

There had to be distinct categories, enough of them to cover a range of statuses but not so many categories that it would be easy for a lay person to become overwhelmed.

This system of classification would not have the level of detail to satisfy a scientific taxonomist. Any public system of classifying psychics had to be intuitive and easy to follow.

Between four and eight elements would be ideal, each one evocative and easy to remember.

Like that, it came to her. The answer lay in the Zener cards, of that she was sure. The Zener cards were a deck used to test for extrasensory perception. Twenty-five cards featuring five different symbols, each one represented five times. Each symbol was easy to recall and remember and certainly wouldn't be mixed up with any of the others.

Cloche pulled out a deck from her desk and selected one representative card for each symbol. She studied all five unique cards for a moment before arranging them in an order that made sense to her.

The first card was the Green Star. By far, this was the most optimistic symbol of the five, she thought. A lone star represented freedom, rugged individualism, and going it alone.

Quite appropriate for the newly formed Psychic State. A Green Star psychic would embody this. They would be the least restricted of the state's psychic citizens. Green Star psychics would be allowed to live on their own terms and free of monitoring – unless something arose that provided cause.

In fact, Cloche anticipated, Green Star psychics would frequently be agents of the State, working in their employ and being afforded additional privileges because of this service.

She made a note of this in a new document, separate from the *Insecta Psychica* manuscript.

The second card in the lineup was Blue River. In truth, there wasn't a literal river on this card but a set of three wavy lines. However, Blue River was prettier than Blue Wavy Lines, wasn't it? It had a certain ring to it and was more memorable.

Blue River psychics would possess a more liminal status, Cloche decided. They'd have quite a bit more freedom than most other designations but would fall short of the Green Stars. Blue Rivers would be allowed to live in their own residences and just like Green Stars would only be monitored if significant cause were discovered, for example, suspicious behavior indicating probable criminal activity.

However, Blue River psychics would not be free to leave their immediate area without a check-in with the authorities, and any approved trips would be subject to whatever restrictions their overseers deemed necessary.

Cloche dutifully recorded this in her notes.

Next in the sequence was Yellow Circle. This could also be called Light Monitoring. Psychics on Yellow Circle status would be bound by a complicated reporting system that included regular visits to a State Sponsor tasked with certifying that they were abiding by all laws and regulations and that the intuitive posed no immediate risk to themselves or others.

Yellow Circle psychics could live in independent housing but only accommodations approved of by the State. Pretty much everything in a Yellow Circle's life needed to be signed off on.

After Cloche had made notes on Yellow Circle, she moved to the second to the last card. Red Cross. This was where the Psychic State would really step in, she thought. Red Cross was essentially Heavy Monitoring. A Red Cross psychic would not be allowed to live in independent housing. Instead they would live at intensive outpatient centers run by the State. Generally, they wouldn't leave the facility unless they had permission. Typically, this would happen due to an issued day pass. Even then, they wouldn't be allowed to leave without the supervision of an official State guardian, who would accompany them wherever they went.

That left the final card. Black Square. This was the end of the road, the most intense government involvement in the life of a psychic. Black Square status meant imprisonment in a State facility. These psychics would be deemed too dangerous to society to have any traditional civil liberties.

Their powers would either be dampened by any means necessary – whether through chemical agents or psychic interference or otherwise – or employed *only* in service to the State on an as-needed basis.

She finished her notes, which had culminated in a compelling letter. She tucked this letter into an envelope and addressed it to her friends in the new government.

Smiling, she summoned a servant to mail it.

There would be two taxonomies, she thought, at least two, maybe more. This simplified framework could seed public policy in the Psychic State, leaving her to document the rest, to explore the nuances of psychic difference.

She turned back to her work in progress, barely noticing the servant's absence as he left with the letter in hand.

The Black Square Option

There are some who would later look back and say that Black Square status was where the Psychic State went too far, that empowering the State to imprison its citizens for no other reason than that they possessed certain gifts was unconscionable, and even if this power had been only responsibly employed that its very existence called into question the motivations and wisdom of the new government.

A just government has no such need, these individuals argue. A just government trusts its citizens, and therefore its citizens trust it in return.

It is a compelling argument, to be sure. However, it is worth noting that it is one made with the benefit of hindsight. Sadly, foresight was in short supply for the leaders of the early Psychic State, despite their wealth of precognitionists and vast clairvoyant resources.

Instead, the new State was tasked with containing potential threats that not only did they not understand but that no government in the world had ever had to deal with before.

Being called authoritarian and viewed as such was an easy bargain for the early Psychic State to make in order to have the protections that the Black Square option afforded them.

from Insecta Psychica: Towards an Intuitive Taxonomy by Cloche Macomber

Sentencing

Before Cloche called the court to order on the day of the sentencing hearing, she took a moment to survey the gathered crowd. At this point, it was mostly familiar faces. She saw the children she'd grown up with and had competed against ruthlessly when they'd been pitted against one another by the adults in their lives.

The faces had of course been stretched and changed by the years and the strange magic of hormones, but they were recognizable nonetheless, etched upon her brain in the years in which she was highly sensitive and impressionable. Their faces were important information in a different time, long ago, when she didn't know the destiny that awaited her and preferred instead to read alone in corners instead of participating in endless mental decathlons.

Minerva's face, however, wasn't in that part of her memory. She thanked fate for that, as it would have made what she had to say next that much harder to say. It was unfair that this poor woman hadn't had the opportunities she'd had, to grow up inside the safe confines of the Coterie, to learn of her truthshaping powers and develop them – and control over them – when she was very young.

What could she have been had she had that opportunity? Cloche wondered.

No, it did no good to dwell on that. It didn't matter. That was not the reality they were working in.

Sighing, she called the court to order and announced the sentence.

"I have read the statement written by the defendant and am ready to lay down my sentence," Cloche said.

"If it were up to me, I would have a different ending written for you. This would go another way altogether. If it were up to me, you never would have had those powers to begin with."

Minerva waited. Her head felt very heavy.

"And if it were up to me, you never would have done what you did. If I had known about you earlier, we could have brought you in sooner or sent someone out to teach you our ways or at least warn you more clearly about the dangers of having the powers you have." Cloche sighed.

"But I didn't know. And it wasn't up to me. So, you did everything you did. You twisted the truth into shapes that suited you, never thinking about the consequences. Never worrying about what would happen because of your actions. You never really understood what you were doing, not only to the people around you but to reality. But that doesn't matter. You didn't need to *intend* to harm reality for you to have done great damage."

"And you *have* done great damage, Minerva. Damage that simply cannot be undone. No amount of restitution or punishment will undo what you have done to reality –and to history. You have let loose something terrible and chaotic. As I stand here, judging you, I have no idea what's going to happen because of what you did, only that it's likely to be great and terrible and to carry on for years, decades, perhaps even centuries from now."

"We are all going to be paying for your enormous crimes for the foreseeable future and many futures beyond."

"I'm sorry to say, Minerva, whether you meant to or not, you have ruined a great many things."

Minerva swallowed hard. She felt herself frozen in place as she listened to the judge speak. It reminded her of being punished as a small child. There was no recourse, no other choice but to stand patiently and listen to the lecture and bear whatever came next, whether it seemed proportional or particularly fair.

"Now that you have been judged guilty, it is my responsibility to sentence you. It is a great burden and not one I take on willingly and certainly not lightly."

"It isn't just that I like you. Because I do like you. I do. You are a good woman, and if none of this whole affair had happened, you would be remembered a different way. You would have been Minerva the Brave instead of Minerva the Liar."

"But it's not just that, it's not just that I like you. I also dread this duty because no punishment I lay down upon you will make things right. Regardless of what I choose, justice will be incomplete, not fully served."

"No matter. Duty requires me to sentence you, regardless of the impotence I face when trying to serve justice in this case."

Cloche paused for a moment, preparing herself to say what came next.

"As such, Minerva Cantor, I sentence you to permanent Black Square status. You will remain imprisoned in the custody of the Macomber Coterie within a psychic-dampening field that inhibits your truthshaping powers until the day that your natural life expires, at which time your body will become property of the Psychic State."

"I'm never leaving?" Minerva asked.

Cloche frowned. She hated having to translate what was already clear into even clearer terms, particularly to someone who would hate the implications of whatever she said. "Correct. You're never leaving, Ms. Cantor."

Moche and Cloche

It had been a long time since Cloche had walked to her sister's dwelling, long enough that going there felt surreal. Perhaps anything would have felt surreal after such a long day. The sentencing hearing in the early afternoon hadn't taken long at all, but the judge had spent most of day hounded by members of the media.

She felt as though she'd answered the same four or five questions at least a hundred times before they were through with her.

But the judge had done her best to entertain the questions politely, even as it seemed that they would never stop coming.

A slight rephrase and a re-ask. Slight rephrase and re-ask. Over and over again, like the reporters were trying to catch her in a lie, one that would only be revealed if she were caught unaware, with her guard down, worn away after hours of repetitive questioning. Well, they would have no such luck.

Let them interrogate her. Let the media ask. She would answer without inconsistency, no matter how much they searched for it.

And ask they did.

The sun had gone down before the final journalists left her. After a quick bite to eat in her chambers, a courier arrived bearing the message. It was time to answer to the most important interrogator of all: Her sister, the mayor.

Cloche's heart raced as she climbed the steep ascent that led to her sister's house – really, a mansion that sat perched atop the highest hill in the Coterie.

The only hill in the Coterie, Cloche corrected herself.

It was the perfect place for a mayor to reside, a vantage point to look down on all her loyal subjects. Perhaps they should call her sister a queen, Cloche thought. It wasn't as though they were having elections anytime soon.

Not now. Especially not now.

Her breath caught in her throat and not simply because of the physical exertion of scaling the path upward. There was so much now that would be frozen in place, as the Coterie was forced to sort out its next move.

There was so much that they hadn't planned for. So much that they couldn't possibly have planned for.

Cloche arrived at the door. She did not knock. She knew she didn't need to, that those who waited for her knew precisely when she would arrive.

Right on cue, a servant opened the door and genuflected. He said nothing, simply bent his head and beckoned for her to follow him to the main sitting room.

Not that she needed the escort, Cloche thought. It had been quite a long time, but she knew the way still.

Moche sat upon a large throne, looming overwhelmingly large as always in both presence and stature.

"Good evening, sister," Moche said.

Cloche bowed before the mayor's bulk. "Good evening."

"I have been informed of the day's proceedings," Moche said.

Cloche nodded. Of course. Her sister Moche had eyes and ears everywhere. It would have been a simple matter for her to keep abreast of the trial, the verdict, and the sentencing, particularly as it was the story of the day and had been all week.

"You've done well," Moche said.

"Thank you, sister," Cloche replied.

"As well as could be done," Moche snapped, a barb in her tone.

Cloche closed her eyes, bracing herself for the onslaught that would surely come. Her sister's ability to inflict mental pain and anguish was legendary. Cloche had been subjected to only a small portion of it as a child, while Moche was still building up her powers. She knew that her sister had grown considerably more powerful since then, and Cloche could not think of a time in her life that she had deserved such punishment more.

I surrender. I will endure this, Cloche thought, miserably, willing herself to believe it fully.

"Don't worry," Moche said. The words instantly eased her anxiety. Cloche knew at once it was a deep command and not merely a suggestion. "You will not be punished. We will all be punished enough before this is all over."

Cloche frowned. "I fear you're right."

"Sister, you're probably wondering why I sent for you," Moche said.

"I am," Cloche admitted.

"I need you to act on our behalf, coordinating with the new government," Moche said.

"The Psychic State?"

Moche nodded. "You have friends there, don't you?"

"A few," Cloche said. "Although I'm not sure what I can do. They're not interested in joining us, and they're not interested in rejoining the United States."

"Of course not," Moche said. "They've tasted their freedom. Naturally, they want to keep it. Although..."

"Although?"

"It's much easier to establish a state than it is to govern one," Moche said gently. "Things happen. Uprisings, unrest, you know... growing pains." She looked at Cloche meaningfully. It would be an easy matter for her to transmit a thought to her sister, but she didn't have to. She communicated everything easily with a glance.

Cloche nodded, understanding her meaning. "You never know what will happen in a young state, do you?'

"It's true," Moche replied, an odd smile curling up the corner of her lips. "And when it does, we'll be there for our friend in need, won't we?"

"Yes," Cloche replied. "Better us than those Eck scum. Or the Skinners or Watsons. They're more money than might anyway."

Moche grinned even wider. "I trust you'll make it happen. That you'll make sure we emerge as the best possible ally."

"But of course," Cloche assured her. She was fuzzy on how exactly she would accomplish this but did her best to project confidence, hoping Moche wouldn't probe further into her thoughts and emotions.

She was in luck. Moche stayed on the surface. "You always were my favorite sister," Moche said to Cloche, before dismissing her with a nod.

"And you," Cloche replied.

It was a long walk back to her chambers, down the hill. While it had been a brutal slog to climb up, walking down it was almost as strenuous, as she strained to counterbrace her weight against forces that pulled her forward. Every step, she risked tumbling down the hill. Preventing herself from doing so took every ounce of concentration.

Cloche was nearly back to her own dwelling before she had the mental resources to consider what her sister had said. A new force had emerged, upsetting the delicate balance between the Families. Nothing she had done overseeing the Minerva incident had done anything to change that reality.

It was daunting, figuring out how to restore some semblance of balance with the unexpected birth of the Psychic State. She felt overwhelmed thinking about it. But she had always been good at solving problems.

"I am nothing if not resourceful," she assured herself as she unlocked the door to her home and slipped inside.

Forever in the Black Square

I am, somehow, less interested in the weight and convolutions of Einstein's brain than in the near certainty that people of equal talent have lived and died in cotton fields and sweatshops.

-Stephen Jay Gould

Gone was the comfortable holding cell Minerva had enjoyed for so many weeks. She'd hoped that she would be allowed to stay where she had awaited and undergone trial, or at the very worse transferred to another unit within the same facility.

No such luck. The new digs weren't in the same building.

And they weren't up to the same standard at all.

Like the basement work camp she'd previously toured, her new home was underground. It was located on the far side of the Coterie grounds, quite a distance from any other buildings. No shops or residences were located nearby. No foot traffic passed by the facility.

The ground level building was merely a guard's outpost, housed in a single-wide trailer. Towards the back of the structure, there was a small elevator that took prisoners to the basement.

Underneath the earth, the real scope of the facility became evident. It sprawled out in every direction. The offices closest to the elevator – the only method of egress – were staffed by a multitude of demotivators.

This made the early journey into her new home arduous. However, they were quickly out of range, and Minerva found herself hopeful.

Rire was no longer assigned to guide her. Instead, she was attended to her new home by four guards who regarded her every move with great interest. Minerva wasn't sure exactly what powers they possessed, but she knew they must be considerable. The longer she spent among the psychic population, the more she was finding she got hunches about the powers of people she was around, hunches that would prove right when she explored them further.

Her guard detail snaked her through a long series of corridors, each of which had a multitude of unmarked doors. Minerva couldn't be sure, but they looked less like cells to her and more like offices.

This made her hopeful. Perhaps her new home would be like that. Less like a cell, more like an office. These were highly evolved people, after all. They would show mercy on their prisoners. She knew it.

Finally, they came to a dead end. Minerva found herself in an incredibly large room with a series of doors on each of the walls. It reminded her a bit of the shower room at the detention center.

She was led to a door that was adorned with runes that she could not read. One of her guards stepped forward and waved her hand in front of the door, which made a hidden control panel flap open. The guard typed in a series of runes, and the door swung open.

"Welcome home," the guard said gruffly. She pushed Minerva in and closed the door.

Minerva noted with great alarm that the resemblance to a shower room didn't end with the door. Her entire dwelling was about the same size. The front room was perhaps six feet square. She had just enough room for her bed and a bit of room to walk around it. There was a second adjoining room of similar size. There was a small bathroom, she noted, in the back room. Her toilet was in her shower. Compared to the size of her prior cell, these quarters were claustrophobic, cramped.

Though she knew it was futile, she pushed on the door that led outside. It didn't budge of course.

"Welcome home," Minerva repeated, sinking down on the bed.

Black Square status. It had been explained to her at length by Espoir, the so-called advocate for her rights, after the sentence had been laid down.

Not that it was terribly complicated or hard to understand. Still, Espoir took Minerva's lack of response to her explanations as evidence that she needed more clarification, and so the advocate spoke for nearly an hour.

Her new home began to hum. Ah yes, the dampening field. That was part of Black Square status, too. It hadn't seemed like a big deal to her when Espoir had briefed her on it. In fact, it had sounded less invasive, less intrusive than the presence of demotivators.

But now that she was in the situation, she could not only hear the low hum but feel it coursing through her, altering her physiology, not only robbing her of any lingering ability that she could push through the natural anti-truthshaping wards found throughout the Coterie but also guaranteeing that she'd never develop new, compensatory powers.

No wonder her guards had been in such a hurry to get away, Minerva thought. The field felt like having tiny intruders crawl through every fraction of her over and over again, rearranging her, scrambling her.

She felt as though she were being continually shaped and reformed every few seconds. An awful feeling.

"A little uncomfortable, particularly at first," was how Espoir had explained it.

Bullshit. What a liar.

As her entire body continued to vibrate, Minerva began to wonder if she were set up. Maybe they were the liars. All of them. These stupid Coterie bitches. Cloche. Rire. Espoir. Rosie. Regina. Change.

And what about her man harem? Her knuckles turned white as she gripped her bed, struggling to shake off the vibrations that coursed through her. Were her boyfriends liars too? Had they set her up? Were they to blame for her being here?

She screamed, but there was no answer. No answer but the humming.

She struggled to make the pieces fit, to explain how she'd gotten here. She built a case in her mind to explain how everyone had betrayed her. It had all started with Chad. She could see that now. It was Chad's fault.

She tried to make the pieces fit. She strained and screamed and fought.

She spent several days wide awake in her cell, fighting the dampening current and straining against the vibrations that invaded her, and yet nothing fit.

The pieces would never quite fit.

"Forever in the Black Square," she found herself muttering. "Forever in the Black Square."

Then she would try again, try once again to overcome the field, or at least come up with an explanation that satisfied her.

And she sat in that cell for the rest of her natural life still trying to truth shape, even if only in her own head.

About the Author

Page Turner is the award-winning author of many books. With a professional background in psychological research and organizational behavioral consulting, Page is best described as a "total nerd." She's been cited as a relationship expert in a variety of media publications including *The Huffington Post*, *Glamour*, *Self*, and *Bustle*.

She clearly can't see the future because she didn't see any of that coming.

Due to her incurable wanderlust, she has lived many places, but these days she calls Dallas home.